Shimon

John Steinberg

2QT Limited (Publishing)

First edition published 2014

2QT Limited (Publishing)
Lancaster, United Kingdom LA2 8RE
www.2qt.co.uk

Cover illustration by Matthew Meadows
Cover illustration © John Steinberg
Image of John Steinberg by Ray Kilby Photography

Printed in Great Britain by Berforts Information Press Ltd.

A CIP catalogue record for this book will be available
from the British Library
ISBN 978-1-910077-04-7

Author's Note

This novel is based on the life of Shimon ben Lakish, better known as *Resh Lakish*, a renowned Hebrew scholar of the third century Common Era. Little is known of Shimon's early life; we believe that he was born in the eastern part of the Roman Empire and became a gladiator or bandit. After a chance meeting at the River Jordan, he gave up his violent past in favour of a life of learning. His meeting with Rabbi Yochanan, their relationship and the argument that eventually destroys them both is recorded in the Babylonian Talmud (Tractate Baba Mezi'a 84a).

All the other characters are entirely fictional, as are the events that are depicted in this novel. My intention is to portray the atmosphere and sentiments of the time through which Shimon lived. If there are any historical inaccuracies in the book, for which I take complete responsibility, I hope that they do not detract from your pleasure in reading about this intriguing man.

Acknowledgments

I would like to thank my family for their unwavering support and for being prepared to share in my adventure.

My thanks also go to everyone at 2QT for agreeing to publish this book and especially to my editor, Karen Holmes, who helped turn *Shimon* into a reality.

About the Author

John Steinberg spent many years in business before turning his hand to writing in 2007. He has co-written and produced two plays for the stage and is also the creator of a series of children's books. *Shimon* is his first novel. John lives in London with his wife and three children.

1

THE HEAT FROM the early morning sun had left its marker. Shimon, his powerful frame already covered in perspiration from the day's labours, wiped the grit from his eyes. Seeing there was no one around, he thrust his rake deep into the earth and pulled his woollen shirt on over his head. The overseer could find another idiot prepared to sweat all day for no money and a paltry amount of food. He wanted something better for himself.

He had slaved long enough – and for what purpose? To work on a piece of land so insignificant and barely arable that it could never support the dozen families who depended on it? To pay the landlord for the privilege of farming it? Angrily, he kicked at a stone.

Shimon had been born into a life of dire poverty. His family had been forced to flee their home in Judea and resettle in this particularly inhospitable part of Arabia Petraea. Jews in exile, they were expected to suffer daily humiliation, grovelling to their masters, grateful for any scraps that might be thrown at them.

It wasn't as if they hadn't tried to better their conditions but peaceful protests had no effect. Then, when a few individuals resorted to more drastic action and a series of disturbances spontaneously erupted around the province, the authorities were quick to take reprisals. Suspects were rounded up and their houses burnt. They had achieved nothing.

Shimon looked across the barren plain, home for the first

eighteen years of his life. It was time to move on.

Who would miss him? His mother was dead and his father was disappointed in him. Apart from learning to read and write, unlike his brothers he showed no interest in studying and therefore, as the eldest son, he would be unfit to carry on the family line of scholars. His twin sister, Miriam, was the only one who cared for him, who understood his thoughts – when she wasn't too busy tending to the sick or helping their Aunt Rivka deliver rich people's babies.

He envied his sister. When they were born, they looked alike but she was the frail one, the one expected to die before reaching childhood. Shimon felt that his parents blamed him for her weakness, as if he was responsible for sapping all the strength that was meant for her. She was the reliable one, the one their parents had always favoured. And she was lucky because, unlike him, she never doubted her faith. She never questioned why God's supposedly chosen people had to endure so much suffering, nor did she ever query the justice of her own unfortunate predicament.

She had always been there to encourage him when he felt despondent; to interpret the meaning of the dreams when they had left him feeling disturbed. But now even his relationship with Miriam was suffering because she had the burden of supporting her useless husband, Avram, who was more interested in studying than earning a living. Shimon felt aggrieved that she no longer had any time for him and he had no one to whom he could vent his anger and frustration.

The hot breeze ruffled his matted hair. He looked at the rake buried in the ground, determined never to return.

✠

'What do you want boy?' shouted the thickset man, a foot shorter that Shimon, who was blocking the entrance to the governor's villa. With his shaven head and fat neck spilling over the collar of his open tunic, he was an intimidating sight. He had once been cut and lost an ear while trying to ward off an attack by a disgruntled slave; the rest of his face was hideously disfigured.

The journey to Bosra had taken Shimon two days. Two days crossing endless fields, his feet blistered and his arms flayed painfully by thorn bushes, with only a crust of bread and a canteen of warm water to sustain him. The only thing that enabled him to continue his journey was his dreams. As he walked southwards, passing scores of well-dressed merchants returning with their wares from the province's most important city, he imagined a similar life for himself. Smart clothes, a small business of his own and enough money to provide for his family.

Now Shimon had finally reached the palatial mansion. As he walked up the perfectly manicured path bordered on both sides by rows of statues and exotic greenery, Shimon experienced a feeling of exhilaration at having entered a different world. He hadn't expected to be met by Spurius, the most senior of the slaves.

'Well?' Spurius asked.

Shimon couldn't answer – his mouth was swollen from dehydration. Everyone in the region knew about Spurius. He ruled the house with fear and enjoyed his reputation as a bully. When Shimon had worked as a bodyguard at the villa a year ago, he had witnessed the senior slave inflicting numerous beatings on his underlings.

'I … er, I —' Shimon tried to speak. With no warning, he was shoved in the back with such force that he nearly lost his footing. Looking over his shoulder, he saw a pack of panting dogs, saliva drooling from their expectant jaws as they prepared to charge at him. Instinctively, he turned to face them.

Just as the leader was preparing to leap, Spurius roared with laughter. 'Away!' he yelled and, picking up a piece of rancid meat from the ground, he threw it over the dogs' heads, diverting their attention.

'Clear off before I change my mind and set the dogs loose on you,' he shouted.

'I was just looking for work,' Shimon stammered, shaken but doing his utmost to regain his composure. 'I've worked for the governor before when he needed extra bodyguards.'

'There's nothing here for your kind, Jew. Go back to where you belong.' Spurius started back towards the house.

Suddenly, another figure emerged from the villa. The governor, Quintus Flaccus, a slightly built, effeminate man, appeared in the courtyard.

'What is going on? I could hear the noise from the bathhouse,' he called out, his high-pitched voice ringing across the open space. 'I do hope that's not another runaway. They always cause trouble.'

'He's just going, sir,' Spurius called. 'Weren't you boy?' he snarled menacingly at Shimon.

Shimon opened his mouth to protest. Then, thinking that neither the governor nor Spurius were going to listen to him or give him a fair chance of getting work, he became despondent. He turned away from the gate.

'Wait!' the governor shouted.

Shimon stopped.

Quintus Flaccus glided over to him on his absurdly small feet.

Shimon held his breath.

The governor looked him over closely. 'Turn around,' he ordered.

Shimon did as he was told.

'Hm,' the governor remarked, not getting too close. 'Filthy. But we may be able to find something for a strapping young lad like him. Especially since the last of the old batch left this morning.'

'Nasty business,' Spurius interjected, ingratiatingly.

'And *Domina* Livia has specifically requested a new houseboy,' the governor continued. 'She does like to have handsome faces around her. I think he'll do nicely.'

'Didn't take her long to get through the last lot,' Spurius muttered, a little too loudly.

'I'm sorry. You were saying something?' the governor enquired.

'No, sir,' Spurius replied hastily. 'Just that you're too good to them. You should have left them to me.'

'You know how I can't abide physical violence. Now, have him cleaned up and get cook to give him a meal. He looks like he could do with one.'

The governor gathered the skirt of his immaculate white linen toga and started to leave. Then he stopped abruptly. 'Does he have a name?' he asked Spurius. Before the senior slave could answer, he continued. 'No matter, he'll be given one of ours.' Then he strolled off, back towards the terrace, happy that he had successfully imposed his authority over his head slave for whom he had always maintained a serious dislike but had been too afraid to dismiss.

Spurius, furious at being overruled by his master, marched up to Shimon.

'You heard him. Now move it!' he shouted. He pushed the boy towards the house. 'Five silver *sestertii* says you don't last the month,' he said with a twisted smile as they entered at the side door.

Shimon, exhausted and overwhelmed by his ordeal, went into the kitchen, a stifling, dirty, smokey room. It was surrounded by dingy servants' dwellings and situated away from the rest of the house. He was given a bowl of soup and a lump of stale bread, his first proper meal for days. He wasn't sure if he was dreaming or whether he really had been given work and a decent place to live.

Shimon was oblivious to the sneers from the other house slaves who had converged like a swarm of ants, eager to inspect their latest prey. Neither did he anticipate the hostile environment that awaited him now that he had entered the governor's household.

2

Marcus Praeconinus was in an implacable mood that hot June morning, having passed another sleepless night plotting to punish those responsible for the delay of his merchandise. His caravan of forty wagons, bulging at the seams with valuables, that had set off from the East four months earlier had just reached Rome. Every taste was catered for with exotic perfumes and spices from India, precious stones from Egypt and ivory from Africa.

Marcus Praeconinus should have been a happy man. Not only was he the wealthiest and most powerful individual in Rome, he was also having a profound effect on the city's economy. He even had the emperor on his payroll. But while his business was booming and Rome was emptying its coffers of gold to pay for its insatiable appetite for his fancy goods, he knew that resentment was growing both among his business associates and his senatorial colleagues. They wanted their share of his substantial profits.

Marcus Praeconinus sensed trouble. His many informers had told him about attempts to undermine his business empire in the East.

His main priority had always been to maintain an uninterrupted flow of goods, which is why he had arranged for his daughter Livia to marry his appointee, Quintus Flaccus, the docile governor of Bosra. As a major part of Marcus Praeconinus's business passed through the province, he needed to feel secure that his merchandise would continue to move unimpeded. Equally important was to maintain the concession of a preferential tax rate, ensuring that only a tiny amount of the huge revenue he generated was paid over to the city tax collectors. This concession could only be granted by the goodwill of the emperor himself. Marcus Praeconinus had to be able to gauge the sentiment of the people and monitor the mood of the Senate so that he could influence their choice should an imperial replacement be needed at short notice.

He had already identified a young man for the role of new emperor: Lucius Antonius Cato, known as Anthony, a handsome young Roman general of Eastern descent. He smiled as he thought of the younger man's ruthless ambition. That alone qualified him admirably for the position of emperor.

Marcus Praeconinus had called in favours. He had also managed to convince the Senate by bestowing upon them a significant amount of largesse that, when circumstances permitted, it would be in their best interests to make Anthony's appointment as emperor a mere formality.

When Anthony was escorted to the bathhouse at the side of the jaded, grubby villa, he found Marcus Praeconinus immersed in his afternoon massage. He wondered why such a wealthy man chose to live in squalor. Anthony had just returned to Rome. Still in uniform and tired from suppressing a series of food riots in the countryside, he didn't relish being summoned to his paymaster's villa.

He was greeted by the scraping sound of a sharp implement being dragged across flesh. Almost overcome by revulsion, he watched the bulbous mass of his host being stripped clean of the masseur's body oil.

'You're late!' Marcus Praeconinus complained, trying to manoeuvre his cumbersome body to face his guest.

'I came as soon as I received your request,' Anthony replied.

'Request? This isn't an invitation to some poxy dinner party,' the older man bellowed.

'Sir, please forgive me, but it took longer to quash the uprising in the countryside than expected,' Anthony replied, wondering how much longer he could tolerate the man's abuse.

'That's what I'm trying to tell you,' the senator said. Suddenly, he waved his arms at the two house slaves who were fussing over him. 'Go on, get out, both of you,' he shouted. 'We've got private business to discuss. And you can take your magic lotions with you!'

One of the eunuchs ducked as Marcus Praeconinus threw an ebony ointment box at him, then turned and ran for the door.

When they were alone, Anthony said, 'I'm sorry, but I don't understand.'

The old senator, wary that someone might be listening, lowered his voice. 'There's a rumour about the people being dissatisfied with the emperor.' He gestured for Anthony to come nearer. A dull thud reverberated around the room as the older man eased himself down from the massage bed to face his guest.

'The plebs are very unhappy about the food shortages and are objecting to paying increased taxes on corn, which they insist should be subsidised.'

The fat man, oil still dripping from his skin, moved nearer to Anthony. 'Beware! Violence could erupt at any time,' Marcus Praeconinus whispered, with a contrived look of concern. 'If we don't act expeditiously, all our interests could be jeopardised.'

Anthony was irritable. He'd hardly slept for the last ten days; he felt grubby and needed a good meal. Yet again he was being forced to listen to stale news from the person in whom he had entrusted his political future. He was convinced that old age must be having an effect: Marcus Praeconinus was beginning to lose his faculties. Anthony just wanted the meeting to end so that he could return to the comforts of his own home.

'Everyone in the city knows that the emperor's days are few since he lost control of the Senate,' he said abruptly. He no longer cared whether he was speaking too freely. 'I'm prepared and ready for the challenge.'

'I've been informed that your regiment will be undertaking joint manoeuvres in the East with the Third Legion,' Marcus Praeconinus announced suddenly.

'That's correct,' replied Anthony, surprised at the unexpected change of subject. He braced himself, suspicious as to what the old man was planning.

'Well, since you're familiar with those parts, you'll be pleased to know that you've been appointed to take charge of the unit. You're to leave immediately,' the senator stated.

'Rome will just have to wait for me then,' Anthony replied, doing his utmost to hide his frustration.

'Be patient. You'll have your opportunity soon enough. In the meantime, you'll be more use to me in the East, finding out why an increasing number of my shipments have suddenly gone missing.'

'How can I be of assistance?' Anthony asked. Perhaps he had underestimated the senator.

'The Third have gone soft,' Marcus Praeconinus announced. 'I pay that bunch of rabble a considerable amount of money for the safe movement of my merchandise. They couldn't even control a bunch of Jews without calling for reinforcements. They need a good kick up the arse! I'm telling you, someone's got greedy and I want you to find out who's turned against me.' His face flushed with his growing anger.

'There are a few influential families that control the trade routes,' Anthony replied, revealing less than he knew. 'But I'm sure that most of them prefer to remain anonymous. They're secretive about their business affairs so it won't be easy to prise any information out of them.'

'Everyone has his price,' the older man replied slyly. 'How much do they want?'

'An initial payment in cash as a sign of goodwill, and probably a percentage on all future shipments,' Anthony said firmly.

'That's thievery!' the old man protested, his face turning crimson with rage.

'That's the way business is done in the East.'

'Haven't they heard of negotiation?'

'Naturally, I will do my best for you,' Anthony said, trying to sound sincere.

'Just wait there,' Marcus Praeconinus ordered and left the warm room, still clad in the masseur's towels. He went as fast as his corpulent body would allow to his study in the main house, where he kept substantial deposits of money for such emergencies. He looked around to make sure that he wasn't being watched, then entered his private room. He got down on his knees and retrieved a heavy iron box hidden behind a large statue. He placed a large quantity of gold coins into several leather pouches, which he took from his writing desk. Then he returned to the entrance of the bathhouse where Anthony was still waiting.

'This should persuade your friends that I'm serious,' Marcus Praeconinus said tersely, handing the pouches over to Anthony. He wouldn't have been surprised if Anthony devised a way of keeping some of the money for himself.

Anthony smiled and nodded his head in tacit agreement, thinking that it might not be too late for the day to be salvaged.

'While you're there, it might also be to your advantage if you get acquainted with my daughter, Livia,' Marcus Praeconinus said, not yet ready for Anthony to depart. 'For a woman, she has a fair grasp of my business affairs, and she's got more sense than

11

that idiot husband of hers.'

Anthony was amused. The senator's lack of scruples obviously extended to his own family.

'She's completely trustworthy and, you never know, you might gain some unexpected benefit,' Marcus Praeconinus added, raising his eyebrows suggestively.

Marcus Praeconinus had another role in mind for Anthony: that of future husband for his daughter Livia. Quintus Flaccus was never meant to be anything other than a temporary appointment until the main prize of having the emperor as his son-in-law came into his grasp.

'Her husband is the governor of Bosra, one of the most important provinces in the empire. Quintus Flaccus has great influence,' Anthony said cautiously.

'He's paid to do as he's told. If he wasn't so obsessed with that religious sect of fanatical Christians that have indoctrinated him, Rome would have less cause to be worried,' the other man snapped.

The two men embraced, Anthony trying hard not to show his distaste as he clasped the senator's folds of sweaty skin. Then Anthony went back down the path to his slaves, who were waiting patiently to return him to the city.

'Remember, you will be my eyes and ears. Rome is depending on you,' Marcus Praeconinus shouted as they left.

Anthony thought that the meeting had ended better than he had anticipated. The old man couldn't have suspected that it was his, Anthony's, family that controlled the majority of the trade routes from the East. In their attempt to protect their interests from outside competition, they had sanctioned the disruption of Marcus Praeconinus's consignments. But since they would now be receiving a share of their rival's operation as compensation, and Anthony had obtained legitimacy for the family business, he would make the necessary arrangements to ensure that the flow of Praeconinus's goods would be unimpeded. Now he and Marcus Praeconinus were partners, it was in his interest to do so.

Anthony strode up to his house, keeping the large stash of gold coins out of sight of the marauding thieves that frequented the streets at night. He would sail on the next boat east; that would give him more than enough time to deal with his business affairs. He had already decided where to put the money to work to his best advantage.

3

Shimon looked at himself in the hand mirror and liked what he saw. Stroking the side of his face, he enjoyed the feel of his smooth complexion and admired his new curled hairstyle. He was happy that there was no longer the slightest resemblance to the desperate farmhand who had appeared, dishevelled and hungry, barely four months ago. Dressed in fine clothes, he displayed all the trappings of a respectable young man who could have passed for an apprentice or artisan.

Domina Livia, the governor's wife, had been responsible for his rapid transformation. His name was now Simon and to complete her requirement of him, she had even taken on a tutor to teach him Greek.

What a difference from when he first arrived! He had waited for what seemed like an eternity for *Domina* Livia's return, not knowing whether she would agree to employ him or would throw him out. She had been accompanying the governor on a tax-raising tour of the province and had remained behind on private business of her father's.

The other slaves had scrutinised him as he finished the scraps of his first meal at the governor's villa.

'You're going to be with those two,' Spurius announced, pointing to Servius and Vibius, two unsavoury-looking individuals, with whom Shimon would be sharing a room. 'Though I don't suppose they'll be too happy giving up some of their valuable space to a Jew. So I'd be careful not to upset them.'

For three weeks Shimon was given the most demeaning task of clearing out the stables. He slept on the floor in the corner of a dingy area next to the kitchen, under the gaze of the other two slaves.

'Something smells bad,' Servius remarked. 'What do you think it is?'

'Must be that piece of cack lying over there,' Vibius replied, pointing at Shimon.

'He should be sleeping with the animals. They wouldn't notice the stink,' Servius jeered.

'Do you think he's got any money on him? He should be made to pay for soiling our room,' the other one said.

Shimon had been provoked enough. Incensed, he got to his feet and approached the two slaves who were antagonising him, determined to teach them a lesson. Vibius pulled out a dagger from under his straw pillow and held it against Shimon's face.

'Go back to sleep, Jew,' Servius said in a loud whisper. 'We don't want any trouble.'

Shimon stood still, just managing to refrain from striking out. He wasn't aware that his roommates had been ordered not to harm him. The governor had placed him under the protection of Spurius and had made the reluctant head slave responsible for his safety, until his mistress's return.

###

Livia knew that she was being used by Marcus Praeconinus so he could take advantage of her position as the governor's wife to promote his business interests. But she would never forgive her father for forcing her to divorce her beloved Lucilius and banishing him, with their daughter, to a remote part of Gaul. Maybe it would have been different if she'd been able to provide a male heir. She would never know.

Her loathing for her father was so great that when he forced her to marry Quintus Flaccus, she put a curse on her husband so that he would never be able to provide Marcus Praeconinus with the successor he craved. Livia regarded her marriage merely as a business arrangement. She had also made it clear from the beginning that she was going to live exactly the way she wanted, and wouldn't hesitate to exploit any opportunity to embarrass her husband.

Livia was feeling particularly mischievous when, without warning, she entered the small anteroom adjoining her chambers, wrapped only in a bath towel. Shimon was dressing for the evening meal, ready to take up his usual position at his mistress's side.

'Admiring yourself again, Simon?' she enquired.

Shimon smiled as he applied a generous quantity of scent to this throat.

'I wondered why I couldn't find you when I wanted to take my bath. You know how much I dislike a female washing me. And as for that foul-smelling oil she covered me with – I had to remove it myself,' she said, pretending to be annoyed.

'Forgive me, mistress,' Shimon replied with too little humility. 'I didn't realise that attending to your bath was one of my functions.'

'You've been neglecting me again. I think you're getting a little too sure of yourself,' Livia said. 'Just because I'm not one of those nubile slave girls that I've noticed make themselves available to you…'

'Mistress, I don't know what you mean,' Shimon protested, turning around and trying hard to divert his eyes from her shapely figure.

'Just remember that I'm the reason you're not still grovelling to that lout Spurius for an extra piece of meat or bowl of gruel. There are plenty of other young men who would gladly have your job.'

'You know how grateful I've always been for the opportunity to serve you,' Shimon answered.

Allowing her towel to fall further from her narrow shoulders, Livia moved closer, her ample breasts brushing against him. Shimon, aroused by the fragrance of her heavily-scented body, felt his heart beat wildly as she reached up and started to massage the back of his neck with her long fingers. He knew he was being compromised but this time he didn't care.

'How long do you think I'm going to put up with your disobedience?' Livia asked, looking into his eyes with a teasing smile. 'Don't you find me attractive? Do you think I'm too old and wrinkled?' She took hold of his hand and placed it on her bosom. 'Or maybe you really don't like women,' she added provocatively.

She placed her forefinger on his lips. Shimon tried to speak but words had deserted him. Any further resistance was futile; he was completely powerless to prevent his mistress from seducing him.

Then without warning, in a totally unexpected change of mood, Livia pushed him away. 'I've no time for any more games,' she announced. 'We're expecting an important visitor for dinner – quite a handsome young man, so I've been told. I need to make myself alluring.'

Shimon was so unsettled by the sudden turn of events that he stood motionless in front of his mistress, not knowing what to do next.

'I should so hate to disappoint him and I can hardly go dressed like this,' she said, exposing herself teasingly to Shimon one last time. 'You can go now. I won't need you for the rest of the evening,' she added coldly.

Shimon looked away, trying unsuccessfully not to let his frustration show.

'Don't look so sad,' Livia said. 'You'll have plenty of time to reflect on how you can atone for your insubordination. Oh, and make sure that the fire is well stoked and there are plenty of covers. I shan't want to come back to a cold bed.'

Turning around, she went out of the room without looking back.

The thought that his mistress would soon be giving her attention to another man incensed Shimon. He had never before felt the intensity of passion that she stirred in him. He was completely beholden to her. Why had he denied himself the pleasures that had been on offer? Next time, irrespective of the consequences, he would willingly succumb to her advances.

What Shimon didn't know was that there would be no 'next time'. The whole episode had been observed by one of the slaves directly responsible to Spurius, who had been conspiring against him since his arrival.

※

Shimon carried out his duties for his mistress, as instructed. Still dressed in his finest clothes, he ate his evening meal alone in the kitchen. That wasn't unusual since the other slaves had made it clear that, as he was a Jew, they didn't want him anywhere near them. He wasn't aware that the arrogance he displayed because of his privileged position only increased their animosity towards him.

He was still aroused by the memory of Livia's voluptuous body. Had he not been so preoccupied, he might have noticed the sound of muffled voices, as the other slaves fabricated the details of the conspiracy they planned against him.

Shimon went to his small room adjoining his mistress's bed-chamber at the other end of the house. He undressed and waited, unable to sleep. At any moment Livia might summon him. Perhaps he would finally get the chance to convince her of his manhood.

For an hour he tossed and turned until finally his eyes closed. He dreamed that the door opened, that his mistress, her golden hair loose over her bare shoulders, slipped stealthily inside, moved towards the bed and reached out to caress his back…

Hard fingers gripped his arm. 'Get up, Jew! Unless you fancy a beating!'

Confused, he opened his eyes and saw Spurius's repulsive features. The head slave was standing over him, brandishing a large wooden club. By his side was another slave.

Pushing away Spurius's hand, Shimon struggled upright. He knew what Spurius was capable of; any sign of weakness would leave him, Shimon, seriously injured. The only way he could defend himself against the other man's viciousness was to confront him.

'You're not allowed to be in here without permission,' Shimon said, as calmly as he could.

'Not who you were expecting?' Spurius growled knowingly. He took hold of Shimon's arm again, his grip tightening like a vice.

'The *domina* is going to have something to say about this. I work for her,' Shimon replied, trying to free himself.

The other slave came forward and took hold of his other arm.

'Not now her husband knows what you've been doing. Forcing yourself on his poor wife,' Spurius exclaimed, shaking his huge head in disgust. 'Just couldn't stop yourself, could you?'

They yanked Shimon from his bed and marched him out of his bedroom, taking pleasure in making him stumble as they dragged him the length of the villa to Quintus Flaccus's private study.

Finally, the three slaves stood before their master.

'But I didn't touch her. I swear I didn't,' Shimon protested.

'Then it's your word against ours, isn't it?' Spurius said, sure of himself. 'Your days here are at an end. I told you that you wouldn't be here long.'

'The *domina* knows I'm not lying. Please, sir, I need to speak to her,' Shimon pleaded.

Receiving no acknowledgment from the governor, who was immersed in signing a pile of official documents, he began to tremble with fear. What was going to happen to him? The thought that he could no longer rely on his mistress's protection, leaving him exposed to the hatred of the other slaves, filled him with a terrible sense of foreboding.

The governor, already late for his guest's arrival, signed Shimon's arrest warrant and threw it irritably at Spurius.

'Make sure he's gone by the time I return from dinner,' Quintus Flaccus said.

He got up quickly from his desk and rushed out of the room without looking back.

4

On a muggy late summer's evening Anthony, protected by three sturdy auxiliary soldiers, marched through the grounds of Quintus Flaccus's residence for a dinner that had been organised in his honour. It had been arranged at short notice through an intermediary on the pretext that, as a Roman general with strong ties to the Senate, Anthony would be able to give assurances on the security of the Eastern trade routes. Recent uprisings by discontented minorities threatened to undermine Rome's interests and the city was starting to feel exposed.

The truth, however, was entirely different. Anthony had been forewarned by members of his family that the governor was going to purge a number of businesses that had been threatened with heavy fines for evading tax liabilities. Those businesses included his own. He needed an audience with the governor so that he could make an agreement that would save him a considerable amount of money. And, Anthony thought as he approached the entrance to the house, dressed in the full splendour of his rank, he was looking forward to meeting Livia. He knew that she was no longer young, and he suspected that he probably wouldn't find her appealing. Nevertheless, if there was opportunity to exploit a relationship with Marcus Praeconinus's daughter, he was going to take advantage of it.

The woman herself was standing by the main entrance, waiting to greet him. Anthony paused before he approached her. The gods were smiling on him; she was more beautiful than he could ever have hoped for. The strands of her magnificent golden hair were pulled back to show the fine planes of her face; her skin was soft and untouched by age. She wore a sleeveless full-length dress of rich red, pleated silk, cunningly structured to accentuate her full figure.

Anthony smiled to himself. Trying to win her affection would be a pleasure as well as a challenge.

'You must excuse my husband for not greeting you,' Livia said with a welcoming smile. 'He's been detained on a tiresome domestic matter, but he will join us shortly.'

As she took her guest's arm and led him into the house, she smiled to herself. Always appreciative of a handsome face, she was pleased by the man who walked beside her. Admittedly, his dusky complexion and black eyes were decidedly un-Roman, but those aquiline features were flawless. And there was a sensuality emanating from him that intrigued and warmed her. This evening's meal would not be the chore she had anticipated.

Together they passed through the heavily scented atrium and entered the panelled dining room with it its garish candelabras and explicit marble figurines. It was obvious to Anthony that the governor had spent vast sums of money decorating the house. As with all wealthy Romans, style was everything.

He was directed to take his place in the middle of the three cushioned couches that were set around a small rectangular table. Livia, reclining on the adjacent sofa, clapped her hands and two servants appeared bearing food. Huge platters piled high with an assortment of mussels, oysters and lobsters, garnished with a variety of vegetables, were placed on the table between them. Two other slaves emerged from the shadows, each carrying a jug of wine. Without instruction, they started pouring the contents into embellished silver goblets in front of Anthony and Livia.

'Rome has flattered us with your presence,' she began, formally engaging Anthony in conversation.

'If you've gone to so much trouble for a total stranger,' Anthony replied, observing the generous selection of food, 'I can't imagine the efforts you'd be prepared to extend to your close friends.' He chose his words carefully; he wanted to charm her but he anticipated that this woman would respond to a challenge rather than flattery.

'My husband likes to entertain. And, after all, it's not every day we have the company of such a prominent citizen of Rome,' Livia responded with a smile. 'How long do you expect it will take to conclude your business affairs?' she asked, wanting to impress upon him that she was well informed about more than mere domestic matters.

Anthony took a small sip of wine. 'Since we took Judea,' he replied, 'the Jews have been a constant source of trouble. Even worse, because of their strange customs which they'd rather give up their lives for than abandon, they don't even make compliant slaves.'

'We've had the same problem in the house,' Livia concurred, having forgotten that her servant Simon was a Jew. 'They don't mix well with the others, although they often tend to be better educated. But I respect their women. They could give many of us a lesson in humility.'

'You seem to know quite a lot about them,' Anthony said.

'There's a woman from one of their villages, a healer. Rivka, I think her name is. She's treated me occasionally for different ailments,' Livia explained. 'Some of her potions and compresses have been most invigorating. It's strange though, I haven't seen her for a while,' she added thoughtfully. 'Maybe she died. She was quite elderly. Anyway, there are sure to be others who can take her place,'

They both laughed and raised their goblets.

'To the gods,' Livia toasted.

'And to my hosts,' Anthony responded, looking into her eyes.

Just then, Quintus Flaccus entered the room with a dramatic wave of his hands. He looked extremely harassed.

'I seek your forgiveness,' he said unctuously. He danced over to Anthony on his tiny feet. 'You must be Anthony,' Quintus Flaccus said, taking hold of his guest's wrist. 'I'm so glad you could come. We have much to talk about.'

Without acknowledging his wife, he positioned himself next to their guest and helped himself to a plate of stuffed quail. He summoned the servants to pour more wine.

'A toast,' Quintus Flaccus announced, raising his goblet. 'To the health of our esteemed guest. May your visit prove fruitful.'

'And may the gods protect you,' Livia added, smiling sweetly, purposely antagonising her husband.

'Yes, well, that's what you *would* say,' Quintus Flaccus muttered, giving her a venomous look.

'Not feeling well, my love?' Livia asked, her smile still firmly in place. 'You are rather pale. Perhaps you should lie down for a while.'

Anthony watched the couple, intrigued and amused by their obvious dislike of each other.

'I shall be fine. Just a little light-headed after some trouble with those wretched slaves,' Quintus Flaccus responded curtly.

'My husband does get upset rather easily,' Livia said, addressing Anthony, who was helping himself to another plate of oysters.

'I do when you denigrate my beliefs,' Quintus Flaccus said irritably. 'The gods, indeed. You know how much that upsets me.'

Anthony decided that it was time to mediate before an argument developed and ruined his visit. 'And what exactly are they?' he enquired. Not that he didn't know. The governor's obsession with Christianity was renowned, despite the need for Christians to practise their faith surreptitiously. Quintus Flaccus hadn't the slightest idea that his secret activity had been meticulously documented.

'Well perhaps I could show you, if you're interested,' Quintus Flaccus replied enthusiastically, getting to his feet, forgetting to be cautious in his enthusiasm about his beliefs.

'If I'm not mistaken, there are more pressing matters to discuss,' Livia said, belittling her husband again. 'And I would be most interested in hearing about them. That is, assuming our guest doesn't object to discussing politics in front of a woman?' She lowered her eyes for a moment, then looked up at Anthony appealingly.

Anthony, amused, didn't need any further encouragement.

Quintus Flaccus sat down, deflated.

'As you are no doubt aware,' Anthony began, looking directly at Livia, and marginalising her husband, 'your province is of great strategic importance to the Empire. However, because of the continuing outbreaks of violence, Rome has started to feel vulnerable. To be honest, the Senate has started to question whether the right authority is in place to ensure that its interests are sufficiently protected.'

Quintus Flaccus jumped to his feet indignantly. 'I can personally guarantee that every measure has been taken to eradicate the problem,' he protested. 'Our Third Legion has even brought in reinforcements, with considerable success. You have my word that calm has already been restored.'

Flushed in the face and beginning to perspire, he reached for his goblet and gulped down the remainder of his wine to try and steady himself. He hoped that his assurance would be enough to end the discussion.

Anthony, seeing that he had unnerved his host, continued his interrogation while Livia sat quietly, enjoying seeing her husband squirm. 'I'm afraid that has not provided Rome with sufficient comfort. You know that there have been several incidents of sabotage of goods destined for Rome in the last month. And with the Saturnalia celebrations in a few months' time, the authorities will not look kindly on those responsible for holding up any more of their festive merchandise.'

Anthony was slyly referring to the sporadic outbursts of violence that he himself had perpetrated against Marcus Praeconinus's consignments. He would threaten Quintus Flaccus with blame for the attacks and thus obtain his complete subservience.

Quintus Flaccus fidgeted uncomfortably, fearing more bad news. 'What can be done to regain their confidence?' he asked, wiping his nose with hand. Anthony thought he sounded as if he were about to cry.

'There may be a solution,' Anthony answered guardedly. 'It appears that the only certain way of protecting the trade routes to Rome is through the co-operation of those in whose interest it is to ensure an unimpeded flow of their own goods.'

'What exactly are you saying?' Quintus Flaccus asked.

'If I may be permitted to speak,' Livia intervened. She had immediately understood the point. 'You're suggesting we have to make those businesses that supply the merchandise responsible for their own deliveries.'

'And how could that be done?' Quintus Flaccus asked.

'Obviously, by offering them sufficient incentives,' Livia replied impatiently. She was embarrassed by her husband's ineptness. He had proved his incompetence in all political matters, but she didn't think it was necessary for him to display his shortcomings in front of such an important guest.

Slowly he began to understand. 'By paying them? Like a form of insurance you mean?' Quintus Flaccus asked, pleased that he was finally beginning to grasp the proposal.

'Or by reducing the taxes due from them,' Livia suggested.

'Only on the receipt of guarantees that they would carry out their part of the agreement,' Anthony said.

The transformation in Quintus Flaccus was immediate. A solution to the problem and the end of a conversation that appeared beyond his comprehension produced a broad smile on his face. He clapped his hands joyfully. 'That's settled then,' he said. Getting to his feet, he sauntered around the room, hugely relieved. 'It won't cost us anything. Most of them haven't been paying taxes anyway. All we have to do,' he said, repeating the words out loud, 'is to place the obligation of maintaining safe passage of the goods back on them.'

Suddenly, his expression changed to one of concern. 'But Rome has passed an edict. They'll never agree to it. Don't forget, the city needs the revenue from the taxes.'

'I have certain influential contacts that, shall we say, might be able to persuade the emperor,' Anthony replied reassuringly. It was still too early to disclose his close relationship with Livia's father, Marcus Praeconinus.

'Would you have any objection if the idea were to come from me?' Quintus Flaccus asked. He strutted back to Anthony with renewed enthusiasm. 'It might help to restore Rome's faith in me. And I would be extremely grateful.'

'If all the other elements of the deal are in place, I might be able to accommodate you,' Anthony replied. It was a small price to pay to secure the man's continued indebtedness.

'They will be, you have my word. I will see to it immediately,' Quintus Flaccus answered.

Anthony knew that his host had practically assured his own demise. After a brief period of calm, greed would again become the norm and the sabotage of Rome's merchandise would resume.

Nevertheless, he had managed to secure a reprieve for his own business and the governor was beholden to him. Now he wanted to focus his attentions on Quintus Flaccus's wife, where he anticipated the prizes would be far greater.

'Regretfully I must leave,' Anthony pronounced, standing up. Reaching down, he took Livia's heavily perfumed hand and pressed it to his lips. He looked into her eyes as he said, 'I must thank you for your most generous hospitality. And for your wisdom that has managed to alleviate Rome's concerns. The city will now be able to rest more easily.'

Livia rose from her sofa and stood close to Anthony, lifting her face up towards him. 'Must you leave so soon?' she asked, disappointed, pouting her sensuous lips.

'There will be other occasions,' Anthony replied. He had no doubt that they had already formed a bond.

He turned to Quintus Flaccus. 'We haven't talked about your "special' interest",' he said, willing to delay his departure for a little longer. 'I would like you to show me,' he said, taking his host by the arm.

'We have to be very discreet because we Christians are not yet a recognised religion and the emperor doesn't approve,' Quintus Flaccus said mischievously.

With one last, lingering look at Livia, Anthony followed the governor out of the dining room. They went through the hallway to a side door, taking hold of torches to light their way.

'You needn't fear, your secret is safe with me,' Anthony said. 'I have some sympathy for your cause. It's completely barbaric to persecute anyone who doesn't worship the Imperial Cult.'

The two men went down a steep staircase into a separate annex. They passed through a narrow corridor at the end of which, tucked away behind a curtain, was a half-height wooden door. Anthony, led by the governor, entered a small room adorned with frescos depicting biblical scenes and images of Christ. The centrepiece was a ceremonial wooden table for celebrating the Eucharist, which stood on a mosaic floor elaborately decorated with geometric patterns portraying more Christian symbols.

'I see that you are quite serious about your religion,' Anthony said, looking around with more than a cursory interest. Knowledge of the other man's weaknesses empowered him. Quintus Flaccus must have bribed a multitude of people to keep his activity secret.

'It's my life, the only thing that has ever brought me any meaning. I've sacrificed everything for my faith,' Quintus Flaccus replied. He pointed to an ancient Hebrew manuscript mounted on the wall. 'Our Lord was a Jew but believed in only one God who controls the entire universe.'

'I might be able to help you gain recognition,' Anthony said. 'And, as a gesture of goodwill, I should like to donate certain Christian artefacts of my own, some of which have great value. I assume you won't object to me visiting occasionally to look at them? I've never been separated from them before, so you can understand that I'm quite attached to them.'

'It would be an honour to have you worship with us,' Quintus Flaccus exclaimed with such a degree of reverence that Anthony thought that he might prostrate himself.

'Now, I really must get back to my unit and inform them of our agreement,' Anthony said. 'There's much to do.'

After he had shown Anthony out of the villa, Quintus Flaccus returned to the house church. He felt reassured that he had acquired a powerful friend who would help fulfil his dream of establishing Christianity as an official religion. In addition, he was convinced that his reputation in Rome would soon be restored; he, Quintus Flaccus, would receive the credit for solving Rome's trade problems. Even his father-in-law, Marcus Praeconinus, would regret underestimating him.

His wife was a different matter. He had become resigned to her indiscretions. It was bad enough that she had resorted to displays of lechery with her own servants without regard to his position as head of the household. However, her disgraceful behaviour, practically throwing herself at his most distinguished guest, was something he could not forgive.

※

In the early hours of the morning, Anthony reached the tavern where he had arranged to meet some business associates. He wanted to discuss increasing his investment in a venture that they were fronting for him. It had, from the beginning, generated so much cash that they needed to find new places to hide it from the authorities.

Armed with the pouches of gold coins that he had brought from Rome, he found his friends engrossed in a game of dice for high stakes. He looked on, eager for his chance to extend his own run of good fortune. The return to his unit would have to wait until the following day.

5

SHIMON WAS SPAT on and jeered by the cauldron of slaves that had converged to view the spectacle as he was led out of the governor's study.

Still in his nightclothes, he was pushed out of the side door of the house into the hands of two waiting guards whom Spurius had summoned.

'Right, you! You're coming with us.' The guards took hold of Shimon under his arms and dragged him barefoot down the steep gravel path, away from the new life he thought he had made for himself. He began shaking with fear, convinced that they'd been ordered to kill him and were trying to find a remote patch of land to dump his body.

'Where are you taking me? I didn't do anything!' Shimon pleaded, struggling to free himself. 'I swear it. Ask the *domina*! She'll tell you. Please, let me go! I'm telling the truth! I didn't touch her!'

'What's it to us? We just do as we're told,' the older guard shouted as he tightened his grip.

'Think he's got some money?' the younger one asked, running his hands roughly over Shimon's cotton tunic.

'Nah! Not unless the *domina* paid him,' the other guard replied.

'Paid you for your services, did she?'

'I told you nothing happened,' Shimon repeated desperately. His eyes began to smart, partly from the pain of being dragged through the streets and partly from the panicky sweat that was pouring down his forehead.

'What's going to happen to me?' he asked anxiously.

'You'll find out soon enough,' sneered the younger guard. 'A pretty boy like you, with your curled blond hair and waxed chest… I reckon you'll be a treat for some of them older ones.'

'What do you mean? Where are you taking me?'

'They'll think that Saturnalia has come early!' The same man laughed, and his companion joined in.

Shimon was led back to the same main road at which he had arrived of his own free will, filled with such optimism, a few months earlier. Now he was being dragged unwillingly in the opposite direction like a common criminal. He couldn't understand what was happening. It was bad enough that he'd been falsely accused of molesting his mistress. It was even worse that she appeared to have forsaken him. If only he hadn't trusted her. If only he hadn't deluded himself that she desired him as a man and realised instead that she was exploiting his position as slave.

He began thinking about his home, his sister Miriam and his family. How he had left them, discarded them, convinced he was too good for them. He'd wanted so much more from his life, more than they could give him. He wished he were with them now.

For a brief moment he imagined that he could get away. He tried to wriggle free from the guards' hold, but they only tightened their grip.

'Ow! You're hurting me,' Shimon cried.

'Tough,' the older guard snarled.

They seemed to walk for hours. Shimon was so tired, his legs buckling. The guards seemed unperturbed by the distance and plodded on, dragging him relentlessly onwards.

Finally they began to approach the outskirts of the capital from where the outline of the city prison was clearly visible in the moonlit sky.

'Not much further now,' the young guard announced. He looked over at his friend. 'It would've been nice to have had a few drinks if we hadn't had to take this extra job.'

'All right for some who don't have a wife to return to,' the other replied resentfully.

Shimon, his feet blistered from walking barefoot, felt his last reserves of energy drain away. 'I can't go on any further,' he cried. 'I need water.'

Ignoring his pleas, the two guards threw him down on his back and dragged him the remaining distance by his feet. Shimon cried out again in agony. 'No more!'

He received no sympathy. 'Sorry, mate, our orders are to deliver you in one piece without any delay,' the older guard said.

'I imagine they'll put together a welcoming committee when they see you,' the other commented jovially.

They had finally reached their destination: a tall, intimidating edifice. It was built of solid stone and reinforced with a massive iron door, making any attempt at escape impossible.

'Right, we're here,' the older guard announced. 'You'll stay here tonight – or what's left of it – until the jailer gets up. You'll be in front of the magistrate first thing in the morning, so you better look your best and hope he's in a good mood. Your life might depend on it.'

Shimon's blood chilled as he was pushed down several stone steps into the foul-smelling prison.

The guard on sentry duty was not pleased to be woken up. He'd been drinking heavily throughout the night and he needed to sleep it off. Irritated and swearing, he shoved Shimon down another flight of stairs to the dungeons.

Shimon was pushed into a cold, dark, damp cell with three other prisoners who were sound asleep. He felt so exhausted from his journey that all he cared about was getting some rest. Instead, he was forced to pass the remaining hours before daybreak manacled to the wall next to a family of flea-infested rats that eagerly took turns to nibble at his swollen feet.

He must have finally dozed off. The next thing he knew, there was a sharp pain in his side.

'Come on, pretty boy!' the jailer called out in a gruff voice. 'You've had your beauty sleep. Shame you didn't turn up earlier last night, I could have enjoyed myself with you.'

Shimon opened his eyes to see a large, repugnant-looking man, his huge stomach unashamedly protruding from his open tunic, prodding him with a stick.

'You're up first in front of the magistrate. Now you don't want to keep this one waiting – he can be a vindictive bastard!'

Shimon tried straightening his arms but then remembered that he was chained to the wall. He felt weak from lack of food and drink and his limbs hurt. The jailer, his breath still reeking of drink, released the manacles and pushed him up the uneven stairs.

Shimon knew that in a short time his fate would be decided. He had already resigned himself to having his freedom taken away and spending the rest of his life in prison. His innate optimism had deserted him and been replaced with hopeless despondency. Chained to the jailer, with the filth from the cell clinging to his aching body, he moved uneasily in silence across the short distance to the magistrate's court to await his punishment.

As he walked up the steps of the austere building, he was viewed with more than a passing interest by a small bunch of individuals disguised as businessmen who were in a heated discussion with the magistrate. Shimon didn't see them hand over a large sum of money to the official who, looking flustered, returned to his room to start the day's proceedings.

Shimon shivered despite the intense heat; his torn cotton tunic was the only remnant of his former status. He gazed up at the short, squat magistrate, who was seated uncomfortably behind his oversized desk. He waited while the man who was about to decide his fate fumbled around in his stained tunic and eventually produced a crumpled list of charges. Then, without looking at Shimon, his voice devoid of any emotion, he made his pronouncement: '*Damnatio ad Gladium.*'

'I'm innocent!' Shimon screamed. 'I didn't do anything! You can't send me away!' He started to wail uncontrollably. But it was too late; the magistrate had already left his seat.

Without any opportunity to defend himself, or for anyone else to speak up on his behalf, Shimon had just been condemned to die in the arena. He couldn't absorb the full implication of the words. The ignominy of being thrown out of the governor's household, his dreams of establishing a new life for himself destroyed, he was numb to any further harm that could be done to him.

He was led away, together with several other condemned criminals who had already received their sentences, to a place that for most of them would be their final destination. He was completely unaware that his real nightmare was about to begin.

6

GAIUS LICINIUS WAS a nasty individual who deserved his bad reputation. Of average height, his once-solid frame had capitulated to an excess of food and wine. His only interest was in satisfying his personal desires. His love of food was only matched by his greed for money and an insatiable sexual appetite for anyone or anything that attracted him.

Licinius was a former gladiator who, by bribing the authorities, had managed to win his freedom and gain a position as *lanista*, the head of the gladiatorial training school. His job was to train a disorganised bunch of outcasts into a highly efficient band of killers. He was efficient – and he was cruel. He provided gladiators who could give the best possible entertainment to the bloodthirsty public that paid his wages.

To Licinius, death was an everyday occurrence that was part of the job. Bereft of any sentiment, he regarded those over whom he exercised control as subhuman scum with a limited life expectancy. He intended to exploit them to their maximum potential before they met their inevitable end.

After less than an hour's march, the convoy of weary men came to a halt. Shimon, dehydrated and unable to feel any sensation in his legs, rubbed the grit from his eyes and looked up. He had arrived at the training school, the *ludus*. It didn't resemble the impenetrable fortress that he'd imagined or the frightening penal institution that he had overheard the other prisoners speculating wildly about. Apart from being larger, its rectangular shape and prominent arches made it look like any one of the municipal buildings that he'd passed on his journey from the magistrate's court.

He gazed at a large circular field in the centre of the complex and at a number of upright posts planted in the ground.

'What goes on over there?' Shimon asked the small, sallow-faced prisoner with whom he was chained, pointing at groups of men paired in combat.

'You'll soon find out, if you're not torn to pieces first,' the man replied, grinning mischievously.

'I don't understand. What do you mean?' Shimon asked, sounding worried.

'Look mate, I don't know who you are or what you've done, but you've not been sent here just to build up your muscles. Most of them blokes won't be leaving here.'

Shimon opened his mouth, aghast at what he'd just been told. Then he remembered the magistrate's pronouncement that had decided his own destiny.

'The lucky ones will end up fighting for their lives in the arena,' the prisoner went on.

Shimon turned around and saw the intimidating presence of the multi-tiered amphitheatre in the background.

'Until it's their turn to be carried out dead to the cemetery. Forgotten about, as if they'd never existed. Probably be me next time,' the man added stoically.

'Why? What are you here for?' Shimon questioned.

'Escaping after I killed a guard. It took them almost a year to catch me. A bloke I paid off informed on me. I've been sentenced to death. But it was worth it to watch that bastard die,' the man gloated, appearing satisfied with the fate that awaited him.

Shimon was ordered into the building and led down the first

of a series of narrow passageways. There was only the minimum of natural light but he could still see the grotesque sexual images that adorned the walls. On each side there were cells, each space no bigger than a cage and barely large enough to house a single occupant. Sleeping accommodation consisted of a hard, straw-covered wooden platform.

As Shimon passed along the corridor, he was greeted by suggestive whistling and the sound of desperate men rattling their prison bars, wanting to be the first to stake their claim on the new young recruit. He was pushed forward by a turncoat, one of the select bunch of inmates who volunteered to discipline their fellow prisoners in return for extra privileges.

Shimon was soon caught up in the misery of the place. He didn't know how he was supposed to survive in such wretched conditions. Discarded by those he had trusted and out of reach of his family, he felt completely alone.

Turning into the next equally murky aisle, Shimon was overcome by the stench of latrines that seemed to penetrate all of his senses. He was going to retch; this was worse than his earliest memory of the open sewers that ran through his family farm.

The turncoat threw him into a tiny cell. On one side of him was a lanky, youth with the face of an angel; he couldn't be more than an adolescent. On the other side was a much older, shaven-headed prisoner with a crazed look in his eyes as if he was just waiting to pounce on his next victim.

'Now you don't want to start upsetting him, if you know what's good for you,' the turncoat warned, slamming the door of Shimon's cell. 'The Beast has his own way of dealing with troublesome neighbours.'

Shimon felt faint. 'I can't breathe! I need water. I beg you,' he implored. His cries resulted in roars of laughter from the adjoining cells. 'Please, someone help me,' he tried again. 'I'm choking.'

This time he received an angry response from The Beast. 'Listen, you son of a whore,' he growled. 'I don't like being woken up. It puts me in a bad mood, see! So if you don't want your balls cut off and stuffed in your mouth, stop your bleating and let me get back to sleep!'

The commotion attracted two guards who suddenly appeared. They found Shimon sitting on the floor of his cell, his hands between his knees.

'You been making a nuisance of yourself already?' one of them accused.

Shimon didn't move.

'He said he needed water,' the other guard said. 'I'll give you water, you useless piece of cack.' Then he grabbed the wooden bucket his partner was carrying and emptied the contents through the bars.

Shimon was completely soaked in slimy excrement. He screamed and tried to protect himself, covering his head with his hands.

'Just kill me now and get it over with!' he cried.

'Silence, scum,' the guard shouted back. 'You'll get your wish soon enough. I reckon the lions are going to have a field day.'

'Nah! I reckon there are other plans for this little beauty,' his partner said, pursing his lips and making kissing noises. 'Anyway, lions aren't particularly partial to Jew flesh.'

Both of the men laughed and strode away, leaving Shimon shivering with cold. He wanted nothing more than to die and end this misery. It had been less than twenty-four hours since his arrest and his spirit was already completely broken.

He could envisage no escape, no release from this persecution and within hours he slipped into a deep depression. Over the next few days, he refused to leave the confines of his cell. He wouldn't even go for meals in the dining room, one of the few privileges available to the men.

For some reason, the youth in the next cell took pity on him. Risking severe punishment, he smuggled in small quantities of food and passed them through a hole in the wall into Shimon's cell. The food remained untouched. Shimon, weak because of his continuing refusal to eat, became obsessed with the thought of taking his own life. It was the only answer: if he was dead, he could come to no more harm. It was the only way he could escape from the hell that he'd been unfairly thrust into. He fantasised about getting hold of a sharp implement.

A few days later, lying in a pool of filth, he contracted a fever and became delirious. He began to hear voices. His mother was calling him, 'Shimon! Shimon!' But when he looked around, it wasn't his mother but his mistress, Livia, beckoning him.

'Shimon!' Again he heard his name being called. This time he was in a field with his sister, Miriam. They were exploring. He had discovered a gold coin.

'What have you found?' she asked, trying to prise his hand open. 'Give it to me!'

He opened his hand and then withdrew it defiantly.

'You have to put it back. It'll only bring us bad luck,' Miriam said firmly. Shimon picked up a handful of stones and started throwing them at her. Now he was running as fast as he could. Soldiers were chasing him. They were catching up with him…

He woke up. His heart was pounding. He tried to open his eyes, but nothing happened and he panicked, thinking that he'd lost his sight. He tried again but still they wouldn't open. Then Shimon heard a man's voice close to him. Was it real or was he still dreaming? Finally, he dragged open his eyes and saw the outline of a large man towering over him. No, this was not a dream.

Gaius Licinius had his informants. He made it his business to know about everything and everybody at his school. He didn't like surprises so he'd had Shimon's every movement monitored since his arrival. It was obvious that the boy lacked the basic skills to survive. And, having heard the ravings of the feverish prisoner, Licinius knew the lad didn't have the courage to kill himself. However, Licinius had secured a deal with the businessmen that he'd met with the magistrate. He knew that Shimon could earn him serious money. It had to be worthwhile enrolling the boy in a brief course of training. Also, the previous games had seriously depleted Licinius's stock of prime fighters and he didn't know when he would be called on to provide the next show.

'All that snivelling. I knew you couldn't do it,' the trainer said. He slid his finger across his throat. 'You haven't got the guts.'

Shimon tried but couldn't muster the strength to lift his head to see who was talking to him. He thought that he'd heard the distinctive gruff voice somewhere before, but in his delirious state he couldn't remember when or where it might have been.

'What do they call you? Come on, boy, I haven't got all day,' the *lanista* demanded.

Shimon sensed by the man's tone that he was no ordinary guard but a person of higher authority.

Completely naked, he got onto his knees and, holding on to the bars for support, slowly dragged himself to his feet. 'My master named me Simon,' he replied in no more than a whisper, his head bowed.

'Now that's not a very Jewish name, is it?' the trainer said, opening the door to the cell. 'This place smells worse than the bloody sewers and by the look of it there's twice as much shit in here.' Gaius Licinius covered his mouth. 'You've had long enough to get comfortable, so get yourself cleaned up and get some clothes. If you're nice and friendly to the storekeeper, he'll sort out something for you. We get all shapes and sizes in here. Some of them have hardly been worn! You don't have any objection to wearing a dead man's clothes, do you?'

Shimon remained upright as the trainer ran his large hands up and down his legs and arms and then over the front and back of his body.

'You're too thin,' the *lanista* said. 'But otherwise, you'll do. No deformities. Nothing that'll stop you fighting.' He laughed cruelly. 'If there had been, you'd be no use to me. You'd just be taking up valuable space. I've seen worse,' he concluded and walked out of Shimon's cell. He slammed the door shut and locked it, then spoke through the bars.

'You're going to be Solly from now on – or for the short time you're still breathing, that is,' the *lanista* informed him. 'Haven't had a Solly before. Perhaps it'll bring me some good fortune.'

Shimon looked at him blankly.

'Your kind, you Jew boys, never seems to fare too well in here. Must be the food that disagrees with you. Sleep well.'

Gaius Licinius disappeared to his own quarters on the floor above for his evening meal.

Shimon ran his hands methodically across the contours of his body, just as the trainer had done. He looked down in horror at his protruding ribs. His previously athletic legs now resembled puny stalks of barley. He was disgusted with himself for allowing his strength, which he could always rely on, to ebb away.

Shimon had lost all sense of time. He seemed to have been in the school for ever. But now he was suddenly able to think more clearly. For reasons that he didn't understand, he had come to the attention of the man in charge of this place, who had made a special effort to visit him.

Shimon was going to look for any sliver of hope to hold on to. Maybe there was a chance he would survive this place. Maybe he would finally get out and prove his innocence. But to do so, he had to pull himself out of the quagmire into which he had fallen.

The next day, Shimon, filthy, naked but with a sense of purpose, left his cell and went to the wash area to make himself look respectable. Apart from a few disparaging remarks from some of the other prisoners, he was relieved to be left alone. Rumours of his illness and his impending demise had spread through the barracks and few of the inmates would risk going near him, convinced that he would still be contagious.

Shimon started to eat again, but it took him several days before his system became used to the bulky foods that made up the inmates' diet. Gradually, he started to put back the weight he had lost and, in a few weeks, making the most of the daily exercise period, he improved his fitness.

One morning, after he'd been at the *ludus* for about a month, he entered the communal dining area. It was already full of hungry men scoffing all the food they could get their hands on. Shimon found a seat and started on his own bowl of cereal. After a few moments, he became aware of a scuffle developing at the other side of the room.

He lifted his head and saw that a fight had broken out. His young neighbour, the one who had brought him food when he first arrived, had been taken hostage by one of the other prisoners named Cassipor.

Without thinking through his actions, but sensing that he couldn't just stand by and see his neighbour so disadvantaged, Shimon got up from his place and ran over to where a small crowd had gathered, excited by the prospect of blood.

'Let him go, he's only a boy,' Shimon protested, confronting his friend's attacker.

'Keep out of my way, Jew. This is no concern of yours,' Cassipor shouted. Remnants of gruel were clinging obstinately to the sides of his mouth. 'This lad's mine.'

He had his arm around the boy's neck and was keeping three other prisoners at a distance with a blade. 'He's mine and anyone who says different will have to fight me for him,' he threatened.

Shimon picked up a wooden stool from underneath the refectory table. He moved quickly and, catching the man by surprise, struck him on the side of his head with such force that Cassipor reeled and fell to the ground.

The young boy freed himself. He didn't acknowledge Shimon or the other men, but ran off without looking back.

Shimon tried to retrieve the fallen blade but a scrawny individual with a withered arm, named Titus, got to it first.

'Grab him,' Titus shouted to Lucius, another prisoner in the group.

Lucius grabbed Shimon in an arm lock, holding him secure.

'I'm going to enjoy cutting up his pretty little face,' Titus threatened. Using his good hand, he swiped wildly at Shimon but missed his target.

Shimon struck out with his foot and Titus lost his balance. Seizing his opportunity, Shimon turned and used his free hand to squeeze his captor's testicles with all his strength. Lucius shrieked in agony and released his grip. Shimon, ignoring the jeers from the increasing number of prisoners who'd come to watch the fight, approached Titus – who was still intent on harming him.

'It's you or me now, Jew,' Titus snarled, brandishing the blade menacingly. He spat at Shimon, emitting a stream of saliva that ran down the side of his opponent's cheek.

Shimon lost control. He leapt at the one-armed man, sending them both sprawling to the floor. Blinded by rage, he started to pummel the older man's face with his huge fists. Such was the strength of his anger, he didn't anticipate retaliation and he didn't see the blow coming that left a deep gash in his jaw.

He got to his feet, barely noticing the blood oozing from the side of his face. He looked to see if anyone else wanted to chance fighting him, but the crowd had already started to disperse, taking their injured friends with them. Despite only trying to defend the young boy from the next cell and being outnumbered, Shimon was blamed for starting the fight. None of the prisoners who had witnessed the episode would defend him. Shimon was carted off to the dungeons. The *lanista* sentenced him to two weeks' solitary confinement.

Using every inch of the cramped space to exercise and maintain his physical condition, Shimon found that the time passed quickly. Even though he had to endure reduced rations, he managed to retain his high spirits. He knew that although the incident in the dining room had left him wounded and led to his punishment, it had raised his stature in the school. The other prisoners had seen him defend himself. They wouldn't be so quick to attack him again.

At the end of his sentence, Shimon was released from the dungeon and strolled confidently back to his own cell. The boy he had rescued was sitting on his bed in the next cell with a vacant expression on his face. His lack of gratitude – of any kind of response – dampened Shimon's good humour. 'I suppose that you want me for yourself now,' the boy whispered.

'What do you mean?' Shimon replied.

'The rest of them don't want anything more to do with me.'

'I thought you'd be pleased I got Cassipor away from you.' Shimon peered through to the bars of the adjoining cell.

'What? You think you've done me a favour? How do you think I've managed to stay alive in here for the past three years?' The boy's voice was full of anger and frustration.

'I don't understand,' Shimon replied.

'It's only because I gave them what they wanted. That's the only reason that bastard *lanista* left me alone,' the younger man continued. 'I was their whore, see. But now they'll think I'm yours. They'll soon get their hands on a new boy and then I'll be disposed of, or worse, torn to pieces in the arena. And I'm not even fifteen!' He started to sob.

'I didn't realise,' Shimon replied.

'You should have left me alone,' the boy whimpered, tears running down his face.

'But they might have killed you!' Shimon protested, raising his voice.

'What do you care, anyway?'

'I can protect you.'

'That's what you all say, until it's your time to leave this world. That's why it's safer for me to spread myself around.'

A moment of silence followed.

'You have my word,' Shimon said, suddenly feeling a strong attachment to the boy in the next cell. 'I won't let anything happen to you.'

7

SHIMON AND HIS young friend, Socrates, became inseparable. They sat next to each other for their meals. Apart from receiving a few crude remarks from the other prisoners, they ate in silence. They were together at exercise time, remaining apart from those inmates whom they suspected would harm them. Most of the fights between prisoners took place at the shared washing facilities and Shimon made it his business not to let his ward out of his sight. He had learnt by past experience that it only took the briefest of moments for trouble to erupt and for a man to end up spreadeagled, moaning on the stone floor, blood gushing from a wound.

Even with the precautions that they took, resentment was growing against Shimon. His relationship with the barrack favourite was the main topic of conversation amongst the other prisoners. It had been blown out of all proportion, of course, to stimulate their vivid imaginations.

'Here, Solly, so how did you get caught?' Socrates whispered in the dark from the other side of the thin wall that separated them.

'What do you mean?' Shimon replied, half asleep.

'Well, I don't suppose, like me, it was for stealing a paltry amount of food from your master because you were hungry.'

'And you're telling me that you got sent here just for that?' Shimon asked, sitting up, astounded at what his young friend had revealed to him for the first time.

'The master threw us out, my mother, father and my four younger brothers. But because I was the one the cook saw helping myself to the kitchen stores, the master gave me special treatment. I can still see him gloating, the mean bastard. "Right Socrates," he says, "it's prison for you." But the prisons were all full, see. They didn't know what else to do with me so I ended up in here.'

Despite his lack of years, Socrates showed surprising promise as a fighter and was particularly adept with the net and dagger. Gaius Licinius immediately saw his potential; this under-age boy in the arena would cater to the more perverse tastes of the crowd. Young flesh was always a popular draw. Licinius made Socrates take the *Sacramentum Gladiatorum*, the gladiators' oath, which bound him to the school and forced his consent to die by the sword in the arena.

Licinius's motives were driven by Socrates' beauty. Within days, the boy was forced to provide sexual favours to some of the more implacable prisoners. They wouldn't react kindly to their favourite being removed and killed, so the *lanista* decided to delay the boy's entry into the arena. Worse still, he had denied Socrates the chance to hone his fighting skills, thus making him unfit for the task should he eventually have to enter the arena.

Shimon believed that he had been in the school for one hundred and twenty days .He had settled into the routine. His physique had been restored to its former strength and his shaven head accentuated his sharp features; in his regulation woollen tunic, he was indistinguishable from all the other prisoners.

But he was not the same as them. Deprived of the closeness of a family, more than anything else Shimon wanted to belong – even if it was as part of this group of dysfunctional individuals whose life he now shared. However, his attempts to integrate were treated with indifference; they made the other men distrust him. In his desire to belong, he had again misjudged his contemporaries' feelings.

The rains had come and the cold mercilessly penetrated the porous walls of the barracks. Shimon had had enough of trying to keep warm, of the boredom, of the interminable routine. He was impatient for his chance to prove his fighting capabilities.

For a few nights he felt particularly unsettled. He was disturbed by something that had taken place: prisoners considered unsuitable to fight were rounded up and led away under guard. Shimon knew that they would never return. There had been a cull of the weakest in this strange and limited society. There would be many more such culls.

Now, surrounded by the thunderous sound of snoring from those who remained, Shimon was fully awake. He wondered what nasty surprises awaited him and whether he too would be taken in the middle of the night to be disposed of. A visit from Gaius Licinius was, therefore, the last thing he wanted.

The trainer was unsteady on his feet as he shuffled up to Shimon's cell. His unkempt appearance and stale breath showed that he had been drinking heavily.

'Now Solly,' he began, oblivious to the fact that he was shouting, 'unlike those other poor bastards who are probably already dead and buried, I'm giving you a chance to save yourself.'

Shimon got up to face the *lanista*, hoping that at last his moment had arrived.

'We're going to give you a sword,' Licinius said. He lurched slightly, and then straightened. 'Now you'd better be careful, because it might hurt someone.' Then he let out a huge roar of laughter.

Shimon's hopes were immediately extinguished. He was convinced that he must be the subject of some cruel joke.

'So if I was you,' the trainer continued, 'I'd stop feeling sorry for myself and get my nose stuck into some of that lovely fodder.

You need to keep your strength up. I want to see you at first light, beating the hell out of that wooden training post.'

'But I've never used a sword before,' Shimon protested.

'At the end of which,' the trainer continued, ignoring him, 'I'll know whether I've got a fighter I can use or whether you'll end up like those other useless bastards in an early grave.'

Shimon realised that he had no choice. He was being given an opportunity to establish himself. He should accept and say that he was ready for any challenge. But something altogether different came out of his mouth.

'I'm innocent,' he exclaimed. 'I shouldn't even be here!'

The *lanista* belched. 'That's not what I hear,' he replied, uninterested. He turned to leave.

'But the charges were all lies! I never did what they said!' Shimon shouted after him.

The trainer stopped, turned around and went back slowly to Shimon's cell. 'Oh, don't tell me … Did they have a grudge against you?' Licinius asked sarcastically, holding on to the bars to stop himself from falling over.

'It wasn't my fault,' Shimon continued. 'The mistress … she … she wanted me …' The events of that terrible evening came flooding back to him.

'Look at it this way, Solly,' the trainer said. 'If you were a slave at your master's house and suddenly you see this handsome young lad enter, uninvited, into your domain, you're not going to be too happy. Then, that young man grabs the most desirable fruit for himself and struts round like he owns the place. Now be reasonable, how would you feel?'

Shimon had stopped listening. He was back in the house, standing accused in front of the governor. A wave of intense anger enveloped him. He wanted to strike out and take his revenge on the back-stabbers who had ganged up on him.

'Will you help me?' he asked of no one in particular. He was so engrossed in his own thoughts that he'd forgotten that the trainer was still there.

'Looks like I already have,' Gaius Licinius replied loudly, managing to attract Shimon's attention. 'You're safer in here,' he added and turned to leave. 'And Solly, you ought to let the *medicus* look at that cut.'

Shimon put his hand up to his face. The wound had never healed properly and he hadn't noticed that a fresh trickle of blood was oozing from it. 'It's nothing,' he said, still troubled by the memory of his arrest.

'If you're lucky, you might even get that young girl that's just been given work. Some sort of healer – or so she says,' commented the *lanista*. 'She's a bit too thin for my liking, but I wouldn't say no. Anyway, from what I've been told, you probably only go for young boys.' Gaius Licinius sniggered. Then, letting out a loud yawn that inflated his huge body to its maximum extent, he wandered off for a few hours' sleep.

Shimon's first thoughts were to share his good fortune with Socrates but since his friend had been denied the same opportunity to fight, he would have to choose his words carefully.

Shimon tapped the code they used to communicate with each other on the wall of his cell. There was no answer. He tried again.

'Socrates!' he whispered. But there was still no reply.

Shimon stretched out on his bed, too excited to sleep. He was finally being given a chance to prove himself, to show those who had doubted that he could survive and what he was capable of.

He must have dozed off because the first thing he heard when he opened his eyes was the screeching sound of cell doors opening and then footsteps. It was morning and time for the first meal.

He called Socrates' name again but his friend didn't reply. Shimon was concerned. Had Socrates been taken in the night?

Suddenly The Beast appeared outside Shimon's cell, his powerful arm tight around the taller Socrates' neck. He thrust his heavily pockmarked face inside and stared at Shimon.

'Pining after your boy?' The Beast enquired. 'Well he's with me now. Surprising what guards will do for a few *sestertii*. I said I fancied a little late-night snack and this is what they brought me. So you don't have to worry.'

'Get your hands off him!' Shimon demanded.

The sight of his young friend imprisoned in the man's arms was too much to bear. Shimon sensed that he was beginning to lose his self-control. He moved right up to The Beast.

'What are you going to do about it, Jew?' The Beast asked. He was totally unprepared for what happened next.

Shimon went straight for the man's face and thrust his second and third fingers deep into his left eye. The Beast screamed. A stream of colourless pulp spurted out, spraying Shimon.

The injured prisoner released Socrates and fell on one knee, holding his blood-drenched face in his hands.

Socrates moved over to Shimon. Still trembling with anger, Shimon approached his victim who was sitting, dazed, on the floor. 'That was a just a warning,' he announced. 'Try touching him again, and you'll find more than just two fingers sticking into you.'

The Beast got to his feet and staggered off. Shimon, his body pumped full of adrenalin, suddenly felt ravenous.

'I should never have let you out of my sight. I should have been there to protect you,' Shimon said contritely.

'That's how it is in here and there's nothing you can do about it,' Socrates replied resignedly. 'You learn to accept it.'

Shimon entered the dining hall with Socrates a pace behind him. He was pleased to have saved his friend and well prepared for his test on the training field. He had forgotten about his own injury.

    That morning, the only patient being attended to by the *medicus* was The Beast.

8

A FEW DAYS earlier, a slight young woman, dressed in a drab, sack-like dress and with her face concealed by a scarf, entered the medical area of the training school. Nobody noticed her. Holding her hand up to her mouth to stifle the sound of her coughing, she presented her credentials to the *lanista*. She was immediately given a trial, assisting the overworked *medicus* in the infirmary dealing with a number of training-ground injuries and several stab wounds incurred by the prisoners.

The young woman was Miriam, Shimon's sister. It hadn't taken her long to trace her brother; it wasn't the first time he'd wandered off, disgruntled, in search of a better life. And since he had always boasted how easily he could earn money through his own efforts, she was not surprised when her aunt Rivka told her that he'd found a full-time position in the governor's household.

Miriam was determined that this time she would not go looking for him. She would let him seek his own destiny. So, to avoid any possibility of a family association between the old woman and her nephew, or any accusations of nepotism, it was agreed that Rivka would stop treating the governor's wife. However, one day, *Domina* Livia urgently summoned the old woman. Rivka realised that something was wrong when Shimon was nowhere to be seen. She overheard two of the kitchen slaves talking about Shimon's arrest and rushed back home to report her news.

That was four long months ago. Four months of torment, when

Miriam had to struggle to overcome her desire to be near to her beloved brother. She wondered how long it had taken Shimon to settle, and worried that he might not have the mental strength to cope with his predicament. She felt his pain and shared his suffering – but she also knew that he had to learn how to look after himself. She would not contact him until the time was right.

Miriam put down her *Tehillim*, closed her eyes and took a moment to reflect. She prayed regularly for his well-being and for the day that they would be reunited. She recalled the long distances she had travelled for her work during their separation. Blessed with the gift of foresight, she believed her brother would eventually be free to lead a long and meaningful life. Because of her frailty, she knew that she would never lead such a life herself.

Miriam looked up. The Beast was standing in front of her, groaning in agony, holding his blood-stained hand over his contorted face. He was her first patient that morning. She quickly applied a clean swab to his eye and he screamed out in agony.

'I'll kill that Jew. Just see if I don't,' he shouted, his pain flaring as she touched his wound.

Miriam continued in silence, methodically applying bandages to the man's face. She was convinced that it was Shimon to whom he was referring. She wondered what could have provoked her brother to inflict such a horrendous injury.

The Beast, still in extreme pain, tottered back to his cell. Even with the loss of an eye, he posed a threat. But the news that Shimon had beaten him that morning had already circulated through the barracks and, as a result, his influence had been irretrievably diminished.

Miriam, still shocked by The Beast's visit, entered the dining room. It was almost empty. She was conscious that she must have seemed a strange sight, a waif-like figure preparing to eat her meagre meal alone.

She had seen enough to realise that her brother's life was in danger and knew that she had to act expeditiously to try and obtain his release.

Miriam returned to work knowing that the long wait to be reunited with her brother would soon be at an end.

As instructed, Shimon was out early on the exercise field practising moves against the stocky wooden training post, determined to prove his fighting capabilities. But instead of finding a sense of purpose, feelings of injustice had started to resurface in his mind.

'Solly, I do hope that you're not going to allow that bad temper of yours to get you into trouble again,' the *lanista* said. 'If you're not careful, your first fight will more than likely be your last. Then all this training will be a waste of my time.'

'Someone needed to teach that animal a lesson and it just happened to be me,' Shimon replied, striking out aggressively. He was irritated that his routine had been interrupted again by the mention of the incident with The Beast.

'Rumour is, you attacked him because he'd taken your boy,' the *lanista* continued. He was in the mood for mischief and making Solly lose his temper again would make the day worthwhile.

Shimon struck at the post with such venom that his wooden sword broke in two, causing a deep cut to his hand.

'Socrates is nothing more than a boy. He never had a chance! You knew he was being passed around the barracks. Why didn't you help him instead of leaving him to fend for himself?' Shimon answered back, throwing the broken implement on the ground.

Once he was under Shimon's protection again, Socrates' life had been made unbearable. The other prisoners molested him purely as a means of provoking his guardian. They were too afraid to confront Shimon directly.

When Shimon was outside training, they took any opportunity to force themselves on the youth and frequently sent him back to his cell in a pitiful state, hardly able to walk. Believing that it was more than his life was worth to reveal the identities of those who had forced themselves on him, Socrates refused to say who they were. Shimon was powerless to intercede on his young friend's behalf.

One day, after being raped continually and left for dead in a pool of bloodied excrement, Socrates gave in to despair. He had had enough. He stole a dagger from the armoury stores during the evening meal. Hiding the weapon in the straw base of his bed, he stayed awake until everyone in the barracks was asleep. Intent on ending his life, he acted swiftly.

By chance, a guard found him the next morning with the blade still implanted in his neck. The rest of the cells, including Shimon's, were empty.

Wild rumours circulated that the boy had been murdered by a prisoner whose advances he had rejected. But Shimon knew that despair had driven Socrates to attempt suicide. If it hadn't been for immediate treatment by the assistant to the *medicus*, under whose supervision he now rested, Socrates would have bled to death. He wasn't aware that it was Miriam's swift reactions that saved his life.

'Listen Solly,' the trainer said, moving close to Shimon. 'I don't owe you an explanation. What I choose to do with you – or anybody else – is my business. Even if I wanted your young boy for myself, there's nothing you can do about it. Now get back to that post,' he growled.

Shimon picked up another training sword from the ground and took a vicious swipe at the trainer. Gaius Licinius displayed an agility that defied his ungainly size. He sidestepped the attack and deflected the blow to his head with his outstretched arm.

'Save it for the arena,' the *lanista* said and turned to leave.

'What are you talking about?' Shimon shouted after him.

'Hasn't anyone told you?' The trainer halted and looked around, pretending surprise. 'It's the emperor's birthday in three days' time. You're going to appear in there.' Gaius Licinius pointed to the arena hovering like a huge grey bowl beneath the gloomy sky. 'That's what all you scum want, isn't it? Well now your prayers have been answered, Solly!'

Shimon stood motionless. 'But I'm not ready,' he said, bemused.

Gaius Licinius swaggered over to Shimon, enjoying his discomfort. 'So I'd be more careful with that big mouth of yours, if I were you. Accidents have happened unexpectedly before the games. You'd better watch your back because you never know who might be lurking in the shadows,' he added with a cruel smile.

Shimon felt his energy ebb away.

'But I've already told you, I shouldn't even be in here,' he protested.

'Guilty, innocent, it's all the same to me,' the *lanista* announced. 'I've got a job to do, see, to provide a tasty spectacle for our discerning public. And if we don't want a riot, I have to make sure they don't feel cheated. So get back to work.'

Licinius put his arm around Shimon with a false show of affection. Then he pointed out a large figure in the distance and said, 'Make sure that you make him sweat before your friend over there decides to end your misery. Oh, I almost forgot,' he added with a contrived look of concern. 'I do hope that you're not going to be asking for special treatment on account of fighting on your Sabbath?'

'Makes no difference to me,' Shimon replied, his gaze fixed on the man who was going to be his first opponent.

'Well, you can never tell with you people,' the *lanista* quipped, and sauntered away from the training grounds.

Later, Shimon was escorted back to the barracks. In a few days, he would be centre stage in the arena, fighting for his life in front of an audience of thousands, all thirsting for blood. He would face a man of far greater experience who would show him no mercy. Only a short time before, he had been determined to avenge those responsible for his young friend's attempt on his own life. Now, as he re-entered the gloomy atmosphere of the barracks and experienced the deafening tumult of men waiting for their evening meal, his mood changed. Ravenous from the day's exploits, Shimon ate alone, not an unusual occurrence since Socrates had been confined to the medical section.

He was so preoccupied with his own prospects that he didn't notice how badly he'd injured his hand when the training sword broke. The skin was flayed and the wound needed medical attention.

In an attempt to clean the wound, he went to the wash area. There he caught sight of the *lanista*, loitering suspiciously.

'Solly, I don't like the look of that,' Licinius bellowed, casting his eye over Shimon's swollen hand. 'I'll get that young woman from the *medicus* to see what she can do for you. Wouldn't be surprised if she was one of your lot,' he continued. 'She does a lot of chanting and praying. Not that it'll do her much good in here.'

On the way back to his cell, Shimon couldn't help thinking that in his eagerness to prove his worth as a gladiator, he'd hastened his own demise. Was he now entering the last days of his life? How stupid he had been in believing that the *lanista* had selected him for special treatment. He was being used, no differently from the rest. He was there merely to make money for the trainer and for those who made a business out of arranging death contests.

Gazing in at the empty cell next to his own, Shimon missed his friend but admitted that the lad was safer under the supervision of the *medicus*. As long as he was there, he wouldn't be able to do any more harm to himself. And he wouldn't be set upon again by the other prisoners.

It had not been one of his better days. Shimon breathed deeply and stretched out his tired frame on the hard bed. His body ached and his hand throbbed but, as he ran his good hand down his muscular arms and powerful legs, he felt strong. Just as he was about to doze off he smiled, recalling the earlier incident with the *lanista*.

If that bastard thought he was going to just lie down and die without a fight, he was making a big mistake. If he had to prove his value, then he would summon all his strength not to disappoint the crowd.

❧

It was late by the time Miriam, armed with her bag of bandages and ointments, left her small room. She was carrying a candle to light the way to the barracks that housed her brother. In order to avoid the other prisoners' attention, she needed to make the journey as swiftly as possible. Even though she'd obtained her orders directly from the *lanista*, she didn't trust him.

So as not to attract attention to herself, she waited for the changeover of the guards on sentry duty. Aware that she might be putting her life in danger moving through a block full of voracious men, she knew she had to make the visit unaccompanied.

Shivering in the cold of the night, Miriam walked quickly through the intricate network of dimly-lit corridors. She had spent such a long time thinking about the things that she wanted to say to her brother to restore the closeness between them. But although her prayers had been answered and they would be with each other again, she realised that she could never disclose the true reason why she had to remain apart from him. One day she hoped that he would understand that her actions had been for his benefit. She just prayed that she could now find the right words to say to him and that they would be well received.

'Shimon!' He heard his name being whispered.

'Shimon!' he heard again. 'It's me! Miriam!' Her small face peered through the bars of the cell door.

Shimon, who had rolled onto his injured hand in his sleep, groaned in agony. Then he opened his eyes and looked up. At first he thought he was dreaming.

'Miriam! Is that really you?' he whispered. 'How did you find me?'

'I came as soon as I could,' Miriam replied, relieved that the darkness concealed the tears that filled her eyes.

Shimon got up from his bed to face his sister.

'I thought that I'd never see you again,' Shimon said.

'The sick needed me,' Miriam began hesitantly. 'I had responsibilities and Aunt Rivka is no longer a young woman.'

She reached for her brother's hand and pulled it gently towards her, carefully applying several of the ointments that she was carrying.

'It was all lies,' Shimon started to explain, wincing in pain from even the slightest touch. 'What they said about the mistress and me. None of it was true.'

'The moment I found out what had happened to you,' Miriam continued, winding several layers of cotton gauze around the wound, 'and realised the danger you were in, I managed to find work with the *medicus* so that I could be near you.' She finished wrapping his hand. 'That should make it feel better. Just keep it covered to give the ointments a chance to work. I haven't got much time. I need to get back before the new guard takes over.'

'I never did what they said, you must believe me,' Shimon

pleaded, desperate for her to believe him. She was his sister, the only person who truly loved him. It was important that she realised that he was innocent.

'You mean about forcing yourself on *Domina* Livia?' Miriam replied.

'How did you know?' Shimon asked, surprised.

'Meaningless gossip,' Miriam responded. 'It's of no consequence. The important thing is that you try and remember everything that happened, even the smallest details, so that I can work on a plan to get you released. We have to move quickly. Now I must leave.'

Under the pretext of packing her bag, Miriam reached into the pocket of her tunic and pulled out a small quantity of silver *denarii*, which she pushed beneath the straw mattress. Shimon would find the coins the next morning; she was sure that he would find a way of putting them to good use.

'They're making me fight, the day after tomorrow,' Shimon said despairingly.

'You must have faith,' Miriam whispered as she was about to depart. 'And most important of all, don't give up on yourself. Remember,' she said, casting her eyes upward, 'there are powers that recognise the injustice you have suffered.'

Miriam passed speedily back through the barracks of sleeping men. She entered her tiny room next to the infirmary and, unable to control herself any longer, began to weep. She had tried to remain strong in front of her brother but the same forlorn look in his eyes, that she remembered so well when their father had beaten him, cut through her like a knife. She just wanted to be able to hold him in her arms and comfort him. To tell him that despite his terror of the ordeal that awaited him, she knew that he would prevail.

Perhaps if she had been there to support him more at home,

he wouldn't have felt so resentful and wouldn't have run off again. She berated herself for not going after him immediately and persuading him to return home. She had not warned him of the likely consequences of entering the governor's household, going into a foreign environment where he was unwanted; where people would take advantage.

Ignoring her tiredness, Miriam passed the remaining hours before daybreak praying for her brother's forgiveness. Let her be granted the opportunity to redeem herself and secure his release.

〰️

Shimon's mood had changed. He lay down on his bed feeling strangely serene. He examined his neatly bandaged hand and smiled as he thought of his sister.

He didn't know if or when Miriam would return but he felt more secure knowing that he was no longer alone.

9

ANTHONY PULLED BACK the thick cover from under his chin and, taking care not to disturb his lover, removed his naked body from the bed. He moved stealthily over to the washstand, enjoying the warm air from the hearth below that had risen through the floor and was permeating the master chamber.

Despite Livia's protestations, he never stayed the whole night, preferring to return to his unit where he needed to consolidate his position as its supreme commander. He also had no desire to be the subject of slaves' gossip or to provoke Quintus Flaccus. Flaccus was a tricky problem; Anthony had engineered the governor's frequent absences so that he could become more intimate with Livia. However, he needed to ensure that the governor still revered him and remained indebted to him.

Anthony and Livia's liaison had started soon after that first dinner. Anthony smiled complacently as he splashed water over his face. The woman was now completely smitten with him; she was already talking about divorcing her husband so she could commit herself completely to her handsome new lover.

Anthony had kept his part of the bargain with her father, Marcus Praeconinus; he had managed to reinstate the smooth flow of future consignments of merchandise to Rome and had also seduced Livia. That had enabled him to obtain a firm grasp of her father's extensive business interests in the east.

More importantly, Anthony's own interests were thriving

and he was generating even more money, raking off substantial amounts from Praeconinus's business. Anthony had established himself as the most powerful man in the province.

Anthony knew that this period of calm was only temporary. The rains had already arrived; it wouldn't be long before bad weather devastated the crops that Rome relied on for its food supply. The plebs would once again be hungry and would vent their anger. Because of Anthony's unrivalled position in the army, and his almost complete control of the trade routes from the East, the Senate would have no alternative but to remove the Emperor Germanicus and appoint Anthony in his place.

In the meantime, he had no reason not to continue to enjoy Quintus Flaccus's hospitality – and the affections of his wife. Anthony smiled again as he started to dress, thinking how easy it had been to persuade the idiot governor. All he'd needed to do was to advise Flaccus that arranging the *ludi* in celebration of the emperor's birthday would be seen as a show of strength and would help to reaffirm his position as governor. The fool had no idea that the money for the three-day spectacle had been provided from the percentage that had been raked off Marcus Praeconinus's business; nor did he suspect that his wife Livia had been instrumental in facilitating the project by bribing the authorities.

Anthony had told Flaccus that he would attend the games as guest of honour so that his presence as the games' promoter would predispose the people to his coronation as emperor. He also intended to enjoy the huge amounts of money that he would make from the gambling activities that he organised outside the arena.

Livia sat up, allowing the covers to fall away and reveal her full breasts.

'Must you leave already?' she asked. 'Are you sure that I can't tempt you to stay?' Beckoning him back to her bed, she exposed her body completely to him.

Anthony glanced at her and smiled, but made no attempt to accept her offer. 'I have to get back to my regiment,' he replied. 'And remember, your husband is returning this morning. It would ruin our plans if he saw us together.'

'May he choke on his own shit,' Livia said angrily. 'Don't you understand? I love you!'

'And I love you, but if you want to be the emperor's wife, you'll need to be patient for a little longer. The gods are with us. Soon we'll be together and you'll never have to see Quintus Flaccus again.'

'What will happen to him?' Livia enquired.

'The assassin's knife can be bought without any questions being asked. If it's suddenly revealed that he is a practising Christian, there won't be too many people upset by his sudden demise.'

'But I thought that you were in favour of the Christians being free to worship that new religion of theirs,' Livia said. She was disconcerted by his sudden coldness; she hadn't realised that her lover was capable of such ruthlessness. She sat back against the pillows and looked closely at him. Perhaps she would have to be a little more careful.

'Nothing – and no one – will be allowed to separate us,' Anthony said.

He would do anything to get what he wanted. Perhaps she'd been unwise to divulge so many details of her father's business. Anthony would have no compunction in using the information to further his own interests.

Anthony finished putting on his uniform and was about to leave. Livia threw back the bedcovers and pulled her cotton tunic on over her head. She wanted to be sure that her lover hadn't detected any uncertainty in her so she decided to accompany him.

Together, they passed silently through the villa as daybreak approached. At the gate, they parted without the usual warmth. They were unaware that Quintus Flaccus had already returned and was praying with several other worshippers in the house church below.

Livia returned to a small private room separate from her bedchamber, where she knew she wouldn't be disturbed. She needed to think. She sat down at a dressing table and began applying a thick layer of whitener to her face. Had she become embroiled in something that, even for her, was too dangerous? Could she cope with such an unpredictable and ruthless man as Anthony? She knew that she was so deeply in love with him that she couldn't allow any feelings of doubt to linger. And she longed for another child.

Livia thought about her daughter Julia. How cruel it was that she had been sent away. She calculated that the girl would now be sixteen. She was sure that Julia was beautiful and prayed that her former husband, Lucilius, would be able to make her daughter understand that she, Livia, had been at the mercy of her father. She was powerless to overturn his decision about the divorce.

She wanted to give Anthony a son but, since she had placed the curse on Quintus Flaccus, the gods had punished her and her menses had ceased. Livia was desperate to rectify the situation.

She held up the hand mirror after giving her face a final examination and got up from her stool, determined to summon Rivka, the midwife. In order to avoid suspicion, she would have to trick her husband into believing that she wanted to have his child. The thought of having Flaccus anywhere near her was revolting but she would do anything to keep Anthony.

Livia summoned the young Greek houseboy who had been employed as her new personal slave. 'Have you found the old woman?' she asked curtly.

'*Domina*, there's still no news of the Jew's whereabouts,' the boy replied. He lowered his head, fearing that he have to bear the responsibility for the old woman's disappearance.

Livia was frantic because Rivka was the only person who might provide a cure. 'Surely you don't expect me to go their village and find her myself, do you?' she shouted. 'Get out of my sight.'

Her raised voice created such a disturbance that it attracted the attention of her husband. His suggestion of finding an alternative midwife was met with so much abuse from Livia that he was seen running from her chamber in fear of his life.

For the next few days, Livia refused to leave her bed until Rivka was brought to her. Rumours about their mistress circulated amongst the slaves. They speculated that evil spirits were consuming her body and that she was slowly succumbing to their will. More seriously, Anthony had stopped visiting. Did he already know that she was unable to bear him children?

The truth was that Anthony preferred the company of her husband, Quintus Flaccus. Together they fraternised with the officials who would be responsible for making the forthcoming games a success.

※

The evening before the games, Anthony, heavily disguised and accompanied by his closest business associates, entered the streets. Crowds of excited people congregated in front of the posters that advertised the following day's games and depicted images of the contestants. The sounds of voices taking bets and money changing hands rang out around the walls of the arena.

Anthony and his men entered the *ludus* through a side entrance. They continued to the first floor of the building for a brief audience with the *lanista*, Gaius Licinius.

'*Salve!*' Gaius Licinius called out to the same men that he'd met four months previously with the magistrate. 'It's good to see you again. Come and have some wine,' he added, already unsteady on his feet. 'You have the whole evening to inspect your merchandise – if they haven't eaten themselves to death first.'

Anthony looked disdainfully at the repugnant individual, thinking that in his festive clothes, he resembled a circus promoter rather than the trainer of gladiators. He immediately regretted that they had done business with the *lanista*. The man couldn't be trusted.

'We haven't got much time,' Anthony replied, trying to make himself heard over the noise of the men below fighting to take their places at the long wooden tables, laden with piles of food and wine.

'I think you'll be happy. We've laid on some juicy contests,' the *lanista* said. He pointed out some of the pairs of fighters who were taking full advantage of the *Cena Libera*. 'The plebs won't feel cheated either, not once they've first been warmed up with a few tasty beast fights.'

Anthony and his associates looked down on the packed dining hall at those who would provide the following day's entertainment. After a few minutes, they departed. Anthony was satisfied. If the men he'd seen attacked each other with the same enthusiasm as the dinner that they'd just demolished, the crowd would not be disappointed by the spectacle.

Anthony left by the same entrance. When they were out of sight of the *ludus*, they discarded their disguises, changed back into their normal clothes and went to a nearby inn for dinner. Anthony considered making his excuses and passing the remainder of the night with Livia. But, remembering that her husband was in residence, he decided instead to accompany his friends for an evening's entertainment at a nearby brothel.

10

SHIMON WAS IN a subdued mood when he found the last place available in the overcrowded dining hall. He had passed the morning on the training field, still preoccupied with seeing Miriam. He felt comforted that at last there was someone who genuinely wanted to help him – even if, as he suspected, she didn't believe totally in his account of his innocence. But he didn't share her belief that her prayers would save him; he knew that salvation would only come from his own efforts.

The atmosphere in the room was a mixture of wild expectation and fear. For many, the waiting was the worst part; realising that each day might be their last. Now, apart from those poor souls who were unfit to fight and whose fate had already been decided, the men, including Shimon, were relieved that their chance had finally come to determine their own destiny.

'Lost your appetite?' a voice growled.

Shimon looked at the man sitting opposite him and recognised Cassipor, who he had tried to prevent from harming Socrates. He remained silent, not wishing to get involved in another incident.

'Don't see why I should care, it's more for me.' The man started eating his way through the huge pile of food laid out in front of him.

'First time is it?' Cassipor asked, appearing not to hold a grudge from the wound Shimon had inflicted to his head. 'Take my advice,' he continued with his mouth full. 'Shovel it in. You'll thank me tomorrow – if you're still breathing, that is.' Then he roared with laughter, splattering remnants of partly chewed food in Shimon's direction.

'Help yourself,' Shimon responded, pushing his own plate towards Cassipor. 'I've been crapping myself since I found out who I'm fighting.' He turned and pointed at his opponent who was sitting at the next table.

Cassipor peered in the same direction. 'You're going to have a treat with him,' he said with satisfaction. 'Shame to waste a pretty boy like you on a piece of dung like that. But don't worry, he'll probably finish you off quickly.'

Shimon realised that he was unlikely to learn anything useful about his opponent. 'So how many have you got through?' he enquired.

'I've lost count,' Cassipor answered, more interested in the new pile of food. 'Anyway, it's of no consequence; I've been damned to die by the sword, so it's only a question of time.'

'What did you do?' Shimon asked.

'I poisoned my master and the rest of his poxy family,' Cassipor said dispassionately. 'He treated his dogs better than us. Death was too good for the lot of them. May they all drown in their own urine, that's what I say,' he concluded, and spat on the floor.

'I'm innocent, I shouldn't even be here,' Shimon announced, surprising himself by his unexpected outburst.

'Listen, pretty boy,' the man said, leaning towards Shimon. 'I've had my eye on you. How about you and me have a friendly game of dice? Unless you can think of something else that I might prefer,' he added suggestively.

Shimon realised that he had underestimated Cassipor's determination to get revenge. He knew that it was highly unlikely that he would leave the table unscathed.

'Got any money on you?' Cassipor asked.

Shimon shook his head.

'That's a pity,' the man snarled. He grabbed hold of Shimon's arm with one hand, while producing a thin sharp blade from the inside of his boot with the other. He pressed the blade against Shimon's face.

'Now you wouldn't want to change your mind, by any chance?' Cassipor asked.

Shimon reached into his pocket and touched the coins that he had found beneath his mattress. He had no idea where they had come from. Wrapping his free hand around them, he felt relief as he pulled out the entire quantity of silver *denarii*.

'That's better!' Cassipor responded. He pulled the blade away from Shimon, placing it on the table. Then he produced a cup and three dice from the inside of his tunic, together with his own fistful of coins.

'The best of three, highest numbers win,' Cassipor declared. 'I can't be fairer than that, can I?'

A small crowd had immediately gathered to watch the game. Cassipor placed the dice in the cup, shook it purposefully and, with a flick of the wrist, sent the three wooden cubes rolling down the table. 'Two fours and a three,' he exclaimed. He handed the cup and dice to Shimon.

Shimon calmly picked up the dice and caressed them in the palm of his hand before placing them in the shaker and rolling them onto the table. Suddenly his apprehension had been replaced with a resolute determination to win.

'Three fours! I don't believe it!' Cassipor shouted. 'Must be Jew's luck.'

The onlookers sniggered.

Angrily, Cassipor grabbed the dice. Without warning, he sent the dice spinning out of their holder. 'Two fours and a six. Go on, pretty boy, beat that,' he challenged.

Shimon, unperturbed and oblivious to the wild glares of the man opposite him, picked up the container and the three dice and in a quick action, rolled them.

'Eighteen. I think I win,' he said coolly. He sat back impassively. Slowly the meaning of his words registered and he felt an enormous release of tension.

The look on Cassipor's face suddenly changed to one of fear. 'Three sixes,' he whispered. '*Fortuna* is with you. You're a bad omen! Stay away from me.' He dismissed the cup and dice with a swipe of his hand. Snatching his blade, he got up from the table and ran off without looking back at Shimon or at the crowd that had already started to disperse.

Shimon drew the pile of coins towards him, realising that he was an easy target for any of the spectators who were still lingering in the corners of the dining hall. He needed to find a safe place to hide his winnings. Trying not to attract attention to himself, he placed the money inside his tunic.

The win had lifted his spirits and increased his confidence. Maybe he would survive tomorrow's battle. He had, however, given no further thought to the source of the money that he had been able to stake. It didn't occur to him that Miriam's influence had already begun to help his cause.

Shimon strode hastily back to his cell. He was astonished to find that Socrates had returned and was sound asleep, stretched out in his own cell. Not wishing to disturb him, Shimon placed half the coins in a cavity in the wall. Then he packed the hole with loose debris to hold them secure. The rest he placed under the straw covering of his bed.

Shimon was desperate to find out why his friend had reappeared without notice. 'Socrates, it's me, Solly,' he whispered, tapping on the wall to try to get his attention.

The boy stirred but didn't raise his head. 'It makes no difference to me,' he said.

'I was worried about you,' Shimon said emotionally. 'No one knew what had happened to you. I didn't expect to see you again. I thought that you'd died.' Tears formed in his eyes.

'You needn't have bothered,' Socrates replied, his voice flat. 'I'm being looked after, see. So the last thing I need is you complicating things.'

'But I thought we were friends.'

Socrates got up abruptly. 'Look, Solly,' he said. 'You've done me no harm but you're not liked in here. There are plenty who'd be happy to see you dead. So instead of worrying about me, you'd be wise to watch your own back because no one's going to risk their life for you.'

Shimon sat down on his bed. He couldn't understand why the person that he cared so much for had, for no apparent reason, turned against him. He thought about what he might have done to cause his friend's change in attitude. They had been such close friends. They ate their meals and exercised together. They knew everything about each other and had shared their hopes and dreams. There was just that one morning, when the *lanista* had summoned him so that he wasn't there when Socrates tried to take his own life. Was that the reason for his friend's coldness?

Shimon fell asleep, chiding himself for not being there to protect his friend when he needed him. He would try his best and atone for the wrong that he had done to him. But that could only happen if he survived the next day's contest. Now he had an even greater determination to succeed.

11

''Ere, Solly! Get off your arse!' the *lanista* bellowed through the bars of Shimon's cell.

'What's the hour?' Shimon replied, still groggy from sleep.

'If you've got any sense, you don't want to go missing the first meal of the day. And I thought you might want to say goodbye to that friend of yours; you know, the one you had such good neighbourly relations with? No bloody use for me with only the one eye. It's a good thing he'll be carried out of the arena because, when the lions are finished with him, he'll have no chance of finding his own way to the cemetery,' the *lanista* joked. 'So move yourself, unless you want to join that useless bunch of bastards that are only good enough for animal fodder.'

Shimon lifted himself off his bed. The image of The Beast's soon-to-be dismembered body flashed through his mind. It hadn't occurred to him that his actions in disfiguring the man would be responsible for his death that morning. He shuddered at the prospect. But The Beast would only be the first of many victims, if he was ever going to be free.

'Anyway, Solly, you've still got young Socrates to talk to if you get lonely,' Gaius Licinius remarked, casting his gaze to the adjoining cell. 'Just make sure you don't get too friendly. See, he's found himself another admirer who wouldn't be too happy if he found out that you were interfering in his private business.'

Gaius Licinius departed, not bothering to look in at Socrates who, as he was playing no part in the day's festivities, remained asleep.

The dining hall was subdued that sunny winter's morning, in contrast to the boisterous atmosphere of the previous night's feast. Shimon had awoken troubled from another broken night's sleep. Faceless images of blood-drenched men still haunted him. In his dreams, they were chasing him from different directions and mocking him. His sister Miriam suddenly appeared, dressed in fine cotton clothes with her hair plaited and her face heavily made up. She was orchestrating the hunt; when he was surrounded and pushed to the ground, pleading for mercy, she pointed her thumb in the direction that signified death. He had awoken in a sweat, not knowing where he was, and thinking that he was again at home with his family.

He wanted to find Miriam and tell her, as he had when they were children, about the nightmares that terrified him, left him distraught and unable to get back to sleep. She had always been there to comfort him and was the only person who could relieve his torment. But she was with him again now, he remembered. Just knowing that she really loved him had given him the strength to overcome the intolerable waiting of the last few days. In a few hours, she would be with him as he faced the biggest challenge of his life. Shimon, his stomach unable to contemplate the prospect of food, rushed again to the latrines to relieve the tension that had been building inside him. But he knew that he had to force himself to eat so that his energy wouldn't be impaired and would sustain him through the coming ordeal.

The alleys around the arena were already full of people. In the early morning sun there was a party atmosphere, long before the official opening of the spectacle. Aromas from the numerous food stalls selling breads, fish, meats and cheeses pervaded the small area. Street vendors selling trinkets and souvenirs commemorating the occasion were doing good business. Some individuals were taking bets on the forthcoming contests, surrounded by excited crowds of people suddenly eager to part with their money. They already had their tickets for the three-day event, and they wanted to indulge themselves in any way that helped them to escape the misery of their mundane lives. Their mood was heightened by the musicians and acrobats, conspicuous in their colourful tunics, whose singing and dancing contrasted perversely with the displays of cruelty and human suffering which were about to commence.

Shimon joined the rest of the band of fighters as the procession gained momentum through the crowded streets. This was the public's chance to see all the gladiators who were going to provide their entertainment, and they took every opportunity to jeer or shout support to the fighters. Men bearing placards providing details of the contestants helped them decide where their loyalties lay.

Shimon walked the short distance in silence, a few steps away from Darius, the man he had been paired against. He was equipped with only a short sword and arm guard; he knew that gave the other man an unfair advantage because Darius had the additional protection of a shield and helmet.

Shimon had a strange desire to talk to Darius, just for a moment, to discuss their shared predicament and to share a few words of comfort before they faced each other. Darius, with his long gangling arms and hunched shoulders, was breathing heavily. He gave Shimon a look of disdain as he approached; it was evident that the ape-like man was in no mood for pleasantries and wanted to be left alone.

The same devious magistrate who had condemned Shimon four months earlier led the procession on horseback. He was accompanied by his henchman, who carried bunches of wooden rods and an axe that symbolised the court official's authority to carry out executions.

The gladiators entered the arena to the tumultuous cheering of the crowd that occupied the upper tiers, anxious for the spectacle to start. There was a thunderous cheer when the governor, Quintus Flaccus, who was credited with arranging the games, took his seat next to Anthony, his guest of honour. Flaccus looked particularly uncomfortable as he acknowledged the crowd.

Shimon was restless, knowing that he would have to wait his turn to fight. He was grateful for the opportunity to use the time in practice fights, hoping that it would ease the stiffness in his injured hand. He entered the small exercise area where he was immediately confronted by the roar of wild animals and shouts of approval from the crowd. The beasts were descending upon the human prey that had been selected to open the day's entertainment.

Shimon shuddered at the thought of what he had been forced into. Then, while his back was turned, he felt a painful blow to his shoulder. His assailant was Darius.

'Sorry, Jew, my sword must have slipped,' Darius said, his large round face erupting into contemptuous laughter.

Shimon saw that it was only a superficial wound. His quick reflexes and the tightening of his back muscles had prevented him from suffering a more serious injury. He responded by grabbing his own sword and aiming it at Darius's head. He caught the side of his attacker's ear and the wound started seeping blood.

'Makes us even, wouldn't you say?' Shimon said, raising his weapon again in a threatening pose. He wanted to take full advantage of the man's injury.

'Solly, that's enough, you'll have plenty of time later,' Gaius Licinius shouted at him, placing the mass of his fat body between the two adversaries. He was furious that Shimon might have already jeopardised the other man's ability to fight. 'I'm contracted to provide a certain number of fighters in good condition, to give the punters what they expect, otherwise I don't get paid. So, Solly, I'm warning you, stay away from him,' the *lanista* ordered. Once again he was apportioning the blame to Shimon. 'Or,' he continued, 'you'll be joining those others who've just been fed to the lions.'

Shimon knew from past experience that the trainer enjoyed humiliating him. Even though the altercation was not his fault it was futile to protest, so he moved away, more intent than ever on proving himself in the arena. The sound of trumpets heralded the main events of the afternoon. Thousands of people responded by cheering as they eagerly awaited the arrival of the contestants.

'Right, you piles of cack,' the *lanista* bellowed. 'Move your fat arses! It's time to show what you can do.'

Shimon drifted to the front of the line. He began to shake with fear. His moment had arrived. Would he come out alive or would he be so badly injured that he would beg the executioner to end his misery? Worse, had he been deluding himself that the bastard trainer was genuinely giving him a chance? Or was he there simply to make a fool of himself as entertainment for the public?

Apprehensively, he covered the short distance into the giant cauldron of the arena. There it was, the fighting pit. Groundsmen were working feverishly, pouring a fresh covering of sand over the pungent-smelling mounds of excrement and congealed blood from its most recent occupants. As the troupe entered the packed arena, Shimon was scarcely aware of whispering under his breath the words of only prayer he knew: '*Hear O Israel, The Lord our God, The Lord is One*'.

Was it the half-forgotten words that affected him? He didn't know, but suddenly he felt calm. Then, as if grabbing on to the heel of this calmness, he experienced a sense of determination, the intensity of which he had never before experienced. Adrenalin began pumping through his veins. He knew that he would prevail.

The crowd rose to their feet while the *lanista* led in the gladiators and the referees who would exercise control over each of the contests. He asked Quintus Flaccus to check the arms that the combatants would use. Appalled by having to witness so much bloodshed, the governor passed the role to Anthony.

Quintus Flaccus felt very unwell. He had already been compelled to leave his seat several times during the proceedings to be quietly sick in the private room that had been provided for his comfort. He was finding it difficult to abide these activities that were so opposed to his Christian beliefs.

Shimon approached his taller opponent. He didn't have the same protective equipment, so he would have to strike first. The two men began to circle each other on the bed of sand, trying to assess each other and looking for the opening that would give them the advantage.

'Come on Jew, what are you waiting for?' Darius shouted. 'Unless you haven't finished crapping yourself.' He laughed, and spat in Shimon's face. The crowd, impatient for one of them to make the first move, started chanting, hoping to incite the fighters into action. Shimon didn't let them wait for long. Wiping away the man's saliva, he lashed out in a lightning strike that caught Darius unaware. It was a direct hit that severed an artery in his adversary's neck.

Darius, spurting blood from the wound, staggered unsteadily on his feet with a look of disbelief in his eyes. Shimon kicked away his opponent's shield that had fallen to the ground and, brandishing his sword in his outstretched arm, he approached his victim for the kill.

The referees, seeing that Darius's wound was too serious

for them to bother summoning the *medicus*, and anticipating Shimon's intent to inflict the decisive blow, rushed to place themselves between the two fighters. They faced the governor; it was his privilege to decide the fate of the injured man.

The crowd were on their feet. '*Iugula*! *Iugula*!' they screamed, demanding the injured fighter's death. Quintus Flaccus froze, unable to sanction the people's request. Anthony had to grab hold of the faint-hearted man's hand and force his thumb upwards, thereby acceding to the wishes of the crowd.

But Darius was not finished. Down on one knee, his whole body twitching violently, he summoned his remaining strength and stretched out his quivering arm to push Shimon's sword away.

Shimon was stunned. He picked up Darius's discarded sword as the other man, in a final act of defiance, grabbed the weapon's handle.

Spitting a mouthful of blood, Darius proclaimed out loud, 'Better to die with honour than at the hand of a Jew.' Then he plunged the blade deep into his own neck and fell, face down into the sand pit.

Shimon lifted his hand in triumph. The crowd responded with cheering and a shower of coins to show their appreciation of the drama they had just witnessed.

Quintus Flaccus presented the successful combatant with the victor's palm. Still in a daze, and not yet able to comprehend that he had won, Shimon failed to recognise the governor. He wasn't aware that it was the same man who had, without compunction, signed the order that had Shimon thrown in prison to fight for his life. Neither did he see Darius being carried out, still breathing, to be given a fatal knock on the head with a hammer by the executioner.

The crowd was now in an ecstatic frenzy, eager for more blood. They were screaming for the next contest. Shimon left the arena, looking everywhere for Miriam, with whom he wanted to share his glorious victory. She was, however, nowhere to be seen.

12

'BEGINNER'S LUCK, EH, Solly!' the *lanista* exclaimed cheerfully, pushing his thick neck through the bars of Shimon's cell. He was still dressed in his festive clothes. He had fulfilled his obligation to the organisers. The three-day event had been a huge success and he was looking forward to his payment – and hopefully a little extra as appreciation of his efforts.

Shimon, still savouring his victory, had been in an exuberant mood until he was escorted back to the confines of the barracks and the realisation that he was still a prisoner. He was angry. Miriam, when he had needed her most, had deserted him. The next time she decided to appear, he would tell her in no uncertain terms that she could go back to Aunt Rivka to tend to the sick, and leave him alone.

The only thought that comforted Shimon was that he would regain Socrates' admiration. The young boy, having heard of his victory, would now look upon him more favourably, and they could become friends again.

'He got what he deserved,' Shimon said after a few moments, not sharing the trainer's ebullience.

'Looks like you will too, unless you get that shoulder of yours patched up,' the *lanista* said. The blow from Darius's sword had flayed the skin on Shimon's back and penetrated deeper that he had realised.

'It's nothing,' Shimon answered, showing little concern.

'Where's Socrates?' He'd expected to see him in the next cell when he returned.

'This is an expensive business', Gaius Licinius replied, avoiding Shimon's question. 'I can't afford to lose any more of my best boys by being careless. I don't want to have to bring in some more Goths because they really are a bunch of animals.' He laughed, his breath reeking of wine.

'So, where is he?' Shimon asked again. Unwilling to be ignored, he squeezed his large hand through the bars and grabbed hold of the *lanista's* arm. 'Tell me,' he demanded.

There was the sound of footsteps and someone approaching. Socrates, on the way back from his evening meal, scurried past the *lanista* and, without even a cursory look at Shimon, entered his cell.

'Solly, I told you were worrying for no reason,' Gaius Licinius announced, pulling his arm free. 'I would hate to interfere,' he said sarcastically, 'so I'll let you two get reacquainted.'

Shimon, confident that he was alone, retrieved his winnings from his tunic. He searched for crevices in the walls where he could stash away the coins. What he didn't realise was that the trainer had not left but had let himself into the adjoining cell for a few intimate moments with Socrates. His needs satisfied, the *lanista* moved his sweat-covered body out of the clutches of his young lover and returned to where Shimon was busy finding a hiding place for the last few coins.

'I'll give you a day at most until you lose the lot,' the *lanista* said, looking greedily at the money.

'That's where you're wrong', Shimon answered back, wondering if despite the darkness, he had been observed. 'I plan to buy my freedom,' he continued confidently.

'I'd keep all that money hidden if I were you, unless you want your throat cut,' the trainer commented, feigning concern for his prisoner's welfare.

'And I don't suppose you'd be the one to inform on me?' Shimon replied suspiciously.

'I'm looking after your interests, Solly! Believe me!' the *lanista* said indignantly. 'I would have thought that *femina* would have at least come and offered you her congratulations,' he continued provocatively.

Gaius Licinius knew everything about those over whom he exercised control. He had established through his informers that the *medicus* had given Miriam compassionate leave. He withheld this information from Shimon because he couldn't risk his gladiator becoming demoralised; he didn't want to attract criticism for providing a disheartened fighter.

Alone in his cell, Shimon felt isolated. The buoyancy of victory had been replaced by despondency. He didn't know when he would have to face the next challenge. His sister had chosen to desert him. Locked away in a stinking cell, no better than the cages that housed the ferocious wild beasts that, like him, had fought for their lives, he no longer had anyone to feel close to.

Early the next day, Shimon's mood was improved by the appearance of an unusually agitated *lanista*. 'Solly, boy! Get up off your arse,' the trainer ordered. Despite the morning chill, pools of sweat covered his eager face. Shimon thought he was about to suffer a seizure.

'You've got an important visitor who doesn't want to be kept waiting,' Gaius Licinius declared, clearly impressed. 'He's come here just to see you!' he added, trying to contain his excitement.

Shimon, rubbing the sleep from his eyes, remained on his bed, unable to imagine who could make the trainer react with such uncharacteristic obsequiousness.

'What he wants with you, I don't know,' the *lanista* said. 'But a good word about me would be most appreciated. See if you can try and oblige me.' Gaius Licinius disappeared so that he could personally welcome the dignitary and usher him to the prisoner.

'Hello, Simon, it's good to see you again.' A high-pitched voice greeted him.

Shimon looked up from his bed. His cell had been unlocked and the individual peering in at him was the same person that he had failed to recognise the previous day. The man's distinctive scent stirred Shimon's senses. He felt a surge of blood as the memories of his arrest came flooding back. He was again facing the man who, without any evidence of wrongdoing, had taken the word of an unreliable slave and had him thrown out of the place that had been his home. And yet, for some inexplicable reason, the feelings of anger and the desire for revenge that had obsessed him for so long didn't resurface. Was his lack of feeling towards the person who had done him such harm a sign of weakness?

'And well done on your victory,' Quintus Flaccus added with contrived enthusiasm, unable to disguise his distaste for his surroundings.

Shimon felt no inclination to reply. He decided that he should wait to hear what the man had to say and learn the real purpose of the visit.

'All that blood and the cruelty to those poor defenceless animals! So barbaric, and all in the name of entertainment. It's not something that I approve of,' the governor proclaimed. His revulsion appeared genuine. 'But we know how you did it, don't we?' Quintus Flaccus gave Shimon a knowing look. 'And we know who's been looking after you, don't we?' he continued, pointing the finger bearing his signet ring high above his head.

'Sorry, sir, I really have no idea what you're talking about,' Shimon responded, thinking that the man was either drunk or had gone mad.

'Ssh!' Quintus Flaccus whispered. 'Remember, the walls have

ears. We have to be extremely careful.' His expression had become serious and his eyes were full of fear.

Shimon was convinced that he was the subject of some perverse joke. He recalled that Quintus Flaccus had been prone to sudden erratic outbursts. Perhaps he had now progressed to a level of extreme delusion.

The governor, trying not to show any reaction to the unpleasant odours emanating from the cell, approached Shimon until they were so close that they were almost touching.

'Simon, you and I have much in common,' Quintus Flaccus stated. 'It is destined that we are meant to be close friends.'

'How do you mean?' Shimon asked, bemused.

'Simon,' the governor continued, 'permit me to speak directly. You have divine protection; you walk with God.' His eyes were full of admiration.

'Divine what?'

'Simon,' repeated the governor, 'you're a Jew!'

'So I keep being reminded,' Shimon muttered.

'You don't understand', the governor said. 'You are one of the chosen. One God. Our Lord was a Jew and he had divine protection,' he whispered, hoping to establish a common bond between them.

'And what happened to him?' Shimon enquired, more out of politeness than interest.

'He was crucified,' Quintus Flaccus replied, encouraged that he had attracted Shimon's curiosity.

'I've tried my whole life to get away from abuse and contempt for being a Jew,' Shimon explained. 'And I don't want to be crucified. I'm much happier without it.'

'Simon, it's not a question of choice,' the governor retorted. 'Once a Jew, always a Jew. You're extremely lucky, and I know that we can bring each other good fortune.'

Shimon began to think that, however bizarre the circumstances seemed, he would have nothing to lose by appearing receptive to the governor's offer of friendship. It might hasten his quest for freedom and his pursuit of a pardon.

'There is, however, a matter of great sensitivity on which I require your assistance,' Quintus Flaccus announced, finally revealing the reason for his impromptu visit. His voice lowered until it was barely audible. 'I want to prove my faith. I want to be like you. Do you know anyone who might be willing to oblige me?'

'Sir, I honestly don't know what you're asking me to do,' Shimon replied, perplexed.

'Circumcised,' the governor whispered. 'I want to be circumcised. You know, without the word getting out.'

'You chose to believe the word of an illiterate bunch of slaves. You had no proof and you didn't allow me to defend myself,' Shimon retorted angrily, unable to restrain himself any longer. 'Now you want my help to get closer to the same God that put me here? What of the injustice I've had to endure?'

Quintus Flaccus reached up and placed his hand on Shimon's shoulder. 'Simon, trust me, you won't be here forever,' he said, trying to sound convincing. 'And it would cement our friendship.'

Shimon pondered for a moment. He knew that Miriam had carried out circumcisions, although on non-Jews it was strictly forbidden. But he had no idea of her whereabouts; yet again, she must have considered that there was something more important than being with him when he really needed her.

'There may be someone,' Shimon offered. The prospect of this powerful man's friendship and gratitude – and the possibility that it could lead to his freedom – was too tempting.

'When can I see him?' the governor responded, his body twitching with excitement.

'Her name is Miriam,' Shimon announced, unsure how the governor would react. 'The *medicus* will tell you where to find her.'

'A woman?' Quintus Flaccus asked, more out of surprise than prejudice. 'Isn't that a little unorthodox?'

Shimon shrugged his shoulders.

'It's of no consequence,' the governor continued. 'I'm truly indebted to you. But remember,' he put his forefinger to his lips, 'this has to remain our little secret.'

The governor, his bird-like face radiating pleasure, affectionately grabbed Shimon's wrist, then turned and glided out of the dank hovel back to the *lanista*, who had been lurking outside, attempting to glean any useful pieces of information.

13

MIRIAM HAD RECEIVED the news of her Aunt Rivka's death the day before her brother Shimon was to face the biggest challenge of his life. Fortunately, the *medicus* had taken pity on her and had persuaded the *lanista* to allow her to return to her family. However, he didn't tell Gaius Licinius that he had agreed to re-employ Miriam when she felt able to return to work.

Not for the first time, Miriam felt compromised, her loyalties challenged. She hoped that Shimon would understand that she hadn't abandoned him – even though she suspected he wouldn't. She had no doubt that he would survive the gladiatorial fight and that her prayers would be answered.

When she arrived back in her village, her aunt's body had already been taken from her home to the small piece of consecrated land where their landlord allowed the Jews to bury their dead. No longer able to await Miriam's return, the family had, in accordance with Jewish law, carried out the burial at first light the day after Rivka died. Members of the old woman's family had watched over her body throughout the night.

Miriam discovered that Rivka had, until recently, resumed treating the governor's wife. Rivka's death presented an opportunity for her to help her brother, if she could gain *Domina* Livia's confidence. Miriam knew that she had to act quickly and present her credentials as her aunt's replacement before it was too late.

At the end of the seven-day mourning period, and disregarding the chronic pain her chest, Miriam set out for the governor's mansion. In the cold February morning, her thin tunic was insufficient insulation against the biting wind that tore through her puny frame. Refusing to submit to her aching limbs, she embarked on the same two-day journey that Shimon had made nine months earlier. She struggled across same overgrown fields, her journey hampered by ground sodden from weeks of continuous rain.

She wondered what type reception she would receive and whether she would find favour with the governor's wife. How similar her concerns were, she thought, to the ones that must have plagued her brother when he wanted to build a new life for himself.

After walking for hours, Miriam was overcome by exhaustion. She'd eaten the small amount of food that she'd brought with her hours before. Then, when she thought she couldn't muster the strength to go any further, the image of Shimon languishing alone behind the bars of his dark cell flashed through her mind. It gave her a sudden surge of energy. She was the only one that he could depend upon. She couldn't fail him.

Travelling through the night, she identified a line of merchants pushing carts laden with produce. She had reached the main road south to Bosra. It was midday when she eventually saw the path that led to the governor's villa.

She was met by the *domina's* Greek servant, who had been sent out every day to wait for Rivka to arrive. He stared suspiciously at the frail young woman standing in front of him and was about to call the guards to have her thrown out, when his mistress suddenly appeared, still in her nightclothes.

'What do you want, girl?' Livia enquired, a stern expression on her face.

'I am here to present myself to *Domina* Livia,' Miriam replied, trying to regain her composure, conscious that it was the mistress that she was standing in front of.

'Who are you? Speak up!' Livia demanded.

'*Domina*,' Miriam started to explain, 'my Aunt Rivka died and there was no opportunity to get word to you.'

'That old woman was your aunt?'

Miriam nodded sadly.

'You're lying!' Livia said accusingly. 'You're just another wretch with a sad tale looking for food and shelter. Now go on your way before I let our head slave deal with you.' She started to go back inside the house.

'I have helped my Aunt Rivka treat her patients on several occasions and have learnt much from her,' Miriam announced, unwilling to be dismissed. 'My name is Miriam. I should be grateful for the opportunity to use the knowledge that I learned from my aunt.'

Livia turned around and saw that the young woman hadn't moved from the place she was standing. She paused for a moment and then her expression became more benign.

'I am sorry for your loss,' Livia replied, with genuine sympathy. Hearing her speak the old midwife's name again, she was prepared to believe that Miriam was telling the truth. 'Rivka was a good woman but I could tell the last time I saw her that her cough was worse. Come here.' She beckoned so that she could examine Miriam more closely. 'She never mentioned you. What did you say your name was, girl?'

Miriam approached the *domina* and tried to remove her shoulder bag to show that she had come prepared with medicines, but her tired legs suddenly failed her. She fell to the ground and remained motionless, breathing with difficulty.

Livia, seeing the slight figure lying prostrate at her feet, panicked. 'Bring water quickly!' she shouted at her servant.

A minute later, the young Greek boy came rushing back from the kitchen, bringing a jug of water and a small drinking bowl.

'Don't just stand there!' Livia shouted at him. 'Make her drink!'

The slave refused to go near Miriam. 'She's a Jew,' he protested. 'It's a bad omen.'

'Get out of my sight, you vile son of a whore,' Livia screamed furiously, sending her slave running into the house. 'And get some bread and oil,' she shouted after him. Then she went over to attend to Miriam herself.

Miriam stirred as she felt water on her parched lips.

'When did you last have any food?' Livia asked her.

'*Domina*, please don't concern yourself with me,' the girl murmured. 'The bag was heavy and I suddenly felt light-headed. Please forgive me for causing you so much trouble.'

'If you're going to treat me, I don't want to see this weakness again,' Livia announced sternly. 'There will be a meal waiting for you in the kitchen when you come here to see me. Is that understood?'

'You are too kind,' Miriam replied. 'You have my word, it won't happen again.' She climbed slowly to her feet.

'Now go!' Livia ordered. 'I shall expect you here at the same time tomorrow. My husband will be away on business and so we won't be disturbed.'

'*Domina*, please allow me to stay. Let me tend to you now and carry out my work,' Miriam pleaded. Livia's treatment could take several months, time in which she would be unable to see her brother again. She wanted to start immediately so that she could return as soon as possible to her work with the *medicus*.

The Greek boy appeared sheepishly with the food and put it on the ground several feet away from Miriam, then rushed back into the house. The young woman began to eat quickly. When she'd finished the last morsel of bread and felt stronger for the nourishment, Miriam accompanied her mistress into the house. She sensed that she was beginning to win the *domina's* confidence but she knew that her ability to help Shimon depended on the successful outcome of any treatment that she gave.

Livia felt comfortable with the young woman; she liked her gentle and submissive manner. She thought that she would be able to confide in her in the same way that she had confided in Rivka.

Miriam was installed in a small room in her mistress's house, inaccessible to any of the slaves who might want to harm her. She passed the following weeks administering a series of medications to bring about the resumption of the *domina's* menses. Despite her efforts, nothing happened. Livia was distraught, thinking that she would never able to conceive. Miriam had to use all her powers of persuasion to convince her mistress to remain calm and allow herself more time to respond to the medication.

Then, a month later, Livia's menses unexpectedly returned. The treatment had worked.

⚶

After the success of the games, Livia's relationship with Anthony had recovered its original intensity. She felt more secure and believed that he would soon ask her to be his wife. Anthony, however, had been summoned to Rome. He was only interested in using the short time he had before leaving to extract from his lover the most confidential details of her father's business so that he could gain complete control of his affairs.

Livia reluctantly agreed that Miriam could treat her husband to cure him of the curse that prevented him from fathering children. However, she hadn't confided in her nurse that it was not her husband with whom she wished to conceive.

Quintus Flaccus was desperate to find the young woman that Shimon had mentioned to him but his search had proved fruitless. The *medicus* at the training school said she'd gone away and he didn't know when she would be returning. Flaccus was becoming increasingly agitated by his condition. Livia had agreed to restore his conjugal rights but his impotence prevented him taking advantage of her offer. He resorted to seeking pleasure in the brothels that were scattered around the city. Unfortunately, not even nubile young women from the more exotic parts of the empire were able to stimulate his sexual appetite. He went home distraught at his inability to perform.

He had no idea that the young midwife standing before him, who had been in his house treating his wife, was the woman that he'd been looking for.

'What are you doing here? I've no use for your potions,' Quintus said irritably and carried on working at his writing table.

'Sir, the *domina* sent me,' Miriam responded respectfully.

'I'm not interested in anything she told you. Ten years of marriage, never letting me anywhere near her and now she suddenly finds out that she can't have children. And you expect me to be sympathetic?' the governor said as if talking to himself. 'Get out before I call the guards.'

'But she can conceive again,' Miriam said. 'The mistress has responded well to her treatment and, with the help of God, there's no reason why you can't have children.'

'What did you say, girl?' Quintus Flaccus sat motionless and looked up at the young midwife, astonished that she had referred to the same one God that he believed in.

'What's your name, girl?'

'Miriam, sir,' she answered quietly.

'You're a Jew?'

'Yes, sir.'

'Well that's a different matter,' the governor replied, his manner suddenly becoming more affable.

'I'm sorry but I don't understand,' Miriam responded.

'I have been trying to find…' Quintus Flaccus began to explain excitedly. He started again. 'A friend recommended a woman who was working for the *medicus* at the *ludus*. He said that she could help me with what I wanted. But it's of no consequence; I'm sure you're equally qualified to carry out the procedure.'

'Sir, I'm only a simple midwife. What procedure are you referring to?' Miriam asked, not revealing that it could only be herself that the governor was seeking. She wondered who could have mentioned her.

'Circumcision,' Quintus Flaccus whispered, leaning forward on his chair, not wanting to be overheard. 'Can you help me?'

'Sir, with respect, there is a more benign treatment, if you will permit me to offer it to you.'

Miriam foresaw great danger. The governor had deluded himself that circumcision would cure his impotence. However, Roman law strictly forbade her to circumcise a non-Jew. But she also knew that the governor could force her to comply with his wishes. She prayed that he would consent to the alternative treatment. To her surprise, he did. Perhaps he was more afraid of the procedure than he believed.

'You must start immediately,' Quintus exclaimed enthusiastically. He began strutting around his study, happy that there would soon be an end to his misery.

Miriam, relieved that the governor had forgone his demand for circumcision, opened her bag and took out several small vials containing different herbs and spices. She measured out the prescribed daily dosage. 'You should notice a difference within a week,' she said. 'Continue the medicine for another month and the symptoms will disappear.'

Quintus Flaccus responded enthusiastically to the idea of the young midwife's treatment. Herbs instead of a blade was a much more palatable solution to his problem. His thoughts focussed on the future, he rapidly forgot his request to Shimon to help him get circumcised. He also forgot the pledge he'd made to help Shimon gain his release from prison.

Miriam's prognosis proved accurate and the governor was cured of his impotence. Flaccus then had no compunction in dispensing with the young midwife's services. He made the decision, without consulting *Domina* Livia, that neither he nor his wife had further use of her services.

Miriam, however, had forged a strong bond with her mistress and established herself as a trusted confidante. She trusted in *Domina* Livia enough to tell her of Shimon's plight and to reveal that she, Miriam, was his sister. Livia said that if Miriam could arrange for her to visit Shimon in prison, she would see what she could do to secure his release. Somewhere deep inside, the autocratic governor's wife still felt slightly guilty about what had happened to the virile young man who had served her.

※

The rains had ceased and been replaced by longer days of warm sunshine. Miriam was free to return to her work with the *medicus*. She sat alone in the kitchen, eating her last meal before the journey to the *ludus*. She sighed; she would have to get used to the squalid conditions of the barracks again.

Gathering her few belongings and the remainder of her meal, she let herself out of the side door of the house and silently made her way down the path to the main road. She had found *Domina* Livia to be a decent woman. The mistress had treated her fairly – and yet she was the same person who was responsible for her brother's plight.

It was midday when Miriam reached the *ludus*. Tired from walking the entire morning and in need of water, Miriam entered the medical section attached to the main barracks to report for duty. She only hoped that the *medicus* remembered that he'd agreed to re-employ her.

'Ah, so you've decided to return, have you?' the *lanista* exclaimed, suddenly appearing from a dark corner. 'Think you can come and go whenever you please? Another one that thinks they've got the ear of our beloved governor?' He pushed his fat sweaty stomach provocatively against Miriam.

Seeing that the man was very drunk, she remained impassive. She hoped that he wouldn't try and force himself on her and would allow her to pass.

'Get out of my way!' the *lanista* bellowed, slurring his words and swaying unsteadily on his feet. 'You'd better go and attend to that Jew friend of yours, if he's not grovelling up the governor's arse again.' Gaius Licinius staggered off back to the young boy who was ensconced in his room on the first floor.

Miriam entered the small space that had been designated for her. She lay her weary body down on the hard wooden platform. She wanted to sleep but the *lanista's* words kept going through her head. So it was true. Quintus Flaccus had visited her brother and Shimon had mentioned that she performed circumcisions. What false hope did he receive in return, she wondered. It distressed her that the governor was using her brother to find a cure for his impotence.

Miriam sat up suddenly as a sharp pain ripped through her. Hadn't the trainer said that Shimon needed attention? Had he suffered a terrible injury in the arena? He could have been lying sick during all the time she was away. She knew that she had to obtain permission to visit him that afternoon while the rest of the prisoners were out on the training field.

⁂

After the first set of games, rumours about the governor's visit to Shimon were quick to reach all parts of the barracks. Shimon felt the change almost immediately. Prisoners who were previously hostile were now content to ignore him. The *lanista* had also become less aggressive even though it was clear that he would use any tactics to derive some personal benefit from his prisoner's unlikely association with the governor. Shimon was feeling good about himself; the governor's visit had raised his expectations of receiving justice to an unrealistic level. More dangerously, he also deluded himself into believing that he had gained the respect of his fellow inmates and especially of his young friend, Socrates.

The one thing that grieved him was Miriam's absence. He could not believe that she had disappeared just before his first battle, that she had left him alone. That she didn't care if he lived or died, preferring to put her faith in God that he would survive. As the weeks passed by, his resentment at her neglect festered, an unhealing wound.

⁂

Miriam obtained the authority she required to visit Shimon and passed swiftly through the infirmary to the prisoners' block. Apart from a few of the older prisoners languishing in their cells, who she supposed were unfit for training, the rest of the barracks was completely deserted.

Shimon was dozing on his side, his powerful legs tucked under his torso. It was the same position that she remembered from when they were children, sharing a bed. Sensing that there was someone watching him, he stirred and saw his sister's small face peering at him through the bars.

'What are you doing here?' he muttered.

Miriam had anticipated her brother's angry reaction and had decided that it would be best to allow him to vent his anger.

'The *lanista* said that you needed attention and I thought that you had been injured,' Miriam answered.

'You disappeared when I could have used some support and now you're suddenly concerned for my well-being? Well, you're too late. I'm not interested. So why don't you go back to help those who need you, because you're of no use to me.' Shimon turned away from her.

'Aunt Rivka died. I had to return home so that I could continue her work,' Miriam explained, trying to hold back her tears.

'Didn't you wonder if I survived? Or were you so sure that your prayers would be answered you didn't bother to find out?' Shimon asked, raising his voice. He eased himself off his bed and moved aggressively towards his sister.

'The sick needed me. I had to be where I was most of use.' Miriam realised that she would have to find some way to convince her brother that she hadn't abandoned him, otherwise she feared that their relationship would be irreparable. She didn't want to mention *Domina* Livia's pledge to help gain Shimon's release, however. There was no guarantee that the governor's wife would succeed.

'I wanted to pray but the words wouldn't come,' Shimon said, having no recollection of the words of divine recognition that had passed through his lips as he was led into the arena. 'I killed a man and felt nothing. That's what this place does to you.'

'I've been treating the governor,' Miriam whispered. 'I know you told him I could help him. There were certain complications and I had to remain until the healing process was complete.' She was trying her best to keep to the truth. It was better that Shimon believed that she had performed the circumcision and that Quintus Flaccus was now in his debt. It might keep his spirits up.

'You could have refused,' Shimon announced, forgetting that he was the one who had recommended his sister to the governor.

'To treat the sick?' Miriam replied.

'But performing circumcision on a non-Jew is punishable by death. If anyone discovers what you have done...' Shimon exclaimed, only now realising that he was responsible for the risk she had taken.

'Don't be concerned, no one will find out.' Miriam couldn't chance telling Shimon the truth: that she had refused to carry out what she had considered to be an unnecessary procedure on the governor. If Quintus Flaccus had offered her brother encouragement about being released in exchange for his co-operation, she couldn't withdraw his hope.

'Don't worry, some good will happen,' she said. 'You will see.' Miriam was confident that the bond she had established with *Domina* Livia would prove fruitful, rather than any false promises from her husband.

'It's really of no consequence. I'm respected in here now,' Shimon said suddenly, his mood changing. 'Now I've made an influential friend, even the *lanista* is treating me differently from the others,' he boasted. 'I only have to win my next few fights and I'll have enough money to buy my freedom. So you really don't need to pray on my behalf any more.' Shimon turned his back on his sister.

Miriam reprimanded herself for underestimating the ordeal that forced her brother to such bravado. Without further comment, she offered him some medication for his injured shoulder that was still paining him, and prepared to leave.

Acknowledging how much her brother had distanced himself

from her, she went back to her work

14

THE FIRST THREE-DAY event proved more lucrative than Anthony expected. Not only were few gladiators killed, limiting the amount of compensation paid to the *lanista*, but the extensive pre-games publicity generated such a demand for seats that the officials could charge exorbitant prices.

Anthony also indirectly controlled the gambling syndicates that operated around the city, where vast amounts of money changed hands during the games. He had accumulated so much wealth that there was scarcely a business in the province where he didn't hold a substantial interest.

As he had predicted, the weather disrupted the crop supply and Rome, its citizens subjected to the spiralling cost of food, was not slow in expressing her anger against the emperor. Marcus Praeconinus, his own goods held up again, sensed that there was now a call for change. He received the approval that he needed from the Senate to have Anthony summoned to Rome, ready to be installed in the Imperial Office.

Anthony didn't have to wait long to achieve his ultimate ambition. By the time his boat had docked on the banks of the Tiber, Emperor Germanicus was already dead.

Anticipating his appointment, Anthony had been careful to delegate most of his business interests to his closest associates so as to keep them hidden from the authorities. But he had not been so prudent in keeping his promises to those to whom he owed favours. He had never considered the price of Marcus Praeconinus's help. Anthony had also underestimated Marcus's daughter, Livia. He no longer considered her part of his future plans.

Anthony's first priority as emperor was to gain the confidence of the people, which meant providing them with enough food to eat at prices they could afford. This he achieved by rescinding the financial concessions the previous emperor had given to the dealers in luxury goods – essentially to Marcus Praeconinus. This allowed the price of corn and other basic foods to be subsidised until supplies were back to their normal level.

Anthony reinstated a strict regime of tax collecting throughout the empire, including on his own businesses, to restore Rome's solvency. He also scheduled a series of imperial games to secure the loyalty of his subjects; these would be held to celebrate his appointment as emperor.

The months of extreme cold were replaced by several weeks of stifling heat that pervaded the barracks. News of the emperor's death had circulated the *ludus* and was greeted with derision by men who had nothing to be grateful to him for.

The *lanista* was the only one whose spirits seemed uplifted. He'd been asked by a group of businessmen who were loyal to Anthony to arrange another three-day spectacle. It was to be even more extravagant than previous games. The trainer was instructed to organise twice the number of fighters and promised that his fee would be increased accordingly.

Anthony wanted full attendance at the arena, since that would substantially increase the profits of the gambling syndicates.

※

Unperturbed that he would be facing another challenge on the following afternoon, Shimon strode into the dining hall, his swagger evidence of his newfound confidence. He smiled at the thought of how, just a few months previously, his nerves had left his insides feeling as if they'd been ripped apart. Having established himself, he had lost the fear that made him susceptible to those who tried to take advantage of him.

Shimon was ravenous after a day of practice fights on the training field and had just piled up his plate with vegetables, when he heard his name being summoned from the far end of the table.

'Simon! Simon!' Looking round, he saw a shrivelled wretch gesturing in his direction. Not recognising the man, Shimon continued with his meal.

'Simon!' the voice called again. 'It's me.'

The person, who was uncommonly slightly built, shuffled along the wooden bench so that they were now facing each other. The man's complexion at first appeared grimy but on further examination Shimon could see that thick layers of charcoal make-up had been applied to create a disguise. It took a moment for him to identify the old man even though his beak-like nose and shrill voice seemed familiar. Shimon stopped eating, shocked that he was being addressed by the governor, Quintus Flaccus.

'Sir, you shouldn't be in this place before the *ludi*, it could be dangerous!' Shimon exclaimed, showing genuine concern for the other man's safety.

'I had you fooled, didn't I? Just my idea of a bit of fun,' the governor said mischievously, indifferent to the warning. 'I hoped we would meet again. I'm pleased to see that you're looking so well. Come.' He gestured for Shimon to follow him. 'We'll go and drink some wine.'

'But it's forbidden for us to leave the *ludus*!' Shimon protested.

'Don't worry,' Quintus Flaccus replied, waving his hands dismissively. 'I persuaded Gaius Licinius that it would be to his advantage to overlook his establishment's most valuable asset going out and enjoying himself for a few hours. There have been some exciting developments. We have much to discuss.'

Their identities protected by the darkness, the two men moved stealthily through the crowded streets. The crowd was excited by the prospect of the games, which would commence the following day. The jangle of money was accompanied by loud cheers of approval and calls of derision as groups of men pushed their way to look at their heroes' images posted on the walls.

The two men entered a noisy inn at the far end of the forum, packed with customers doing their best to quench their thirst in the sultry night. They found spaces at a small corner table and, almost immediately, a large jug of wine and two cups were slammed down on the wooden surface in front of them.

'The plebs are drunk again,' the governor remarked. 'If it were my decision, I'd cancel all these disgraceful displays of cruelty.'

Quintus Flaccus produced a crumpled poster from his decrepit tunic. Shimon recoiled, horrified at the image of himself and his giant opponent. He felt his throat tighten; in less than twelve hours, he would again face a vicious adversary who was intent on killing him.

'The problem is, there would be rioting in the streets if we interfered with their right to attend their precious games,' the governor said, filling his cup. 'And there's even less chance of stopping their gambling. They just pay the fine if they get caught. Where they get the money from, I can't imagine.'

Shimon, tired and preoccupied with the next day's challenge, wanted to get away from the governor and return to the barracks to sleep. 'I thank you for the wine,' he said, not wanting to cause offence, and stood up.

'You don't understand.' The governor clasped his child-like hand around Shimon's solid forearm, ready to reveal the purpose of their meeting.

'I do have to leave', Shimon reiterated, this time with more conviction.

'Simon, it's what we've been waiting for,' Quintus Flaccus announced, ignoring Shimon's protests. 'A royal patron who'll give us respectability. You must meet as soon as possible. He is certain to make an appearance tomorrow.'

Shimon, sensing that he had little choice but to let the man continue, sat down again.

'Simon,' the governor whispered, drawing himself closer to Shimon, 'the new emperor is sympathetic to our cause. You know, one God? Just imagine no longer having to meet secretly, like common criminals. The new emperor Anthony is our salvation. With his support, it's only a question of time before Rome adopts Christianity as the official religion of the empire.' Quintus Flaccus appeared so ecstatic that Shimon thought the man was about to have a seizure.

'It's so exciting,' the governor continued. 'And you, Simon, have helped to make it happen. I knew that you would bring us good fortune,' He reached out and touched Shimon's hand.

'Sir, you did mention that you would be willing to help with my release,' Shimon reminded the governor. He still believed that Miriam, at great risk to herself, had performed the governor's circumcision.

'Yes, yes, when the opportunity presents itself,' the governor replied dismissively. 'But now I really do have to go. With all these celebrations, you must forgive me, I'd almost forgotten that you will be appearing tomorrow,' he said, glancing at the poster and scrutinising Shimon one last time. 'May *Fortuna* be with you. Not that you'll need her.'

Quintus Flaccus slid out of the tavern into the warm evening and joined the streets teeming with people who provided him with the perfect cover to disappear into a nearby brothel. Now he was cured, he was going to take full advantage of the pleasures that his impotence had denied him. He chuckled at the cleverness of his deception. The Jew had already proven a good omen. His destiny was to remain in prison. He, Quintus Flaccus, would continue to derive benefit from the boy's divine protection.

Shimon, still needing to feel optimistic that his close relationship with the governor would ultimately prove beneficial, strolled back to the barracks, planning how to defeat Gallipor, his next day's opponent.

He expected to be confronted by the *lanista*, eager to know why the governor had wanted to see him. The only sound that he heard, however, was that of men groaning or screaming out in pain, reliving past experiences or having nightmares about the following day's ordeal.

Socrates, who never usually returned from the *lanista's* quarters until the early hours of the morning, was asleep in his cell. Shimon and Socrates had re-established their friendship. The younger man knew that Shimon's influence with the governor had enhanced his reputation with the other prisoners, so he was unlikely to be harmed. However, it was also rumoured that, with the recent influx of new young Greek boys from Sparta, the trainer was becoming tired of Socrates. He might soon end his protection. The *lanista* had, however, given Socrates an opportunity to save himself and enrolled him in the same gladiatorial training as the other novices.

Shimon, feeling the effects of the wine and the intense heat of his cell, soon fell into a deep slumber. He started to dream. The disfigured face of The Beast suddenly appeared. The partially dismembered body began moving towards him with such clarity that it was as if he was standing over him. Shimon felt a huge claw-like hand reach out for him. The Beast picked him up effortlessly and carried him away across his shoulder like a sack of corn. He dumped Shimon in a cart filled with laughing corpses making the short journey to the cemetery.

Shimon stirred. He placed his hand on his heaving chest. The loud beat of his heart told him that death hadn't come. Then, from out of the shadows, a woman dressed as a prostitute appeared and silently entered through the open gate of his cell. Without making a noise, she began to undress and lay down next to him. Shimon, suddenly feeling the warmth of a female body, opened his eyes.

'Not the one you were expecting?' Livia asked, her teasing eyes bearing down upon him.

'*Domina*?' Shimon mumbled her name under his breath. He was completely bewildered.

'I never had an opportunity to say a final farewell. Now I'm compensating for my oversight,' she said, manoeuvring herself expertly on top of him.

'But how did you manage to get in?' Shimon asked, breathing heavily. His mistress's distinctive fragrance aroused him. He felt her perfectly formed body, now locked perfectly onto his. He was back in the governor's villa, alone with the *domina*, slowly succumbing to her will. Nothing had changed. He tried to rekindle the months of resentment that he'd felt towards her to stop himself giving in to her.

'You would be surprised how persuasive I can be.' She touched his lips with the tip of her long elegant forefinger, her face beaming with the pleasure of her deceit.

'You must be mad!' Shimon exclaimed, without any of his former deference.

'Just my chance to get a little excitement,' Livia replied with a wicked smile. She leant forward and began massaging his neck and shoulders with oil that she had brought with her.

'So you haven't come because of me? You didn't want to absolve yourself of guilt for the injustice I suffered?'

'Dear boy, surely you didn't expect the slaves to tell the truth?' Livia laughed. She found Shimon's naivety endearing. 'Or did you think, perhaps, that I would be prepared to compromise my husband's position for a young houseboy, even one as handsome as you?'

'And that's all I was to you? Entertainment? A thrill?' Shimon said, breathing heavily. He could no longer resist her as his body was gripped again in a wave of ecstasy. They lay together, the mistress and her former servant, their bodies entwined for that moment as lovers.

The first rays of light broke through the small opening in the roof above. It would soon be daybreak and time for the first meal. Shimon needed to sleep.

'The debt has to paid in full,' Livia whispered provocatively, using all her strength to roll her former servant on top of her. 'Now get back to work,' she ordered. Wrapping her slender legs around him, she began to writhe with pleasure as he thrust deeper inside her.

Livia had achieved her purpose. She dressed quickly. Careful not to wake Shimon, she took a small vial and collected droplets from his sweat-drenched body, which she placed into the fold of her toga. His scent was worth savouring. She then left the tiny cell without looking back.

Miriam was waiting for her. The two women hurried away from the barracks to the meeting place, where Livia's most trusted servant was waiting to return her to her residence.

'Most satisfying, my dear Miriam,' Livia proclaimed, revelling in the experience of the last few hours with Shimon. 'You have fulfilled your obligation and now I shall have to find a way of ful-filling mine. Do not fear,' she added, as she was helped onto her horse, 'the secret will remain between us.'

Miriam lowered her head, acknowledging the commitment they had made to each other.

'Be assured that I shall contact you soon. Look after yourself,' were Livia's parting words as she rode away.

Neither woman knew that they had met for the last time.

15

'SOLLY! GET YOUR arse off that bed!' the *lanista* bellowed. 'It's time to show them what you can do!'

Shimon, exhausted from his encounter with Livia the previous night, had slept past the first meal of the day and been absent at the morning roll call.

'Can't think what's been going on in here, but it smells like a bleeding brothel,' the *lanista* commented suspiciously, standing at the open door of the cell. 'That *femina* been looking after your needs, has she? Don't blame you not wanting to go with them prostitutes. Never know what you might catch!'

'I don't know what you're talking about,' Shimon answered, while confused images of the previous night's escapades flashed through his mind. He moved his hand over the contours of his broad chest and smelled Livia's distinctive fragrance. No, it wasn't a dream.

He sat up, rubbing the sleep from his eyes, and tried to restore the circulation to his aching limbs. He felt relaxed and strangely unperturbed about his afternoon fight. But he had awoken ravenous and needed to eat. He must replenish his strength to give him an advantage over what might be an uncompromising opponent.

'You'd better be especially vigilant, Solly, because this one isn't going to roll over and die just because he gets a few little cuts and a few bruises,' the trainer warned. He enjoyed instilling fear in his boys. 'I want a good fight. We wouldn't want to disappoint our lords and masters. Which reminds me,' Gaius Licinius continued. 'I trust you'll remember to give me some credit for your special treatment.' He was not willing to lose an opportunity to enhance his reputation. 'Rumour is that your friend the governor is best mates with that new emperor, Anthony. If he decides to honour us with his presence, he won't be happy with a feeble performance. So you see, Solly, you'd better put on a proper show because a lot of eyes will be watching you, if you know what I mean. Now move yourself!' Gaius Licinius shouted as he left to get dressed for the occasion.

Shimon took a few coins from the stash that he'd hidden away and went to the dining hall. In return for a bribe, the kitchen hand could always be persuaded to break the regulations and open the food stores. It had taken a while, but Shimon now understood how to survive the harsh conditions of the *ludus*. The respect that he'd achieved for his fighting, together with his close relationship with the governor, had made his life easier.

For the first time, he had money he'd won by his own efforts. But he had no doubt that he would need to accumulate a significant amount of cash to buy his freedom. Meanwhile, he had to focus his attention on defeating the man nicknamed in the barracks as The Giant.

※

When he entered the arena, Shimon enjoyed the tumultuous reception of the massive crowd. He glanced at his shadow projected on the scorching ground by the mid-afternoon sun. At nineteen, he was already a man. Aware that he was only being exploited for his natural athleticism and uncanny physical strength, he had finally received the recognition that he had always craved.

The crowds in the packed arena, impatient for the sight of first blood, were jeering at the two men in the pit who were still attempting to get the measure of the other. Shimon, pumped up with adrenalin, approached his opponent confidently, his sword gripped in his hand. He could sense fear in Gallipor's pig-like eyes and knew that despite the greater protection that his net and trident afforded him, he had to be the one to strike first. But he had misjudged the agility of the larger man.

His overconfidence led to a temporary loss of concentration. He was knocked off balance with a blow to the head from the base of the other man's three-pronged spear. Slightly dazed and seething with anger at being caught unprepared, Shimon got up swiftly from the sand and immediately lunged at his opponent who was standing a step away. He managed to grab Gallipor's net and then, entangling the huge man's body in his own snare, left the bewildered giant unable to move.

The crowd, many of whom were now on their feet shouting their approval, demanded more humiliation. The net tightened around Gallipor's neck and he made violent choking noises as he was pulled towards his captor. Shimon, his sword drawn, was ready to inflict the final blow.

But the crowd wanted more. They wanted him to extend the man's agony. He acceded to their wishes and mercilessly dragged Gallipor around the perimeter of the arena. The crowd howled with derision. What they didn't know was that the twisted net had created a noose around Gallipor's neck and had already done its work. The Giant was already dead.

Shimon, victorious again, paraded in front of the cheering crowd. The people were happy to show their appreciation by throwing a multitude of coins of different dominations in his direction.

Shimon had expected the governor to present his award, since Quintus Flaccus was representing the absent emperor. He was disappointed to find that Flaccus had left his seat and delegated the function to a magistrate. The same corrupt magistrate who had sentenced Shimon to a life in the arena.

Weighed down by pouches filled with his prize money, Shimon raised his arm high above his head and gestured his appreciation to the crowd. Gallipor's body was carried out through a narrow cutting and dumped in a pile with the rest of the day's defeated. Perhaps it would be claimed for burial by his grieving family and friends; the likelihood was that it would not be.

※

Shortly before the games began, Emperor Anthony sent a message to Quintus Flaccus, saying that he could not present the *ludi*. Perhaps it was the thought of witnessing such barbarity again that made the governor ill. He immediately started vomiting and had to summon his physicians. He was helped from the arena, leaving the corrupt city magistrate to preside over the remainder of the three-day spectacle.

As he lay back on a couch after they had treated him with a calming herbal infusion of chamomile and lavender leaves, Flaccus wondered why he was yet again in the invidious position of hosting another set of games. Had he overestimated the man in whom he had confided so much? Was Anthony, for some unknown reason, avoiding him?

Flaccus knew that his wife was besotted with the new emperor. He had chosen not to discourage their relationship so that he could rely upon Anthony's continued support for his Christian sect. But now he was feeling aggrieved. His life had been made intolerable by Livia's obsession with that wretched midwife and her treatment for her medical condition. It was not for his benefit that she was so desperate for a cure.

Quintus Flaccus was convinced that Livia and Anthony were conspiring against him and intending to undermine his position as governor. He knew that he had to act quickly to foil them, even if it meant seeking the counsel of the father-in-law he had always loathed, Marcus Praeconinus.

⚑

It was early evening when Shimon returned to the *ludus*. There had been no respite in the heatwave that had gripped the province for the last month. The protracted hours of daylight ensured that one long day seemed to roll effortlessly into another. He had lost all sense of time and it was only the change in the seasons that indicated how long he had been interned.

The day had gone exceedingly well and Shimon was looking forward to sharing a substantial evening meal with Socrates. He would enjoy telling the boy the details of his victory.

Shimon was about to set off for the dining hall when he was confronted by a furious Gaius Licinius barging into his cell.

'Turning your back like that on a man that could kill you for a measure of molasses,' the trainer bellowed at Shimon. 'Are you trying to make me look like a fool?'

Shimon was bewildered at the extent of the *lanista's* bad temper. His face was flushed with anger.

'I didn't expect…' Shimon began.

'Listen, you big-headed bastard,' the trainer shouted. 'I've dedicated a lot of time and effort into making you what you are, and I don't expect you to piss it away with a performance that's more suited to the fucking circus.'

The only plausible explanation Shimon could assume for such an unwarranted outburst was that the games promoters must have reneged on Gaius Licinius's fee. He waited for the trainer to finish venting his frustration.

'And don't talk to me about your influential friends who are always so busy up each other's arses,' Licinius ranted. 'If they'd bothered to be there, they probably wouldn't even have noticed that you won.'

'But the crowd,' Shimon protested. 'They were roaring their approval.'

'Didn't get value for money,' the trainer retorted. 'And from where I was sitting, there were many of your public would have preferred for you to have been the one dragged out to the grave-yard!'

He stood back and folded his arms. 'Solly,' he said, 'you've seriously disappointed me.'

'I won, didn't I?' Shimon replied, suspecting that he was not being told the real reason for the *lanista's* belligerence.

'You would be wise to start saying your prayers,' Gaius Licinius remarked, shaking his head. The trainer departed, looking unusually despondent, leaving Shimon to finish burying his winnings and to contemplate his warning.

❀

Miriam winced at the pain in her chest. She suspected that she didn't have long to live. She wanted to spend that short time close to her brother.

Later that evening, without the authority of the *medicus*, Miriam passed quietly through the crowded barracks. She was oblivious to the noisy jeers and obscene gestures of desperate men; she was not concerned about her own safety.

Miriam had passed the Sabbath praying for Shimon's safe return and to somehow find a way of restoring the closeness they had once enjoyed. The desire to protect him had been rekindled;

it had overwhelmed her in its intensity. As she had when they were children, she wanted once more to hold his head in her hands when he was woken up by nightmares. She had been the one to console him when he got the blame because he had been born strong and healthy. She wanted him to understand that even though they had little money and life appeared unkind, they could reap rewards of a far more valuable nature.

She could see that her brother had matured, even if he appeared to have lost much of his sensitivity. He had endured great suffering. He had learned to look after himself. She was proud of him. With the help of God, he would be free one day to follow the meaningful life for which he was destined, and where his true qualities would become evident.

When she arrived at Shimon's cell, her brother was lying on his back with a defiant expression.

'Still here? That must be another miracle.' Shimon looked up at his sister from his bed.

'I'm pleased that you appear in such good spirits,' Miriam replied after a short pause. 'I've heard that you've developed a good reputation, especially with the younger prisoners,' she continued. She was aware of the speculation about Shimon and the *lanista* vying for Socrates' affections; but she had nursed that young man when he was near to death and knew how much he admired Shimon. She was convinced that the rumours were merely another attempt to discredit her brother.

'You mean Socrates,' Shimon responded. 'The older men are always trying to force themselves on him and he's only a boy. They think that I want him for myself but they know better than to start a fight with me.'

Miriam could sense that it would be unrealistic to expect her brother to suddenly abandon his bravado so that they could recreate the bond they had always shared.

'So you know how to look after yourself?' were the only words that she could think of saying.

'You have to in this place,' Shimon answered. 'It helps if you have important friends.'

'Provided you can rely upon them.' Miriam understood that Shimon was referring to the governor. She knew that she risked alienating her brother but she had a responsibility to warn him about the erratic nature of the man he was convinced was concerned for his well-being.

'The governor and I are close friends,' Shimon announced, in an attempt to impress his sister. 'He even wants me to meet the new emperor,' he added.

'Even now that his health has been restored?' Miriam probed.

'What do you mean?' Shimon asked. It had not occurred to him that Quintus Flaccus's friendship was only dependent on Shimon helping him to be circumcised.

'There were other ailments that caused him to doubt his manhood,' Miriam divulged. She realised that Shimon had failed to grasp the true nature of the man. 'He needed my attention, and I was already treating other members of his household.'

'*Domina* Livia?' Shimon gasped.

Miriam nodded.

'Does she know you're my sister?' Shimon asked, getting to his feet. 'Did she mention me?' He was desperate to know whether the *domina* had said anything about visiting him surreptitiously.

'The treatment was successful and she wanted to keep me employed. We had grown quite attached.' Miriam purposely avoided the question.

'And the governor?' Shimon asked.

'He paid me well but as soon as he'd recovered, he said there was no further need for my services.' Would this make her brother recognise the callous nature of his so-called benefactor?

'But you did all that was required of you!'

'We can't depend upon other people to help us,' Miriam warned. This was her last chance to make her brother face reality.

'You obviously don't understand. I've brought him good fortune, he said so himself. It's only a question of time before I'll be granted my freedom. He gave me his word!' Shimon sounded less sure of himself.

'I'm only saying that you need to be wary of whom you trust because when we're of no further use, we are easily forgotten,' Miriam said. 'Just remember, there will always be those who appear to display great compassion but only want to take advantage of you to promote their own interests.'

'I don't need any more of your words of advice,' Shimon said angrily. 'I've managed to survive well enough without your interference and I'm quite capable of making my own decisions. So why don't you just go back to your precious work and leave me alone?'

Shimon turned his back on the frail young woman, making it abundantly clear that their meeting was over. Miriam, with a terrible sense of guilt, allowed herself one last lingering look at her brother and then moved silently away. She hadn't accomplished her objective; she knew that she had failed him.

Returned to her tiny room, she took some paper and a pen from her bag. Deeply upset, she started to write a letter to her brother. She hadn't noticed that the *lanista* was waiting for her.

'I thought I warned you last time about visiting your Jew friend without my permission,' Gaius Licinius snarled. 'You obviously can't get enough of each other can you?' The trainer grabbed hold of Miriam and shoved her against the wall. The young midwife, trembling with fear, mumbled a prayer as he rammed his bulging body up against her so she was unable to move.

'Well, I hope he left some for me,' he sniggered as he ripped off her clothes and mercilessly forced himself on her, placing his thick hand over her mouth to snuff out her muffled screams.

Then, leaving the midwife's almost lifeless body on the floor surrounded by a pool of blood, the *lanista* placed the letter from Miriam's bed inside his open tunic and staggered off.

16

THE EMPEROR'S MEASURES to secure the support of his subjects proved unsuccessful. The early months of Anthony's office were dominated by strife and rumblings of discontent in the Senate. Rome's insatiable appetite for luxury goods showed no sign of abatement and unenthusiastic tax collectors, threatened with intimidation by those wealthy individuals that had most to lose, failed to impose the new levies that would have replenished the city coffers. The city could, therefore, no longer provide affordable food for its citizens and was vulnerable to serious unrest.

The emperor, preferring to remain in the city, had become involved with Julia, a fiercely ambitious young woman. She was Livia's seventeen-year-old daughter who had been sent to Rome by her father, Lucilius, to find a husband. Her beauty meant that there was no lack of suitors. An intermediary loyal to Marcus Praeconinus had introduced her to the emperor and he was immediately attracted to her. She had the same passion that he'd found in her mother. Anthony didn't hesitate in making her his mistress.

The emperor had other important matters to occupy his time. Anthony had lost interest in the East, which might have gone unnoticed had he not also lost the respect of the influential Third Legion on whose support he depended for his appointment of emperor. He had also been replaced as the most powerful man in the province by two families that had previously competed with him for control of Rome's trade routes. As a result, a major part of Marcus Praeconinus's business had now been lost to a ruthless group of individuals with no allegiance to Rome.

Marcus Praeconinus was determined to exact his revenge on Anthony, the man he had patiently cultivated for imperial office. Not only did he intend to retrieve the substantial sums that had been stolen from him, but he also had no compunction about exposing the emperor's relationship with Julia. When his daughter, Livia, discovered that she had been cast out in favour of her own daughter, Marcus Praeconinus was certain she would co-operate fully with an investigation against Anthony.

No longer being able to rely on the influx of funds that had been extorted from the trade routes, the emperor's gambling syndicate was deprived of its main source of income. The governor, Quintus Flaccus, was applying pressure to wipe out betting, an activity that he regarded as an evil addiction among people with barely enough money to eat.

It was decided, therefore, that the group that now controlled all the major gambling activity in the province would privately sponsor one final *munera*, after which they would disband the operation and divide up the spoils. The *lanista*, Gaius Licinius, would be given short notice to provide even more exotic attractions and stage contests of unprecedented violence between the gladiators. This would encourage the public to place bets with as much of their money as they could.

Shimon endured the monotony of the following weeks not knowing when he might have to fight again. He was still enjoying his fame. Now a veteran with successes to his credit, he had gained the reluctant acceptance of his most hardened adversaries.

His relationship with Socrates, free of sexual impropriety, had deepened. The two friends passed many hours planning the lives they would lead after they had obtained their freedom. Shimon even offered his young friend part of his money, so that they could start up a business of their own. The distraction of their dreams helped them, even for a brief interlude, to escape the tedium and loneliness of their everyday existence.

The dry season had ended and the first rains had arrived. Shimon left the dining hall in high spirits. He'd forgotten about his disagreement with Miriam weeks before and assumed that her continued absence was because she was busy assisting the *medicus*. During their evening meal, he enjoyed impressing Socrates again with his victory over The Giant and his young friend never tired of hearing all the gory details.

Walking ahead, Shimon didn't notice that Socrates was lagging behind him, nor was he aware that his young friend had just given the signal to a man with a thin blade who was in hiding, waiting to attack him.

'I told you that I'd come looking for you, didn't I, pretty boy?' the assailant said, with a look of hatred on his face, bustling Shimon into his cell and holding the weapon up against his victim's neck.

It was Cassipor, the man who had lost to him in the dice game many months ago. Shimon knew that Cassipor would fight to the death to retrieve his money.

'So you'd better tell me where you've hidden the cash,' the man threatened, tightening his grip.

Shimon was having difficulty breathing. Making use of his free arm, he dug his elbow hard into Cassipor's ribs. As the other man gasped and drew back, Shimon grabbed hold of a jagged piece of ceramic tile on the floor of his cell.

'This makes our fight fairer,' he said.

'A Jew with guts,' Cassipor sniggered, trying to hide the pain that Shimon had inflicted.

Shimon lunged at Cassipor with such ferocity that he was stunned. The injured man, bleeding from a huge gash on the side of his face, fell to his knees, clutching his wound and groaning like an animal waiting for a merciful end to its pain. But the fight wasn't over. Unwilling to accept defeat, Cassipor lashed out, his blade making a deep incision in Shimon's leg.

Shimon cried out, feeling the metal rip through his thigh muscle. Mustering all his strength, he picked the bigger man off the ground like a sack of barley and threw him out of the cell.

'Next time, I'll kill you,' he shouted. Cassipor staggered off, holding the lacerated skin on his face.

Socrates had witnessed the entire incident from only a short distance away. He returned to his cell deprived of his reward for informing Cassipor about Shimon's stash of money.

Shimon tore off a strip of his tunic and tied it tightly around his leg to stop the bleeding. He teetered unsteadily through the winding corridors of the barracks, knowing that he needed immediate medical attention. Going to Miriam, he recalled their last difficult meeting and regretted that it had ended acrimoniously. It had been his fault. Now he had a chance to rectify the damage.

'I'd stay away from the infirmary, Solly, if I were you,' the *lanista* called out. 'Lost another bloke during the night. And that idiot *medicus* told me we'd got rid of it. I can't afford you catching dysentery.'

Shimon ignored the trainer's warning and tried to push past him but Gaius Licinius placed his bulging body in the way to prevent him passing.

'So who have you been upsetting this time?' the *lanista* asked, glancing at the wound on Shimon's leg that was seeping blood.

'That piece of cack Cassipor. Did you tell him about my money?' Shimon snarled.

'I swear on Jupiter's stone, I never told anyone,' the trainer replied, indignantly.

'Just a coincidence that he attacked me, then?' Shimon was convinced that the man was lying.

'I don't know who told him. Honest I don't.' Shimon appeared to be so angry that the *lanista* feared that he would harm him. 'I wouldn't betray a man with your influence. Or should I say, someone that used to have your influence.' He grinned slyly.

'What do you mean?' Shimon asked.

'Your friend the governor?' the *lanista* queried. 'He's not been around much recently, has he?'

'He's a busy man.'

'Busy licking the emperor's balls,' Gaius Licinius retorted with his usual crudeness.

'And you're talking out your arse,' Shimon answered back, angry that his association with the governor was being challenged.

'Flaccus was only ever interested in dragging our beloved emperor into that religious sect he's obsessed with,' the trainer continued. 'That's the real reason why we haven't seen him in months. Solly boy, accept it, you've been dumped!'

'Meaningless gossip,' Shimon said.

'Listen, Solly, people tell me things – for a price.' The *lanista* rattled a few coins in the pocket of his tunic. 'Like about that *femina* of yours,' he added after a short pause.

'What about her?' Shimon asked.

The *lanista* smiled, enjoying the power that he now wielded over Shimon.

'Tell me!' Shimon shouted, becoming agitated.

'No need to be so hasty.'

'Where is she?' Shimon demanded. 'I need to find her.'

'What's it worth?' The fat man grinned.

Shimon, ignoring the excruciating pain in his leg, jostled the trainer out of the way and moved towards the entrance of the infirmary to find his sister.

'Solly, she's not in there.'

Shimon turned around.

'She's dead,' Gaius Licinius said, without displaying the slightest emotion.

Shimon's jaw sagged. His body went limp. 'It can't true, you're lying,' he said, shaking his head. Tears started to well in his eyes.

'Swept away in the plague,' the *lanista* declared. 'I've lost some my best men.'

'Did she suffer?' Shimon mumbled, recalling how frail she'd appeared the last time he saw her.

'It certainly wasn't quick,' the *lanista* replied. 'She was always concerned for all the other poor bastards and made sure that they were given the medicines before she thought of herself.' Even he seemed moved by Miriam's selflessness. 'No, I can definitely say that it wasn't a painless death,' he repeated.

Shimon started crying in earnest. He felt as if one of his limbs had been severed and his heart was heavy with remorse.

'Why couldn't it have been me?' he mumbled to himself. He had rejected her. Turned her away, the only person who cared for him. He was the cause of her pain. If he hadn't been so blind and allowed himself to be taken advantage of, he wouldn't have been sent to prison and she wouldn't have needed to come looking for him.

He wandered around the barracks in a daze, unwilling to accept Miriam's death. He was sure it was only a bad dream; that she would be there when he woke up as she always had been when they were children. He staggered back along the winding corridor, unable to absorb what was being said to him by the men that marked his path back to his cell. He collapsed on his bed and covered his head with his hands as he tried to escape the nightmare that had been forced upon him.

The next morning, the *lanista* came looking for Shimon. ' 'Ere Solly. Stupid to get upset over a woman,' he said. 'I've got a new bunch of slave girls arriving any day now. You can have one of them if you like. The plebs are going to love watching them hacking each other to pieces.'

'That's all they are to you,' Shimon said. 'Just another pound of flesh to be put on display for your bloodthirsty customers. You're a heartless bastard.'

'Listen Solly. It's a business like any other.' Licinius began to justify himself. 'All I'm doing is giving the people what they want. Could be sacks of corn, could be bodies, it doesn't make any difference to me. If the merchandise is in good condition and ripe enough to be consumed, that's all I care about. And I haven't noticed you turn away from your adoring public and refuse to take their money. Remember, we're all the same; we look after ourselves.'

Shimon stood up and rubbed his injured leg that had become numb. He approached the *lanista*. 'Unlike you, I didn't volunteer to be here and can't just leave when I've had enough,' he answered curtly.

'Solly, you don't know anything about me. But I know about you. I've been where you are, and fought where you've fought. Like you, I realise that this life is a pile of shit. We both have masters to please who we owe our lives to. Unfortunately for you, it's me. Now,' he said, adopting a more business-like tone, 'talking of the price of corn, your friend the governor wants to arrange another *munera* because his loyal subjects are unhappy about the recent food shortages.'

What the trainer didn't reveal was that Quintus Flaccus's endorsement had only been obtained after he'd received threats to expose his religious practices unless he gave his approval for the games. Realising that he had no alternative, the governor gave the authority for the spectacle to be staged.

'So Solly, here's something for your leg.' The *lanista* handed Shimon a piece of gauze. 'There's some lotion on it that I got from the *medicus*.'

Shimon untied the piece of cloth that was sticking painfully to his wound and applied the new dressing to his damaged limb.

'You'd better hope it heals quickly because we've only got two weeks before the *munera*. We can't possibly have one of our veterans not fully fit,' the *lanista* announced. 'I thought you'd like to know who you're going to be fighting,' he added slyly.

Shimon, still preoccupied with his sister's death, showed little interest.

'Well, I hope that young Socrates is more enthusiastic. You're his first match.'

'You can't do that!' Shimon protested.

'I thought you'd be happy slogging it out with your biggest admirer,' the trainer replied cynically.

'But you can't make him fight,' Shimon pleaded. 'Does he know?'

'He will, when you tell him,' the *lanista* said. 'You might also ask your boy if he knows why Cassipor just happened to appear looking for all that money you won.'

Shimon, still struggling to accept the dreadful news that he was being forced to fight his closest friend, was unwilling to contemplate that Socrates might have been implicated in his attack.

17

SHIMON COULDN'T TELL Socrates about the dreadful fate that awaited them. Soon they would be facing each other, leaving one of them dead or badly injured. The thought of any animosity between them was too painful to contemplate.

For a week, Shimon suffered headaches and blurred vision that had left him increasingly lethargic. Unable to train with his usual vigour, he remained alone in his cell for long periods.

'Solly, I'm getting worried about you,' the trainer called out, seeing Shimon curled up on his bed. 'Get up and onto that training field or you'll only be good enough for target practice.'

Shimon had difficulty moving his arms and legs, which felt as if they had been fastened down with weights. He could barely identify the distorted features of the *lanista*.

'Come on, Solly, move yourself,' the trainer repeated, trying to force Shimon out of his bed. 'You wouldn't recognise young Socrates. He's got all this aggression that he's been waiting to unleash. It looks like he's really got a grudge against you.'

'What did you say to him?' Shimon asked, lifting his head, finding it an effort to talk.

'Didn't have to say anything, Solly,' replied the *lanista*. 'Some of his other acquaintances did the job for me. I don't think they were very complimentary about you. I'd wager that you'll see a completely different boy from the one you have fond memories of,' he added spitefully.

'You turned him against me.'

'The crowd wants to see a fight to the death, not some girly pantomime. He just needed a little encouragement.'

The deluge of rain that penetrated every crevice of the barracks was accompanied by a period of severe cold. Extra exercise periods were arranged to raise the men's low morale. Shimon, still struggling to rid himself of the malaise that had gripped him after his sister's death, had only regained a modicum of his strength. He was not fit for the impending challenge.

On the day of the games, Shimon joined the procession for the opening ceremony in a near stupor. He couldn't feel any normal sensation in his arms and legs; it was as if he was treading air. Not knowing how, he reached the arena. Suddenly he found himself in the fighters' pit, having to contend with a biting wind against his face and the intimidating roar of thousands of people.

Unsteady on his feet, and with only his shield for protection, he suddenly felt the presence of his opponent bearing down on him. Devoid of his usual agility, Shimon couldn't manoeuvre his cumbersome body. He knew that there was no possibility this would be a fair contest. Instead, he left himself exposed and Socrates, scorn evident on his once-angelic face, was quick to take advantage.

The younger combatant unleashed a series of blows at his former friend. Shimon, unable to move, managed to cover his head as his shield received the brunt of the punishment. He was sure that he was going to die.

Then, just as his battering had reached its climax, Miriam suddenly appeared before Shimon's eyes. She was standing in the place of the man who was beating him. Now he could only hear his sister's voice giving him instructions and shouting words of encouragement.

Her words rallied him. With a combination of belief and determination, Shimon stepped back from Socrates' onslaught. He had to exert all his resolve to save his life, which had suddenly assumed a vital importance.

The crowd, still sensing an early kill, continued to goad Socrates. But Shimon, striking out wildly, succeeded in knocking the sword out of Socrates' hand. The boy moved backwards, trying to retrieve his weapon, but as he moved he slipped and suffered a deep cut to his leg from his own blade that was partially submerged in the ground.

The young fighter's strength slowly dissipated as his lifeblood began to drain out of him. He didn't know that his sword had been dipped in poison to ensure him a certain victory over his more experienced opponent.

Looking up at Shimon, Socrates' face again resembled that of an innocent young boy begging for forgiveness.

Shimon was stunned. How had he inflicted a fatal wound on his friend without realising it? He looked down at the sword in his hand and knew it wasn't possible. His confusion, his listlessness – had he been drugged for the last few days? By whom?

Socrates looked up at him, wide-eyed, lying prostrate on the blood-drenched sand. With a great effort, he lifted his head and with his lips quivering, he whispered the *lanista's* name.

'Gaius Licinius,' were his final words.

Shimon bent down and cradled Socrates' head. But it was too late, for the friend whom he had loved as a younger brother lay still in his arms.

Shimon felt numb. He wanted desperately to cry out, to express the deep sense of loss that penetrated every part of his being. Instead he just remained beside the body, unable to react.

Refusing to take the victor's salute, Shimon got up and walked away without presenting himself to the governor. He was led out of the arena, accompanied by the jeers of a crowd unhappy with the outcome and voicing its disapproval. They had been cheated of a decent performance.

※

The games proved a financial disaster for the organisers and sponsors. The gambling syndicate, unable to pay out the vast amount of money it owed to the people with whom it had placed bets, promptly disbanded its operation and disappeared. Many of its associates were forced to flee into hiding, including Gaius Licinius who, fearing for his life, didn't dare to return to the *ludus*.

Unrest was also spreading through the empire and the authorities were blamed for depriving its citizens of food. In Rome, there were a number of serious disturbances and attacks on the city's municipal buildings and occupants. Most of the people's anger was directed against the emperor; they believed that he had abandoned them.

Marcus Praeconinus had his own grievance against Anthony. Having paid substantial sums for the information, the aged senator now had irrefutable evidence that it was his protégé who'd been responsible for the sabotage of his merchandise. This, together with the fact that he was being blamed by the Senate for pressurising them to endorse Anthony's appointment, meant he had no alternative. Anthony would have to be removed as emperor.

A week later, the deed was done. The emperor was discovered stabbed in his bed, in the arms of his seventeen-year-old lover.

Shimon found the monotony of the empty weeks that followed almost impossible to bear. He chose to eat his meals and attend exercise periods alone. To alleviate his boredom, he pretended that Socrates was still in the cell next to his own. He began communicating with his friend through the break in the wall that separated them, reliving the happy experiences they shared together.

Although Shimon had not yet been imprisoned for two years, he couldn't remember life before the *ludus*. He was resigned to his existence and no longer felt a burning desire for justice. Instead, he reconciled himself to passing the rest of his life locked away, oblivious to the outside world.

One morning, Shimon was awoken not by the usual rant of the guards but by a visit of an entirely different nature.

'Simon, it's me. I'm in trouble,' the governor announced, appearing at Shimon's gate, his face taut with worry.

Shimon didn't respond.

'You must help me,' Quintus Flaccus insisted.

Shimon glanced over at the man gripping the bars of the cell with his small hands

'What do you want?' he asked abruptly. He no longer had any faith in the governor's friendship. 'I have nothing to say to you.' His tone expressed the contempt he felt for the man he was looking down upon.

'Simon, please, my situation is extremely grave,' the governor begged.

'Makes no difference to me,' Shimon answered dismissively,

and returned to his bed.

'But I'm relying on you,' the governor insisted desperately. 'You're the only person who has the power to save me.'

Shimon recalled the months he had languished alone in his stinking cell, his hopes unrealistically raised by the governor. He had been deceived into thinking that this man, who had condemned him without proof, would keep his promise to help him.

'Go and ask the emperor for help. Or has he rejected you too?' Shimon responded.

'He's dead, and I'm afraid that I might be next! I need you to protect me!' Quintus Flaccus said.

'You should be more careful who you make friends with,' Shimon said, aware from rumours that had circulated around the barracks that Anthony had been assassinated by one of his slaves while he was sleeping.

'You don't understand,' the governor replied, still sounding supercilious despite his predicament. 'The new emperor has passed a decree that places all Christian lives in danger. You have the blessing of the Lord. With you beside me, I shall be safe.'

Shimon almost laughed. The man was begging for his help.

'Simon, I made a vow to you a long time ago. Well, now I'm fulfilling it,' the governor said sanctimoniously.

Shimon glared at him without speaking.

'You told me about that Jewish girl? You said that she could help me,' the governor said. 'You must remember! I promised that if circumstances permitted, I would try to have you released.' He was fidgeting nervously with his signet ring.

At the mention of his sister, Shimon moved menacingly towards the little man. The governor's face went pale.

'I remember that when she'd helped you and she was no further use, you threw her out,' Shimon answered scornfully. 'And I didn't get out of this place.'

'I didn't,' the governor stammered. 'I mean it wasn't as you say. She was paid well for her work...'

'And now you just happen to have conveniently remembered your promise?'

'Yes, it's the truth.' The governor had begun to perspire profusely. He was so agitated that he feared he might faint.

Shimon understood how stupid he had been. Miriam had tried to warn him not to trust the governor, but he chose to ignore her words. He felt a pain deep inside, that his stubbornness had caused the rift between them that he would never be able to heal. Tears appeared in his eyes as he thought about their last acrimonious meeting. He just wanted to be able to ask her to forgive him.

'But you have to help me,' the governor repeated.

'I don't think you're in a position to make any demands,' Shimon replied. 'You made a vow that you had no intention of keeping – until now, when your life is in danger. I suggest you ask that Lord of yours to fulfil his promise of divine protection and see whether He keeps His word. Now I think that you should leave.'

'I'll do anything,' Quintus Flaccus begged. He began to snivel. 'Surely you can appreciate that I wouldn't demean myself like this if I wasn't desperate?'

'What are you offering?' Shimon asked, his interest unexpectedly rekindled.

'Your release,' the governor replied. 'Isn't that enough? You have to understand, I didn't have a choice. Do you think that you're the only one that shouldn't be in here? Your mistress, that wretched woman, always taunted me, flaunting every young man that attracted her. You try and keep the slaves' respect under those conditions. And I had to think of my position.'

'Grant me a pardon,' Shimon demanded.

'But I'd be ridiculed,' the governor replied, shocked at Shimon's presumption.

'That's not my problem,' Shimon answered.

'I don't suppose that I have an alternative.' Quintus Flaccus looked dejected. 'I'll make the arrangements. You will be working for me,' he stressed, recovering his poise after a brief pause. 'I'll instruct the other slaves to stay away from you and if they cause you any trouble, they'll be got rid of. You have my authority to do whatever's necessary to ensure my protection.'

Shimon was aware of the irony of his situation. He had been given his freedom by the same man who hadn't hesitated to deprive him of it two years previously.

'The new emperor has drawn up lists of our followers and has ordered us to abandon our beliefs by showing allegiance to the Imperial Cult,' Quintus Flaccus disclosed. 'I've cancelled all my public appearances and official engagements. An assassin could strike at any moment. You'll leave here in the morning. I trust that I can rely on your discretion to keep our conversation private?'

Then, gesturing nervously with his hands, he slid away.

18

'RIGHT, SOLLY, GET yourself up! Unfortunately I've been told you're going to be leaving us,' shouted the same turncoat guard who had escorted Shimon when he first arrived at the *ludus*. 'And you'd better put these on,' he added, throwing fresh clothes at Shimon. 'Looking at you, anybody would think that you've been locked away for years and the key has been thrown away. Can't have you leaving us smelling like any old vagrant, especially where you're going, can we? It would ruin our reputation.'

Shimon swung his powerful legs off his bed, yawned and rubbed his eyes.

'Pity that you won't be here to see the new *lanista* who's arriving today. Rumour is he's from Germany and from what I hear, a proper bastard. Makes the old one look quite tame in comparison,' the guard said, and left Shimon to make his final preparations.

Shimon looked at the open door. He felt almost reluctant to leave the place where he had been imprisoned for almost two years. In a strange way he'd become attached to its routines and its brutality.

He retrieved the money that he'd carefully hidden away and walked through the dimly-lit corridors of the barracks for the last time. Two of the governor's slaves were waiting to escort him back to the villa from which he'd been summarily ejected.

Impulsively, he put his hands out in front of him, expecting to be manacled. He hadn't yet absorbed the fact that he was a free man. As he moved slowly away from the *ludus*, Shimon stopped every few paces and looked behind him, convinced that the guards were pursuing him and would drag him back to the barracks. Gradually, as the *ludus* disappeared from view and they approached the open road to Bosra, his mood changed.

He began to reflect on the experiences of his lost youth. He couldn't believe that he was the same person as the naïve boy of eighteen who'd left his family, believing that he was entitled to a better life. Imprisoned for two years, subjected to the worst forms of human degradation, he no longer knew who he was. In the *ludus* there was little difference between life, which was no more than a pathetic existence, and death, which was a welcome release from it. Yet, against all expectations, he had survived. Now he was about to re-enter an unknown world, he felt unprepared for the adjustments that he would have to make. How would he cope with being free again, having to think for himself, making his own decisions? He had become used to rigid routine, where his concerns were limited to the next meal and remaining sufficiently alert to protect himself from his adversaries. His apprehension increased with every step that he took.

Shimon put his hand in his pocket to check that his money was still there. It represented his only security; it was the only thing that separated him from the impoverished youth who had made the same journey many lifetimes before.

Continuing up the familiar winding path as dusk descended, he noticed that the villa had lost much of the grandeur that had impressed him. The brickwork looked faded; the building resembled a mausoleum that had been allowed to fall into disrepair rather than the official governor's residence.

He was led through the side door of the house. His body tensed; any moment he expected to be confronted by Spurius, the head slave. Inside, he recognised only a few faces. None of the slaves remembered him and Spurius was no longer there.

Shimon was shown to the same small dingy room that he had been forced to share with two others when he had first arrived looking for work. Now he was its only occupant. He wouldn't have any difficulty remaining vigilant, for he had learnt not to trust anybody.

He felt hungry since he had left the *ludus* before the first meal, and decided to go to the kitchen to find something to eat before reporting to the governor.

An ungainly looking man was sitting alone at the long wooden table in the middle of the room, hunched over a bowl of gruel. Shimon helped himself to a portion from a large metal pot that was still simmering on the stove and sat down.

'Do you know where I can find the master?' Shimon asked.

The man seemed oblivious and carried on with his meal.

'The governor has instructed me...'

'I know who you are,' the man replied, looking up at Shimon. 'The master is where he always is these days, locked away in his study. Thinks that will stop an assassin's dagger.' He laughed out loud.

'My job is to ensure that doesn't happen,' Shimon announced.

'May *Fortuna* be with you. Because she abandoned the bloke who was here before.'

Shimon guessed that the man was referring to Spurius.

'What happened to him?' Shimon asked.

'Found murdered in the bushes. Left a trail of blood from over there,' the man said, pointing to the same door where Shimon had entered a short time before. 'It wasn't as if he didn't deserve to die. He was a nasty individual. I'm just surprised that it didn't happen earlier. The governor wasn't too upset either. He never liked Spurius. Wouldn't be surprised if he was the one who arranged it.'

'And you replaced him?' Shimon enquired.

'I'm his younger brother, Appius. Same mother. We didn't know our fathers. I don't suppose you know *Domina* Livia,' Appius continued. He leaned across the table so that he was facing Shimon. 'Apparently,' he whispered, 'she and Emperor Anthony were lovers – when they weren't arguing and throwing things at each other. But the mistress was so badly affected by his death that she's never recovered. Now she just comes and goes whenever she pleases. Hasn't been here for weeks. Rumour is that she's been seeking the comfort of a number of young Greek men.'

Shimon wondered if his mistress knew that he'd been released from prison. He often thought about the night of passion they had shared and that she had showed no remorse for the injustice he'd suffered.

What Shimon and the other slaves didn't know was that Livia had been recalled to Rome by her father the senator, Marcus Praeconinus, to give an account of her business dealings with the emperor. The senator, concerned that his interests had been compromised and had come under the control of clans hostile to Rome, was determined to retrieve all the money that had been stolen from him. Livia had also been forced by her father to seek reconciliation with her daughter Julia, since Marcus Praeconinus was convinced that Anthony, attempting to impress his young lover, had divulged confidential details of his extensive interests in the East.

The old man had underestimated his granddaughter, however. Her loathing for him was even greater than her mother's; Julia had refused to disclose any information until Marcus Praeconinus agreed to finance her permanent move to the capital city.

Shimon finished his meal and went out of the kitchen. He walked over to the other side of the house to his master's study;

the last time he was in that room, he was pleading for his life. The door was open but the room was empty. There were plates of half-eaten food and a makeshift bed; the governor had obviously been using the study as his refuge.

Just as Shimon turned to leave, the dishevelled figure Quintus Flaccus appeared from behind his huge wooden desk.

'What are you doing here?' the governor asked in his high-pitched voice.

'Sir, I want to know where I should begin,' Shimon replied.

'If I knew that, I wouldn't need you, would I? Emperor Decimus wants me dead and it's your job to make sure that he doesn't succeed. Is that clear? Now get out!'

Shimon left the governor's study determined to do everything possible to identify the vulnerable parts of the two-floor villa that could be used by an assassin. Over the next few weeks, with the help of Appius who had established that the new member of the household was not a threat to his position, Shimon learned everything he could about the other slaves and made a list of likely suspects. He relayed his findings to Appius. Shimon was satisfied that the head slave was not one of those who might attack the governor.

One evening, when the rest of the household was asleep, the governor quietly entered Shimon's room.

'Simon, have you any news?' he whispered. The strain of being confined to his study was evident on his troubled face.

'The assassin is most likely to come from within the household,' Shimon replied.

'Who is it?' Quintus Flaccus enquired nervously.

'I'm not certain. Any of your slaves might have been bribed to kill you.'

'Get rid of them all!' Quintus Flaccus shouted, not caring that he might be overheard.

Shimon got up from his bed. 'Sir, I've found nothing certain so far. Getting rid of them all would not solve the problem.'

'Which one has turned against me?' Quintus Flaccus said, waving around his thin arms like a petulant child. 'I know you suspect someone. Tell me.'

Shimon was embarrassed by the man's lack of self-control. 'Eventually, one of them will make a move and then we will act,' he replied, attempting to offer some reassurance.

'*Fortuna* has abandoned me,' the governor whined.

'I thought these challenges were a test of your faith,' Shimon responded. He was impatient with the man's hysterics and spoke more abruptly than he intended.

'What do you know about faith?' the governor snapped.

'Perhaps it might be safer if you spent longer periods in that small room at the end of the corridor,' Shimon suggested, referring to the house church hidden away under the stairs.

'You were not supposed to go in there' the governor replied, shocked that Shimon had been in his prayer room.

'I'd keep it locked if I were you,' Shimon recommended. 'I'd say that behind those precious statues is a perfect place for someone to lie waiting for an unsuspecting person at prayer. You might consider disappearing, just for a short time until the situation becomes calmer.'

'What, so that bitch can continue taunting me with her affairs,' the governor responded angrily, referring to his wife. 'Now she's coming back from Rome, it would please her to have me out of her sight. Even with all those healer's potions, Livia wasn't able to give me a son. I should have divorced her long ago. I thought Anthony was my friend but he only used me to get to her father's money,' the governor ranted. 'If he'd been genuinely interested in promoting Christianity, he'd still be alive. And now you're suggesting that I have to go into hiding just because I want to be free to practise my beliefs. Not that I can possibly expect you to understand.' He glared at Shimon, as if he was to blame for his predicament. Petulantly, Quintus Flaccus turned around and marched out of the room.

Shimon believed that poison would be the most likely method an assassin would use to kill the governor. He therefore concentrated his investigations on the cook, whom he had found to be a particularly resentful individual. Using poison in the governor's food, the man was in a perfect position to carry out an assassination undetected.

Domina Livia was expected home the next day. The kitchen staff were told to prepare a banquet to celebrate her safe return. The fuss and chaos that surrounded such an event would give his suspect the opportunity he was waiting for if he did indeed plan to poison his master.

Shimon awoke early and, after the first meal, which he ate alone in the kitchen, he hid in the pantry where he could watch the cook at work. He knew that he risked being detected by the other kitchen slaves, but he wanted to catch the perpetrator before he had a chance to act.

He didn't have to wait long. The cook began preparing the food for the celebration. Then, after a few minutes, he produced a vial from his tunic and quickly poured its contents into a grimy iron pot that was boiling on the stove.

Shimon leapt out of his hiding place and pounced on the cook before he had a chance to escape. The governor was immediately informed and rushed, partially clothed, into the kitchen as the cook was bundled into the hands of two of the guards.

🙖🙖

For the next few days, Shimon remained vigilant to ensure that there were no further attempts on his master's life. He was particularly careful to vet the new slave who was employed to supervise the kitchen.

His job was complete. Assuming that he was now free to leave the villa, Shimon was gathering up his belongings after his evening meal when he was surprised by the unexpected appearance of his mistress.

'The cook!' Livia announced incredulously. 'Who would have believed it?' Livia was holding the empty vial in the palm of her slender hand. 'So you think my husband can now rest easily?'

'I'm not aware of any further threat,' Shimon replied, noticing that she seemed strangely forlorn.

'You must leave immediately,' Livia suddenly informed Shimon, recovering her poise. 'Your life is in danger.'

'What do you mean?' Shimon asked.

'My dear boy, all is not what it seems. My husband is going to send you back to prison.'

What was she talking about? She was obviously unaware of the governor's commitment to free him. 'But the threat to his life has been removed. He promised me my freedom,' Shimon said.

'There was no threat,' Livia announced.

'I don't understand. I saw the cook myself. He was putting poison into the master's food.'

'What you thought was poison was nothing more than harmless spices,' the mistress said, smiling.

'But the cook? He's been dismissed! If you knew he wasn't guilty, why didn't you say anything?' Shimon asked, concerned that an innocent man had been arrested and that he had been instrumental in some kind of conspiracy.

'It was convenient,' the mistress responded. 'Despite his extra privileges, he was always the most resentful of slaves. There's no doubt that eventually he would have committed a crime,' she said assertively.

'I don't understand,' Shimon admitted.

'My husband would never have released you.'

'But he thought that his life was in danger from the emperor. He told me so himself,' Shimon protested, unable to grasp what was being revealed to him.

Livia moved closer to Shimon and placed her hand affectionately on his shoulder. 'I gave an oath to Miriam. I knew that she was your sister. I agreed that if she could provide a simple service, I would try and compensate you for the injustice you suffered. I would make sure that you were released.' She smiled at the memory of her late-night visit to the barracks.

Shimon recalled the events of that evening. He now understood the reason his mistress appeared so desperate to see him again, but was astonished that his sister would consent to such a ploy.

'But since my husband was the only one who could obtain your release,' Livia added, 'it had to be his idea.'

'So you made him believe that he was about to be assassinated?' Shimon asked.

'So that I could keep my word to your sister. I've warned him that unless he wants to incur the wrath of his Lord on the household, he must keep his pledge and set you free. But, as you know, my husband can be erratic, so collect your things and leave the house quickly before he comes looking for you.' Livia smiled before leaving Shimon for the last time.

Shimon saw that she had left a small pouch in the corner of the room. Looking inside, he found a few gold coins. It was his mistress's way of helping him start a new life.

Heeding her warning, he left his small room. Not wanting to attract attention, he let himself out of the side door of the house and proceeded swiftly down the path away from the governor's villa.

19

SHIMON REACHED THE main road and started the long journey northwards, back to the home that he had left two years ago. Then, remembering that Miriam would not be there to greet him, he halted. There was nothing for him to go back for. Miserably, he sat down at the side of the road and put his head in his hands.

After a while, he dragged himself to his feet. He had to go somewhere. Trying to suppress his feelings of despondency, he carried on walking towards the city. What was he going to do for the rest of his life? He needed to find work but he had no particular skills. Certainly nothing that anyone would pay for. He looked at his massive hands. Fighting was all that he knew.

For now, he had enough money for food and lodging. Something would happen, he assured himself.

A few hours later he reached Bosra and found an inn that offered basic accommodation. He paid for a small room and for the first couple of days did little more than sleep. His nightmares had become more intense and left him exhausted. On the third day, he paced restlessly around the small chamber. He was bored. He had to find some direction in his life.

He passed the next few days wandering the streets outside the arena, trying to recapture the atmosphere, that addictive mixture of fear and exhilaration that had once energised him.

One cold, bright afternoon the crowd outside the forum was particularly frenetic. The place was bustling with people, some listening to the official's announcements while others were glancing at the daily news displayed on the public notice boards.

'Hello, Solly. I didn't expect to find you loitering around here,' a familiar voice called out. 'Come and join me for a drink and you can tell me your news.'

Shimon turned around and saw Gaius Licinius pointing at him. Before he had a chance to consider the offer, the man grabbed his arm and led him to the inn that he had been to once before with the governor.

'So you're a free man now? Who'd have thought it? What have you been doing with yourself since you left the school?' asked the *lanista*.

'I found work,' Shimon responded warily. He knew that the man opposite could never be trusted.

'Let me guess?' the *lanista* said, leaning closer. His foul breath indicated that he had already been drinking heavily. 'Your friend the governor made you an offer that you just couldn't refuse?'

'We came to an arrangement,' Shimon replied.

'He made a nice comfortable nest for you both, did he?' the trainer asked, filling up his cup with wine. 'Must have been like a tug of war with the *domina*, and you in the middle.' He grinned lasciviously. 'Come on, Solly, I don't like drinking alone.' Gaius Licinius poured some of the watery red liquid into Shimon's goblet. 'Made you feel good, did it? Both of them fighting for your affection – or were you the dessert at those dinner parties they share with their fancy friends?'

'You're drunk.' Shimon got up from his place, eager to get away from the trainer.

'Wait, Solly!' Gaius Licinius shouted loudly. 'There's a lot you don't know.'

'Like what?'

'What's it worth?' the *lanista* asked.

Shimon sat down again, his curiosity stirred.

'You've made plenty of money and I'm a businessman,' Gaius Licinius explained. 'I don't give away information for free. So, come on!' He put his hand out to Shimon. 'Make it worth my while and then I'll tell you things that you wouldn't believe.'

Shimon produced a few *denarii*, which he slammed on the table. It was worth taking a chance if he could find out more about the governor's strange behaviour. And he wanted to understand all that had happened over the past few years.

The *lanista* looked at the money disdainfully, poured himself another drink and put the coins in his pocket.

'They only got rid of me because I knew what they were doing. All that bloody money.' He shook his huge head resentfully. 'They couldn't spend it fast enough. She was the clever one, Livia; her and that Emperor Anthony were involved in it together.'

Shimon moved irritably in his chair. The *lanista* was rambling. Had he wasted his money?

'Naturally, Rome and her father Marcus Praeconinus believed they had command of the situation but Anthony was ambitious,' Gaius Licinius continued. 'That's why he wanted your *domina* for himself, so he could take control of her father's business. And that idiot governor Flaccus was blind. He couldn't even see what was going on in his own house. He was more interested in getting the emperor to give his consent to that new religious sect that had converted him.'

'None of this is of any interest to me,' Shimon said, and got up again.

The *lanista* helped himself to more wine. 'Don't you want to know how you were just able to walk away from the *ludus*?' he asked.

Shimon stopped and looked at the trainer curiously.

'Thought you might be interested,' Gaius Licinius said, indicating that he was keeping the most valuable information until last.

'The governor needed my help,' Shimon told him emphatically.

Gaius Licinius roared with laughter, amused at Shimon's naïvety.

'I suppose you had a private word with your Jew God,' he joked. 'And He said, "Don't worry, Solly boy. I'll make sure that none of those blokes you're going to face will give you any trouble. They'll just take one look at you and lay down and die."'

Shimon didn't understand what the man was talking about. Was it because he had had too much wine? Or was the trainer trying to swindle him out of a few more *denarii* by implying that he had more information?

'Money is why you're still alive and not in the graveyard with those other worm-infested corpses,' the *lanista* said.

'You've gone mad,' Shimon declared, but was sufficiently curious to let the man continue.

'I only wanted what was rightly mine,' the trainer explained. His face was flushed and he was beginning to slur his words. 'I made them a fortune through the games. But then, they suddenly changed their plans. They said that things were becoming uncomfortable. They wanted to get rid of me!'

'How many times do I have to tell you?' Shimon replied angrily, leaning his powerful body across the table. 'None of this is of any concern to me!'

'Those blokes you fought were paid to lose and anyone telling you different is a liar. Their families were grateful for the money.'

'What do you mean?' Shimon asked, bewildered. 'Paid by whom?'

'Large amounts of money from an unknown source finds its way to this bunch of influential businessmen including, you've guessed, Emperor Anthony. See, they know that with the help of my specialist knowledge, they can treble their investment and more by betting on the result of the fights.'

'You're telling me the fights were fixed?' Shimon demanded.

'You couldn't lose unless you tripped and fell on your bloody sword.'

'You're lying!' Shimon suddenly felt unsure of himself.

Gaius Licinius sat up straight, all signs of his drunkenness gone. Sensing Shimon's vulnerability, he now sought to take full advantage of him.

'Solly, you might be interested in this new business venture of mine. We could be partners,' he suggested. He touched Shimon's arm. 'All we have to do is organise the fights so that the right man wins. No one gets hurt because they're only exhibition contests. But the crowds love them. Together, we can make a fortune.'

'That's why you weren't surprised to see me,' Shimon remarked, too absorbed in the trainer's revelation to listen to what he was now saying. 'You came looking for me, didn't you?'

'Look, Solly, I don't want any trouble,' the trainer said, trying to sound more conciliatory. He sensed that he might have underestimated the younger man's reaction – and Shimon's size and power made him a frightening adversary. 'All I'm saying is that you were lucky to get out alive.'

Shimon was feeling increasingly uncomfortable. He wanted to get away but it was as if he was being forced against his will to stay and hear the rest of Gaius Licinius's revelations.

'The syndicates had their money on Socrates, so they were furious when he was poisoned by his own sword. He was supposed to have killed you.'

'And he nearly succeeded,' Shimon responded sourly.

'A number of people were getting suspicious because you kept on winning. So the syndicate dumped you in favour of your young friend,' the other man explained. 'And when you killed him, they lost a fortune. They thought that it was my fault, so I had to disappear or to risk a dagger in my back. When Anthony was murdered, the men who controlled the money were deprived of their main benefactor. They were out of business, which meant that I could come out of hiding.'

'So you're telling me that your friends took bets on me to win. And because I'd been drugged – and I'm sure you knew nothing of that!' he retorted contemptuously, 'they were going to make huge amounts of money on my death, since I was incapable of defending myself.'

'You've upset a lot of people,' the *lanista* answered, undeterred by Shimon's aggression. 'There are plenty of people who would be happy to see you dead. That's why you'd be wise to consider my offer.'

'And you expect me to believe that you're telling me all of this because you're only concerned for my health?'

'I've got no grudge against you, Solly.' The trainer grinned.

'That's not very comforting, since you didn't think of warning me that my fight with Socrates was going to be my last,' Shimon replied.

'The syndicates would have had me killed,' Gaius Licinius protested.

'And I suppose you think you deserve my sympathy?'

There was a short pause, then the *lanista* reached across the table and grabbed Shimon's wrist. 'So, Solly, you and me. We got a deal?' he asked. 'I'll wager you can't wait to start fighting again, showing off that lovely body of yours.'

'Get yourself another boy,' Shimon told him firmly. He pulled his hand away and ran out of the inn in the direction of the forum. He didn't want to believe what he had just been told. He didn't want to accept that he hadn't won the fights fairly.

Gaius Licinius followed him out of the tavern. 'Shame about that *femina*,' he shouted, trying to catch up with Shimon. 'She had a message for you, see!'

Shimon stopped. The *lanista* had followed him into a narrow alley. Shimon grabbed him by the throat, lifted his feet clear off the ground and pinned him against the wall. 'You're not worthy to mention her name, you vile piece of cack,' he growled. 'So if you have anything to say, you'd better be quick because I've got no conscience about killing you. The chances are that I might quite enjoy it.'

'It's just a letter,' the trainer replied hoarsely, his voice indistinct as Shimon tightened his grip around his throat. 'She said it should be given to you, but only if you came looking for her,' he lied, trying to save himself.

'Why should I believe you?' Shimon wanted to know.

'I can't breathe,' the man complained.

'Then consider yourself a dead man!'

'Please, I'm telling the truth,' Gaius Licinius pleaded. 'I was going to give it to you, honest, I was!'

'And how much extra money would you have wanted for it?' Shimon demanded.

'It's yours; you can have it for free if you let me go.'

Shimon released his grip from the *lanista's* neck but kept his arms stretched out either side of his victim so that he couldn't escape. The trainer, suspecting that he had only been given a temporary reprieve, fumbled inside his stained tunic and produced a crumpled letter, which he handed to Shimon.

'Now can I go?' he begged, still trapped against the wall.

'What have you done with her body? Take me to where she's buried.'

'How am I supposed to remember? It was a long time ago,' the *lanista* protested, trying to extricate himself.

'It's not that long since you took such pleasure in telling me what had befallen her,' Shimon said, wishing that he'd inflicted the final blow on the pitiful wretch. 'Now move yourself! I want to see my sister's grave and you're going to take me there.'

He pushed the fat man a few paces ahead of him. The two men travelled a short distance through a maze of narrow streets. The entrance to the cemetery was concealed beside the arena.

'It could be anywhere in here. Be reasonable,' the trainer pleaded.

'Then you'd better start digging,' Shimon replied.

The *lanista* staggered over several mounds of earth that hadn't yet settled until he stopped in a far corner of the field.

'Here it is,' he announced, sounding pleased with himself for finding the place. He pointed to a small grave set a short distance away from the rest.

Shimon approached the man and, forgetting the strength that had always flowed effortlessly into his limbs whenever he was provoked, he grabbed the *lanista* by the neck.

'Don't ever let me set eyes on you again, unless you want to suffer the same fate as all those poor bastards whose deaths you caused.'

He pushed Gaius Licinius away forcefully, into one of the newly-dug graves. Struggling to get to his feet, he didn't notice the thin-bladed knife that he always carried concealed beneath his tunic fall to the ground.

As Gaius Licinius scurried away, Shimon picked up the knife and absent-mindedly put it into his pocket. Then he sat down by his sister's grave and took and opened her letter.

My beloved brother, I suspect that by the time you read this letter my soul will have departed from this world and hopefully will be in a better place. Please don't blame yourself. It was destined when we were born that my purpose would be fulfilled at a young age. I accepted my fate, as you must now, for you have a long and meaningful life ahead of you.

I did what I could to release you from the injustice you suffered but I failed. If you can find a way in your heart to forgive me, I beg you to take my remains for a proper burial to the Galilee, to the land of our people where, God willing, I shall be able to find eternal rest.

Until we meet again, your sister Miriam.

Now Shimon knew what he had to do.

He hurried back to the forum to find a market stall where he could purchase some materials to cover the body that he would take to its final destination. Then he returned to the cemetery. With his bare hands, he began penetrating the hard-crusted surface of his sister's burial place.

It was dark when, exhausted and covered in dirt, he recovered Miriam's partially clothed remains.

Shimon wrapped her carefully in a cotton shroud and then placed her small body into a large sack. Tears running down his face, his sister lying at his feet, he bitterly regretted the disappointment he had brought to her during her lifetime.

Shimon placed the letter in his pocket and started on the long journey to fulfil his sister's final wishes.

20

TRAVELLING DAY AND night for four days through high mountain passes and across flowing streams with his sister's remains over his shoulder, Shimon walked the same road that his ancestors had taken from Jerusalem more than a century before. He looked down on the rolling green valleys and the vast expanse of blue water of Lake Kineret, and saw that he had eventually reached the Galilee.

He felt calm now as if, even in death, Miriam was still there to guide him. They had been reunited and he no longer felt alone. He would find a suitable burial place for her and then return to the land of his birth to look for work.

As he went down the side of the mountain, the sun appeared to drop out of the sky in front of him, making the remaining descent more treacherous. Shimon, suddenly feeling vulnerable, used his spare hand to feel inside his tunic. The *lanista's* dagger was still there. Looking around, he saw only small farms and flocks of grazing sheep; there was no apparent danger.

Stopping at the side of the lake, he refilled his canteen with water. He was filthy from his journey and, removing his soiled clothes, he stepped into the lake to wash the grime from his body.

After he had dried himself using his tunic, and put the damp garment back on, he continued around the lake. The terrain became flatter; spread out in front of him were the Hebrew burial grounds.

Shimon placed Miriam's body down carefully on the conse-crated land. He chose an easily identifiable area at the edge of the boundary wall, then he started moving earth away to create a final resting place for his sister.

Once the hole was deep enough, Shimon picked up his sister's tiny shrouded body and placed it in the ground. He felt an over-whelming sense of melancholy. The last four days had brought them together. He had never left her side. Now it was as if a part of him was being wrenched away forever.

Ashamed that he didn't know a eulogy for the dead, he put his hands over his eyes and repeated the only words he knew: '*Hear O Israel, The Lord our God, The Lord is One.*'

His grieving process had finally begun. He lay his aching limbs down next to his sister's burial place and, ignoring the hunger in his stomach, soon fell into a restless sleep.

'Who are you? Why can't you leave me alone?' Shimon plead-ed. He was completely naked. A huge man was wrestling with him, trying to gain an advantage over him and throw him to the ground. The two of them were alone in a sandy pit. The only sound was his own voice amid the eerie silence of the arena which was packed with people.

'But you're not prepared,' the faceless man replied, his voice sounding strangely distant.

'Who are you?' Shimon repeated, unable to match his much stronger adversary.

'It is who you are that's important,' the man answered, refusing to relax his grip.

'What do you mean?' Shimon asked his captor.

'Who are you?' the voice repeated.

'Let me go! You're hurting me.' Shimon felt a sharp pain in his leg as he struggled to free himself.

'You have a debt to pay,' the man said emphatically.

'Show me your face!' Shimon shouted, using his last reserves of strength to try and break the vice-like grip that was crushing him.

'It's not for you to see.'

'Then why don't you kill me?' Shimon responded.

'You've had your chance to die,' the man replied. 'Now you must live!'

'But I don't know how,' Shimon cried.

'Then you must learn!' the voice roared.

The figure suddenly turned around and Shimon saw that it was Miriam. He opened his eyes, feeling disorientated and needing a moment to adjust to his surroundings. Grimacing from stiffness, he got up slowly from the ground, still troubled by the dream that continued to haunt him. It was early morning and seeing no one about, he shuffled away from the burial place, in search of food.

Shimon followed several different paths that ran alongside a winding river. He picked apricots and almonds from the trees that covered the fertile area before it flowed into the lake. He felt strangely calm. For a reason that he didn't understand, he felt comfortable in this place. Gazing in every direction, he was astounded by its natural beauty.

21

Esther was busily weaving in her house, her hands sore from fulfilling the orders for clothes, when she saw the wild-looking stranger in the distance. She was tempted to interrupt her work and tell her brother Yochanan about him but she knew that he would have just started the evening service and could not be interrupted. When he finished, he would hold study sessions late into the night, so she decided it would have to wait until the morning.

The academy was home to thirty young, gifted students who had devoted their lives to religious studies. Yochanan was its principal, the *Rosh Yeshiva*. He had opened the school when he moved there with his younger sister five years earlier from Sepphoris, the place of their birth less than a day's journey away. In that time the school had become the most important institution in Israel for the handing down of religious laws.

As Esther ate her evening meal, she wondered about the wild-looking man. It was rare to see anyone in the vicinity who was not connected with the academy. Where had he come from? Where was he going? And why was he walking so purposefully?

Tired from her labours, Esther went into her small bedroom to sleep. Her brother regularly worked on his texts throughout the night and she knew he wouldn't return until daybreak.

The next morning she left the house early, still preoccupied with the stranger and whether he had gone away. Before taking the steep path to the farm that supplied all their daily needs, she felt a strange desire to cleanse herself in the river that ran down the valley.

Shimon had also spent the night close to the river. Not sure where he would go next, he was still sitting beneath a tree when he saw a barefoot young woman approaching in his direction. She was carrying a small book and appeared to be mumbling to herself.

It wasn't until she was a short distance away that she noticed the unfamiliar figure sitting on the ground. Panicking, she ran off quickly into the bushes.

'Wait!' Shimon shouted, without moving. 'I don't want to harm you.'

But she had already gone. Even from that one fleeting glimpse, he had seen that she was very beautiful. Her oval face and almond-shaped eyes stirred his senses. Who was this lithe girl with a crimson kerchief? Where was she going?

Shimon wandered aimlessly along the river without hope of seeing the girl again. Entering into the thickest part of the undergrowth, he heard the sound of splashing water. A sense of foreboding enveloped him. Had the girl slipped into the river when she ran away from him?

He followed the sound to a secluded pool. He saw a figure a few yards out from the bank, submerge then rise to the surface, then submerge again. Convinced that the girl was drowning, Shimon ripped off his tunic and jumped in after her. He swan rapidly towards the figure – and was confronted by a burly, clean-shaven man.

'Should I regard it as a compliment or do you jump in after anyone that you find appealing?' the man asked.

'You're not who I expected,' Shimon replied, trying to hide his embarrassment.

'Who did you expect?' the man asked, submerging himself again in the clear water.

'I... I...' Shimon responded, relieved that it wasn't the girl but unsure how to explain his actions.

'Well then, I'm sorry to disappoint you,' the man replied, turning his back on Shimon and lifting his massive frame out of the river.

'You should be more careful,' Shimon said, remaining in the water. 'The current is strong. You might have drowned.'

'You must forgive me for causing you any trouble,' the man replied. 'I obviously hadn't appreciated the hazardous nature of a simple bathe.'

'I made a mistake.' Shimon waded through the water and climbed effortlessly onto the riverbank. 'I've got a long journey ahead, so let me pass,' he said as he retrieved the clothes that he'd thrown off.

'Wait!' the man called out in his deep voice, putting out his huge arm to stop Shimon from leaving. 'If it's any consolation, I do have a sister who is apparently even more beautiful than me.'

Shimon glared at the man. Was this the brother of the woman that he had seen.

'Would you tell me where I might find her?' Shimon asked, with no attempt to hide his eagerness.

'Forgive me,' the man replied, 'but any man whom I introduce to my sister must first prove himself worthy of her.' He appeared unsurprised by Shimon's question.

'Prove themselves worthy to whom?' Shimon asked.

The large man remained silent and started to dress. Shimon, sensing that he had been rejected, was incensed. 'Look, I don't know who you are. I don't wish you any harm. Just tell me where I can find the girl and I'll be able to start my journey.'

'Being jumped on by a stranger, although an interesting experience, is not exactly what I intend for my sister,' the man replied. He appeared unimpressed by Shimon's size and obvious strength. 'Although I must admit, it does show a certain passion.' He smiled and suddenly began singing, as if the entire incident had lifted his spirits.

'Where I come from if you see something you want, you have to take it before anyone else does,' Shimon stated, trying to justify himself.

'So what brings a man like you to these peaceful parts?' The man gazed at Shimon's heavily scarred body.

Shimon hesitated, not trusting him sufficiently to divulge the true purpose of his journey. 'Family business,' he replied vaguely.

'I'm intrigued,' the man said. Now fully clothed, he wrapped a woollen shawl around his colossal shoulders.

'You wouldn't understand.'

'You never know.'

'It's of no consequence,' Shimon said, reluctant to speak of his anguish in coming here to bury his sister. 'There's nothing here for me. I'll be going.' He started to walk away.

'You've had a hard life,' the large man called out after Shimon.

'I survived,' Shimon replied, separating the bushes to clear a path for himself.

'I'd be interested to hear about your experiences,' the man said. He started to follow Shimon up the steep incline of the riverbank. 'It's not often that someone like you just suddenly appears and makes such an immediate impression.'

'I need to find work,' Shimon said. He was flattered that someone was showing a genuine interest in him. Perhaps this man could help him after all.

'So where will you go?'

'I shall return to the land of my birth. Maybe I can find something there.'

'If you have no definite prospects, there's always a place here for someone with your, how should I say, physical attributes. The land provides us with all our needs. We always need help to work on it.'

'And what could possibly tempt me to stay here?' Shimon enquired.

'An honest day's endeavours in return for food and shelter. What more can a man ask for?'

'I can't say that it sounds appealing.'

'This is a place of learning,' the man announced.

'You mean a school?'

'But only for those with ability. Should you decide to devote that same strength that has clearly enabled you to survive life in the physical world to learning, you would be welcome.'

'So you are a teacher then?' Shimon asked. He watched the man as he passed the fringes from the corner of his shawl through the fingers of his right hand.

'I didn't realise it was that obvious,' the teacher replied with smile.

'I abandoned learning a long time ago. I'll go my own way,' Shimon said. He set off, leaving his companion gazing after him.

'Should you decide to return, the offer will still be here,' the man shouted, raising his arm in a farewell gesture. Slowly he began to walk in the opposite direction, all the while reciting a prayer for his visitor's safe return.

22

ESTHER SAT IN front of the hearth trying to warm herself, still enthralled by her earlier adventure. Her heart was beating wildly after she saw the young man and he attempted to pursue her. Eventually, realising that he was no longer behind her, she had immersed herself in her own secluded part of the river.

A few moments later, a short distance away, she overheard her brother in heated discussion with another person. Was it the wild man with his long hair and piercing gaze who had made a chase for her? Wanting to find out, she moved towards them, hidden by the undergrowth.

The sound of the two men's voices grew louder as she approached. She watched, captivated, as the massive bodies circled each other like two predatory beasts. Never before had she seen a man of such intimidating power; his fighter's stance seeming to conceal an anger that was waiting to erupt . At the same time, she was amazed at her brother's indifference to the danger that he was courting. It was as if he was laying down a challenge to the stranger.

Esther retreated to her own part of the stream, leaving her brother and the stranger to continue sparring on the riverbank, not knowing whether she would ever see him again.

Now back home in the kitchen, she placed the last remaining log on the fire to keep the dwindling flame from extinguishing and thought about her brother.

Even when they were children, he had been filled with a competitive spirit. He always needed to prove himself the best at whatever task or studies he was involved in. After the death of their beloved parents, their grandfather had taught him to be a blacksmith and he had been apprenticed. But Yochanan had always considered the life of a blacksmith dull and the world of business to be beneath his dignity. When against her wishes, he sold all the land they'd inherited to fund a life of religious study, what choice did she have but to follow him? He was the only close family she had.

She had wanted to marry Yochanan's best friend, Raphael, but had given up that chance of happiness to help her brother establish his own school. Now she was waiting for him to fulfil his obligation and find her a husband.

There had been suitors, but none had proved themselves sufficiently worthy. The *Rosh Yeshiva* had strict criteria for her potential husband: he had to be a suitable study partner. Since all the men who had sought to marry her had failed to achieve the intellectual standard that Yochanan required, Esther was never given the opportunity to make her own assessment of them.

✲

It was midday when the teacher returned to the house. The meeting with Shimon had left him feeling high spirited.

'Brother,' Esther began as soon as he entered. 'You know I try not to complain, but how much longer can we be expected to endure such hardship? We had to go without our own food again last *Rosh Hashanah* so that your students were not deprived. We have no money and the farm can't produce enough for our needs. The new governor, Quintus Flaccus, is even less sympathetic than his predecessor. It's said that he's one of those New Christians and blames the Jews for a grave misfortune that he suffered. He won't delay sending his tax collectors to demand the two *denarii* from all of us so that we can continue to practise our beliefs. And if we can't pay, the academy will close and we will have to send the pupils away.'

She started to cry, struggling to keep warm by the dwindling hearth.

'The students contribute what they are able,' Yochanan replied, not appearing overly concerned.

'You have thirty mouths to feed; surely the students should be encouraged to learn a trade? Are we not told that study of *Torah* without an occupation is wrong and eventually leads to sin? Most of your students are already betrothed, and when they leave here they'll have their own responsibilities.'

'It is our duty to support them during their studies. The physical world can wait for them,' the *Rosh Yeshiva* answered dismissively. 'I will not be distracted from our main purpose. Our role is to provide rulings according to the Law of Moses that will ensure our people not only continue to survive but also flourish in a land of learning. And now they are waiting to be told which of them I shall appoint as my assistant.' Yochanan got up from his chair.

'Who have you chosen?' Esther enquired, knowing that the successful candidate would inevitably suffer the same fate as his predecessors. Unprepared for the commitment they would be expected to show to their master, they would soon be dismissed. Their reputations would be diminished to such an extent that maintaining their place in the academy would become untenable.

'Ah!' Yochanan exclaimed with his usual ebullience. 'You'll just have to be patient.' He stretched out his huge arms.

Then the master left for the study hall and his students, who eagerly awaited his arrival.

Although the rains had ceased temporarily, Esther pulled the covers over herself to keep out the cold that still permeated the poorly insulated house. She knew what to expect when she challenged her brother's conscience about the sacrifices she'd made for his benefit. She wished now that she'd carried on her nurse's apprenticeship.

Yochanan had shown great compassion when he accepted Isaac, a married man from a poor family, into the academy. His wife soon conceived but became sick. A midwife who had travelled a long distance to attend to her aunt's son at the next village had to be summoned. When the nurse arrived, Esther asked whether she could help deliver the baby and proved particularly adept at her work. The mother was saved but unfortunately the child died, leaving the husband distraught and unable to continue with his studies.

Esther remembered that the young midwife, only a few years older than herself, had refused payment for her services. Esther had been so impressed with the young woman that she hoped that she would be offered a position as her assistant. Yochanan had also appeared captivated by the midwife's dedication. She was a very spiritual woman and they shared many common interests.

Yochanan had not shown any interest in women since the end of his marriage some years ago. He had married young, and his wife gave birth almost immediately. However, she soon grew tired of his absorption in his studies and the lack of money that made their lives so hard. She never saw her husband, and felt that she was denied a chance to build a life with him. After eighteen months, she demanded a divorce and Yochanan, unwilling to be distracted from his work, agreed to her wishes. He never referred to her again. Yochanan wanted a relationship with his son but the mother had turned the child against him.

Miriam, however, seemed to delight him with her knowledge

and spirituality. The two had spent many hours together, often disappearing to the lake to talk. Had Esther not known her brother so well, she would have suspected that a relationship was developing between them. But one day, without warning, Miriam left. Yochanan was quieter than usual for a while but gradually his normal ebullience returned.

Yochanan refused to let Esther leave the school. He said that she was already carrying out valuable work and couldn't be spared. Esther suspected, however, that he didn't want her to go because he dreaded the prospect of loneliness. He had tied her to him, even if it made her unhappy.

Esther often thought about that young woman from a distant place, dispensing goodness and care to the needy who, in different circumstances, would have become her teacher and valuable friend.

⁂

The school, a flimsy rectangular building, was situated high in the valley overlooking the Sea of Galilee. The largest of a pair of abandoned farmhouses, it had been converted into an academy. One part comprised a sparsely decorated dormitory with basic sanitary facilities, and the other a study hall with a small dining area. Esther supplied food for the thirty students, obtained from the nearby farm and prepared in her own home.

The study hall vibrated with the sound of pairs of students vying with each other to prove their arguments. Silence fell when the master, dressed in a ceremonial white robe that accentuated his already giant stature, entered the room. His devoted followers rose to their feet; they were waiting to hear who would be appointed as their teacher's study partner.

'My pupils,' the master began with a look of satisfaction because he was again the main focus of their attention. 'I am pleased to see that you've been diligently reviewing your studies. Through your efforts, the academy's standard of excellence will be upheld. But it is not enough to confine yourselves to the arguments of the sages if you are unfit to apply their rulings in the physical world.

'I am looking for a rare individual, one who is prepared to make the ultimate sacrifice. A person who will devote himself, unconditionally, to providing me with the tools to engrave the laws that will be passed on to future generations. These will ensure the survival of our people.

'If you feel that you are unable to show that level of commitment, ask yourselves whether you should save your families their hard-earned money and seek another vocation. In seven days it will be the festival of *Purim*, the time when our people endorsed their relationship with the Almighty and were saved from destruction by the Persians. A time for celebration, when you will be informed of my decision.'

The teacher left his young protégés, stunned by his proclamation, and went back to his home.

23

SHIMON, DEVOID OF any real sense of purpose, travelled back along the same path through the valley. He took a longer route around the lake so that he didn't have to pass his sister's resting place; the pain of her burial was still too fresh in his mind.

As he started his ascent into the mountains, he thought of his encounter with the man and his words of friendship. Had he been too hasty in declining his offer? Without Miriam waiting for him, what reason was there to return to a place that was full of painful memories? A place to which, even if it used to be his home, he no longer felt any attachment?

He fantasised about the olive-skinned girl, the crimson scarf covering her black hair. He wondered if he would ever see her again. Shimon put his hand in his pocket. His money had dwindled to a few coins. Why would she be interested in a pauper? he asked himself.

What he needed was to start earning a decent amount of money again. He would either enrol in the *ludus* as a volunteer or join a band of travelling fighters that put on shows in different market towns. Then he would return to the Galilee, worthy of the girl, and try to claim her for himself.

※

Shimon arrived back in Bosra several months later. He had found temporary work as a labourer on a high mountain pass after he helped the farmer gather a flock of sheep that had escaped from their pen. The owner was grateful for his assistance and Shimon needed little persuasion to remain. The job provided him with enough to eat to rebuild his strength and a set of new clothes. When the old farmer suddenly died, leaving only his wife and disabled son to look after the farm, Shimon agreed to prolong his stay until they were able to find a replacement for him. Finally a cousin had arrived at the farm to take over, and Shimon was free to leave.

Shimon entered the city indistinguishable, or so he believed, from any other citizen on its busy streets.

His mood was completely different from when he left months previously. He wandered to the arena, curious to assess his reaction. How would he respond when he saw the place that had absorbed every moment of his life for two years and which had nearly succeeded in dehumanising him?

Shimon gazed up at the theatre that brought exaltation for the few but the demise of many more. He felt nothing. No longer did he thirst for the excitement of the fight, nor did he pine for the crowds' adulation. It was as if he had willingly forfeited the competitive advantage that had kept him alive during his imprisonment. Shimon turned around and walked back to the forum. He had finally freed himself from the hold the past had over him.

He went back to his old rooms above the inn. Every day he slept late but woke unsatisfied because of the nightmares that continued to plague him.

For the next few weeks he lived a life of solitude in a place where he no longer belonged. He helped out on a few market stalls to earn a few extra coins to pay for food and his lodgings but the desire for anything more had deserted him. He was content with a simple existence.

Shimon wasn't aware, however, that his return had been keenly anticipated and had been reported by the innkeeper to members of the same syndicate that had lost vast amounts of money on his final contest. The syndicate paid heavily for information about his whereabouts; they wanted their revenge. They planned to attack Shimon soon after he arrived in the city but never found the right opportunity to carry out their deed undetected.

Then one evening, two men followed Shimon into a dark alley by the side of the inn on his return from his evening meal.

'There he is,' the smaller man shouted to his mate, once he was sure that he'd identified their victim.

They ran at Shimon with their daggers drawn and bundled him against the wall, out of the sight of any possible witnesses.

'What do you want?' Shimon cried out, panicking at the thin blade that was held menacingly against his throat.

'Not so brave now, are you, Jew?' the taller assassin asked scornfully.

'Now you know what that young boy Socrates felt before you plunged your sword into him,' the smaller man added, reinventing the details of Shimon's fight with Socrates to justify his own violent intent.

Shimon remembered the *lanista's* warning. He realised that the two killers had been sent by the crooked gambling syndicate with whom the trainer had been involved.

'Cost a lot of people their hard-earned money, you did. But now you're going to pay them back. Understand?' The second man held his weapon so close to Shimon's side that he flinched in pain as the steel tip penetrated his skin.

'So come on Solly, hand us all that money you stole,' the first assailant said, enjoying the intense look of fear on their hostage's face.

Images of the barracks and the fights with The Beast and

Cassipor flashed into Shimon's mind, accompanied by unwavering determination to survive. He lifted his knee and buried it deep into the groin of the smaller of his attackers, causing the man to lunge wildly at him and miss his target. Then Shimon used all his force to strike the other perpetrator hard with his elbow, shattering the bones in his face.

Now free to retrieve the trainer's dagger from inside his tunic, Shimon was ready to fight for his life. The first assailant could not be deterred and thrust at him a second time, but Shimon was too quick and cut the killer's throat. Unwilling to meet the same fate, his mate ran away, having failed to accomplish his mission.

Shimon wiped his dagger clean on his tunic that was already soaked from the wound in his side. Holding his hand over the spot to try and stem the flow of blood, he knew that he urgently needed medical attention. His only hope was to try and get to the *ludus*, a short distance away, and seek the assistance of the *medicus*. The man had always treated him fairly.

Shimon staggered away and entered the barracks, trying to avoid the attention of the new *lanista* or any of the guards. He was fortunate since the *medicus* happened to be on duty that evening.

'Please, you must help me,' Shimon implored the surprised practitioner. Those were his last words before he collapsed unconscious on the cold stone floor of the infirmary.

⁂

'Solly!' the *medicus* called out, his kind face overcome with worry. 'You must leave immediately.'

Shimon had woken in great pain from the wound in his side and discovered that it was heavily bandaged. 'What's the hour?' he asked, still groggy from the sedative he had been given to help him sleep.

'It's nearly light. Here take this,' the *medicus* said, offering his patient a cup of sweetened water and a piece of bread. 'Now the bleeding has stopped and the healing process has started, you must go,' he repeated nervously.

'No one knows that I'm here,' Shimon answered.

'The *lanista* has ordered everyone out on the training field and he'll be here any moment. He's already reduced our food because he's convinced that his men get too comfortable in here. Gaius Licinius is even more of an animal than he was before.'

Shimon look aghast at the mention of his old trainer.

'Four weeks after you left, the bastard strolled back in here as if he'd never been away,' the *medicus* continued. 'What happened to the new one, I've no idea. One morning he'd just disappeared.'

Shimon now understood the urgency. He remembered their last acrimonious meeting in the forum when his trainer appeared so surprised to see him. Gaius Licinius had obviously earned so much money that he found a way of getting rid of his replacement. Shimon speculated that the devious individual had secured an agreement with the syndicate that they wouldn't harm him if he could guarantee to deliver the person who ruined their business. Shimon shuddered at the thought that the *lanista* wouldn't rest until he was dead.

'The way he took advantage of that *femina* still haunts me,' the *medicus* exclaimed, shaking his head, disgusted. 'You remember, that poor young Jewish girl? She treated you, if I remember correctly.'

'She died in the plague,' Shimon said, repeating what his trainer had told him.

'That was afterwards.'

'What do you mean?' Shimon questioned, alarmed that his sister might have been subjected to further suffering.

'Gaius Licinius forced himself on her. Afterwards she became withdrawn. It was almost as if she had lost the will to live. I was the one who found her.' The *medicus* shook his head sadly.

Shimon began to shake with anger. Still wincing with pain, he manoeuvred himself carefully off the bed and reached for the *lanista's* dagger from the inside of his tunic.

'I'm going to kill that bastard!' he screamed. He now understood why Miriam, unable to cope with the shame that she had to endure, didn't visit him again and passed her remaining days alone.

'If he sees that I've been providing you with shelter, he'll have me carted away with those other poor souls that have outlived their use, so please hurry,' the *medicus* pleaded, thinking only of himself.

Shimon touched Miriam's letter. Remembering her words of hope, he knew that he would have to combat his inclination to seek revenge.

Shimon thanked the doctor, who refused the offer of payment for his care. Still in a lot of discomfort, he moved unsteadily out of the *ludus* before Gaius Licinius had an opportunity to search the area.

Not daring to return to the inn to retrieve his belongings, he hurried out of the city where he had escaped death. Unsure about his future but certain that he had fought his last fight, he followed the same route that he had taken months earlier.

Dressed only in the basic clothes that the *medicus* had risked taking from the stores at the *ludus*, Shimon soon found himself unprepared for the hazardous trek back to the Galilee. He had failed to consider the dramatic change in weather conditions brought by the onset of the rains. As he climbed into the mountains, he was exposed to the biting cold.

Shimon tried to divert his mind from the difficult journey that he had undertaken. He thought about the teacher's beautiful dark-haired sister and imagined that she would be there waiting for him by the river. How foolish he had been to leave the place so hastily.

A further day into his travels, the wound in his side again seeping blood, Shimon collapsed on a remote snow-covered path. He was convinced he was going to die.

He was disturbed by the gentle prodding of a blunt implement. Shimon believed that he was back in the dungeon in the city prison and it was the jailer waiting to escort him to be sentenced at the magistrate's court. He opened his eyes, for a moment unable to focus on the youth standing over him resting on his wooden staff. Slowly he recalled that it was the same disabled boy whose family he had worked for previously. He must have travelled further than he thought and had unknowingly passed the entrance to their farm.

With enormous effort, using the youth for support, Shimon walked the short distance to the boy's home. The boy's mother and cousin were still grateful for the help he'd given them the previous year; they gladly looked after Shimon until he regained his strength.

Despite the dreams that continued to plague him, often leaving him exhausted, he recovered his strength sufficiently to resume his journey. The days had become longer and warmer so travelling was less arduous.

Now that he was able to think more clearly, he started to question why he had returned. What could a place that was so different from the only world he knew offer him? Tempted to turn around and go back, he instinctively felt for Miriam's letter that he had guarded so carefully. As he touched it, he knew that he had to continue. As he started to descend the mountain, all feelings of doubt disappeared.

Shimon gazed at the fertile land around him and again felt drawn to the place. Almost a year after he'd arrived carrying his sister over his shoulders, he'd returned to the Galilee.

24

'FAMILY BUSINESS?' THE man suddenly called out.

Shimon, again feeling the need to be close to Miriam, turned around. He saw the familiar figure of the teacher staring at the sack in which he had carried his sister's remains. Shimon had just retrieved it from where he'd hidden it by the side of the grave after he'd buried Miriam.

'How did you know I was here?' Shimon replied, surprised by the man's arrival.

'We live in uncertain times so it's in our interest to remain vigilant. But it's evident that you wouldn't possibly consider harming us,' the teacher replied.

'I've been busy,' Shimon said hesitantly, trying to avert his gaze from the individual whom he sensed was scrutinising him.

'You don't owe me an explanation,' the man remarked, seeing Shimon's unease.

'I've done some bad things.'

'Show me a man who hasn't,' the teacher replied glibly.

Shimon saw that the teacher was smiling at him. He was soothed by the warmth that radiated from the man's handsome face. Suddenly, he felt completely at ease in his company.

'My life has not been one that I'm proud of.'

'So your conscience has been troubling you and that's the only reason you returned?' the man asked, sounding disappointed.

'All that time on your own can send a person mad. You start

imagining things until you no longer recognise what's real. The same dreams always repeating themselves, never letting you get any rest.' Shimon moved erratically as he spoke, as if still tormented by some burden that he had to bear.

'Perhaps you've begun to realise that it's time for some new challenges,' the man remarked, impressed by Shimon's willingness to talk about himself.

'But the past still won't let go.' Shimon sat down on the ground, sounding despondent.

The large man positioned himself opposite him, on top of a prominent boulder. 'Dreams can often accentuate a particular anxiety but can also prove to be part of its cure,' he said.

'You don't understand!' Shimon exclaimed, getting to his feet. 'At the beginning, I'm fighting the same faceless man who wants to force me onto the ground. I can't get out of his grip and when I struggle to free myself, he injures me. He could easily kill me, but it's as if he's giving me a chance to save myself.'

'Then what do you see?' the teacher asked curiously.

'My sister's face,' Shimon replied, staring vacantly at Miriam's grave. 'The man just disappears.' He picked up a handful of pebbles, which he placed carefully on the grave.

'I'm sorry for your loss,' the teacher said with genuine compassion. The gesture signified that Shimon had suffered a personal bereavement. The teacher got up from his place to comfort him.

'I don't need your sympathy. You didn't know her.' Shimon stepped a few paces back, unwilling to share his sorrow. 'If you're about to tell me that she's now found her reward and eternal peace, I'm really not interested,' he continued, more curtly than he had intended.

The teacher stood close to him but remained silent, giving him an opportunity to reflect. He knew the importance of timing when giving words of comfort to the bereaved.

After a long pause, he said, 'My name is Yochanan.'

Shimon, who had started to reveal his most private feelings to a stranger, was suddenly consumed with doubt. And yet, he felt strange warmth towards this man. I want to trust him, he thought. Perhaps he can help me rid myself of the demons that threaten to destroy me.

'We're all connected in one way or other and I share your pain,' Yochanan said, putting his hand affectionately on Shimon's shoulder.

'I don't suppose you know how it feels, losing the only person that ever loved you.' Shimon looked down on the small mound of the grave that had now developed a covering of thick grass. 'All my sister ever wanted was to help those who couldn't look after themselves. She gave out free potions. She wouldn't take any money for them. She said it was better that they went to the poor. Not that she could afford to be so generous when we rarely had enough to eat.'

'She was obviously a remarkable young woman,' Yochanan said carefully. He, too, had known a woman like that: the young woman who had tended to his student's wife. He looked more closely at the young man. There was something familiar about his features, something that he recognised. Could it be...?

'She never had enough time for me though,' Shimon said, shaking his head sadly. 'I was never able to match her expectations. But she always knew if I was in danger.'

The teacher recalled his own last meeting with the exceptional young midwife for whom he had developed such a deep respect. He had rarely encountered such a combination of profound wisdom, love of God and dedication to the well-being of others. But there had also been a sadness in her, almost as if an essential part of her had been torn away, rendering her incomplete. Yochanan thought often of her and remembered their time together. She had asked for no reward for the treatment she had offered the student's wife, other than a small favour; that if Yochanan ever met her brother, he would try to help him.

'We were born together,' Shimon explained. 'And even though she was the frail one, she was the one that attracted attention.' Tears welled in his eyes at her memory. The grief, which he had tried to suppress for so long, poured out of him. 'She provided the food for the family,' he continued. 'Wealthy people trusted her to deliver their precious children and they paid her.'

Shimon rummaged inside his frayed tunic and produced Miriam's badly stained letter. 'This is all I have to remember her by.'

'May I see?' Yochanan requested.

Shimon passed the crumpled note to his companion, who read it carefully.

'You travelled a long distance to carry out her wishes,' the teacher commented, his attention still focussed on the letter.

Shimon stood silently with his head bowed.

Yochanan recited a psalm of comfort for the mourner and then, drawing Shimon towards him, embraced him. 'Come, you must be hungry. Let us get some food and then I'll find somewhere for you to rest before you decide to leave again.'

Yochanan escorted his companion out of the burial grounds. He felt excited by the challenge of transforming a man of such immense physical power into a more spiritual person. He was also aware of his duty to the midwife. First, though, he had to convince his visitor to remain in the Galilee.

The two imposing figures passed along the side of the lake and continued the short distance towards the small house that the master shared with his sister.

'Where are we going?' Shimon enquired suspiciously.

'It's not far,' the teacher said. He had to raise his voice because the wind had come up, making his shawl flap around like some huge canopy.

They went into the dwelling, its sparsely decorated living area offering little comfort except for a wooden table and two chairs. Shimon could see a weaver's loom and spools of flax by the window, the only place where there was any natural light. The fire in the hearth was still smouldering. Someone had been busy working until recently.

Yochanan pointed at the empty workbench. 'The barley is now ripe for harvest and my sister is occupied in the fields,' he announced.

Shimon's heart began beating faster. Would the girl, the memory of whom had helped him through the ordeal of the last few months, soon be here?

Yochanan returned with a meagre portion of food, washed his hands, mumbled a few words of prayer and then summoned his guest to the table. 'It's Passover,' he said, holding up the unleavened bread then pushing it towards Shimon. 'A celebration of the delivery of our people from the hands of our oppressors. A time of hope, the new harvest.' His voice was enthusiastic and he searched for a glimmer of acknowledgment from his visitor.

'Her death was my fault,' Shimon said, still preoccupied with his sister and showing no interest in the food. 'I'll never be able to forgive myself.'

'You judge yourself harshly,' Yochanan replied, with his mouth full.

'There was bad feeling between us,' Shimon explained.

'And you didn't have an opportunity to ask for forgiveness?' Yochanan was curious about his companion's extreme sense of guilt.

Shimon shook his head. 'In prison, you soon learn that there's nothing unusual about death. I didn't find out what had happened to her until months later. The worst thing was not being able to see each other, except when I got into a fight – and the *lanista* only sent her to me to stop me from bleeding to death. When my sister discovered that I was in the *ludus*, she persuaded the barrack doctor to give her work so that she could be near enough to help me.'

'Only a very special person would be prepared to endanger their own life for the sake of another,' Yochanan said.

'I just wanted to tell her how sorry I was. But I was too late. She'd got sick again and was too frail to withstand the illness that had affected the whole *ludus*.'

'But with the help of God, you were able to find her,' the teacher said quietly.

'Only after nearly murdering that evil bastard of a trainer to find out where they'd buried her.' Shimon started to tremble with anger. He could never forgive the degradation that Gaius Licinius had imposed on his sister. He just wished that he'd killed the piece of scum when he'd had the opportunity. Then, at least, he would have avenged her honour.

'But now you're together again.'

'For a while,' Shimon answered. 'As long as I am here.'

'You can't keep on running away.'

'We're from different worlds, you and I.' Shimon got up from the table and gazed outside at the hills and mountains. His anger had dispersed, replaced by an inner calm.

'You never know, eventually those worlds could become one,' the teacher responded.

Looking outside at the grandeur of the scenery, so far away from the stinking city streets, Shimon felt a sense of humility. He was wrong. He and Yochanan were part of the same world, part of something so awe-inspiring that it made him feel totally insignificant.

He recognised that he was in a very special place.

25

THAT EVENING, ESTHER returned exhausted from a full day's labour in the fields. She was in high spirits. The barley crop was more than sufficient for their needs. They would be able to sell the surplus in nearby markets and support themselves for a few more months.

As she entered the house, she noticed two drinking cups on the table. Yochanan had been entertaining a visitor before he returned for his night of study. For a second, she wondered if it was the stranger. One of the students had told her that morning that an unkempt, intimidating man had been seen near the farm. If it was the stranger, she wondered whether Yochanan had persuaded him to stay. The only place that could provide adequate shelter was the sheep barn, which she had passed on her way home. Perhaps he was already there.

Esther ate her meal, preoccupied with thoughts of the wild man. Perhaps she would look for him the next day.

✿

'I trust you slept well?' a voice bellowed from the entrance of the barn. Behind him, the sky was bright with sunshine.

Shimon looked up and saw the shrouded figure of Yochanan towering over him like some huge praying mantis. He rubbed his eyes and, despite the early hour, attempted to adjust to his new surroundings.

The array of distorted faces that passed through his mind when he was asleep had, once more, left him feeling disturbed. In his dream, he was being pulled in different directions by the *lanista*, who was laughing at him, and then by his sister, whom he wanted to touch and bring close. But as he reached out for her, she just drifted through his fingers.

Shimon's mouth felt dry and he was grateful for the pitcher of water and piece of dry bread that Yochanan had brought him. Impulsively he felt for Miriam's letter, wanting to touch her words. He panicked when he realised that it was missing.

'Is this what you're looking for?' the teacher asked, holding out the missive. 'Please forgive me, I must have forgotten to give it back to you,' he added, not in the least embarrassed.

Shimon took it back, grateful for its safe return.

'Why do you believe that you're responsible for your sister's death?' Yochanan asked, making a cushion of grain for himself on the floor of the barn opposite his guest.

'I was the one who placed her in danger,' Shimon replied hesitantly. He chided himself for allowing the teacher to retain his private correspondence and felt aggrieved that the fellow considered it entitled him to carry on the previous day's discussion. 'If I hadn't been in prison, she wouldn't have come looking for me. She suffered terribly in that place before she died.'

'Doing what she did best,' the teacher added.

'What do you mean?' Shimon asked.

'You said that she was a healer. She knew the risk she was taking when she went into the *ludus*. You didn't cause her death.'

Becoming agitated, Shimon rose to his feet. 'It was my fault that I took all the strength that was meant for her when we were born. That's what my parents said to me.'

'You felt that your parents abandoned you?'

'It was as if I never existed,' Shimon responded dolefully.

Yochanan pointed at the ground and slowly the younger man sat down again.

'And you resented her because of that?' the teacher asked softly.

'Yes!' Shimon blurted out. 'No! Look, I don't know. I'm just confused.'

Yochanan moved nearer and, looking sympathetically at his troubled companion, began to explain. 'Children born at the same time often have more complicated relationships and conflicting emotions than other children. But it's clear that your sister cared for you deeply. She saw in you something that you couldn't see in yourself.'

'But, she never told me...'

Yochanan put up his hand to stop Shimon from interrupting. 'Your sister was obviously a wise woman,' he continued. He was certain that the midwife he'd been so fond of was the young man's sister. 'She may have been aware that she'd fulfilled her purpose on this earth. But with her passing, she has instilled in you the same inspiration to fulfil the purpose that God intends for you. That is her gift to you.'

Shimon, upset by what he was hearing, stood up again and began to pace the enclosure.

'Do you think she'd have forgiven me?' he pleaded.

'Dear friend, your sister was also seeking your forgiveness.'

'That can't possibly be true.'

'She was aware of your suffering and probably felt responsible for what happened to you. But she also knew that you and she had to separate so that you could become independent and pursue your own life. That would have affected her deeply.'

'So why didn't she say anything?' Shimon asked.

'She must have exercised great restraint. But she knew that, for your sake, she had to remain silent.' Yochanan paused and took a long drink of water from the jug resting on the ground. 'The faceless person that you are fighting is your conscience. The injury that you said he caused you is self-inflicted because of your deep sense of guilt.'

'I don't understand,' Shimon said.

'The guilt that is your burden – it's because you were the one who survived. Your sister's legacy to you, what she's attempting to impress upon you, is that you must choose life. That's her message.'

'I'm sorry but I really don't know what you're saying.'

'It's in the letter,' Yochanan replied, indicating that he wanted to retrieve it to justify his hypothesis.

Shimon took the note from his pocket, as he had done on numerous occasions.

'Now look carefully,' Yochanan said. 'The lines contain the Hebrew letters that, together, make the word for life. And the numerical value of these letters adds up to eighteen, which is the bearer of good fortune.'

Shimon pondered for a moment and then remembered the game with Cassipor, the night before his first contest.

'Three sixes on the dice!' he exclaimed. 'I was born on the eighteenth day of *Nissan*.' In his enthusiasm, he didn't question how he could suddenly recall the Hebrew date.

'That happens to be today,' Yochanan said, his face bright with joy at his friend's discovery. 'Now are you beginning to understand?'

Shimon rushed out of the barn into the fresh morning air. He felt a tightening in his chest and his head hurt with everything that had been said. How could someone who didn't even know his sister understand more about her than her own brother? And what right did a stranger have to tell him what she expected of him?

Shimon had heard enough. He quickened his pace, determined never to return. Unconsciously, he took the longer route around the lake to avoid having to pass Miriam's grave. But somewhere, deep inside, he was unable to dispel an overwhelming feeling of shame that he was running away again.

He stopped suddenly, acknowledging that he was no longer that person. He needed to find out more about himself. Who he really was – and more importantly, what type of person he could become.

Shimon turned around and went back. Yochanan had anticipated his reaction and had been content to wait for his prediction to be justified and the young man to return.

Shimon found the teacher swaying gently, immersed in prayer. Then, without any form of acknowledgment, the teacher returned to his cushion.

'Feeling better?' he asked.

'The letter and the numbers on the dice, it has to be a coincidence because there are still so many things that don't make any sense,' Shimon replied, breathing heavily and recognising that he still needed further explanation of his past.

'Haven't you ever questioned how it was that you survived?' Yochanan asked, beckoning Shimon to sit opposite him.

'I nearly didn't survive.' Shimon's mind drifted back to the last time he saw the *lanista*. What pleasure the trainer had taken in telling him that the fights had been fixed. That he had not won his contests fairly and had merely been manipulated by the syndicate. Gaius Licinius had enjoyed destroying everything that Shimon had thought he'd achieved.

'Being at the mercy of that evil bunch of bastards, I shouldn't have had a chance.' Shimon leaned towards the teacher, angrily. 'And I wouldn't have had, if those crooks hadn't taken a load of money on the first two fighters, and then paid them to lose. So it's a little hard to persuade myself that I was saved by the hand of God when the truth is, it was only the power of money.'

'That depends on your perspective,' Yochanan said.

'When the money stopped flowing into their business, my fate was sealed.'

'So it is even more miraculous that you survived,' Yochanan countered.

'I survived only because my sister was eventually able to persuade the *domina* to help me. Which is what she should have done when I was first thrown out of the governor's villa,' Shimon replied, still feeling resentful.

'I would say that after you were falsely accused, too many coincidences went in your favour to be attributed to mere good fortune.'

'How could you possibly know that?' Shimon asked.

'Do you remember the story of Joseph?' the teacher asked. 'After he was sold by his brothers? He was also falsely accused by Potiphar's wife but it was his destiny to remain in prison in Egypt so that he could be instrumental in bringing about the redemption of our people.'

'How does that relate to me?'

'Your sister Miriam realised that the only way she could be certain that you would be able to carry out the life intended for you was for her to stay close to you. The fact that you were imprisoned gave her that opportunity.'

'Are you saying that even though I was innocent, she expected me to be incriminated and sent to prison? That's impossible,' Shimon protested.

'Dear friend, your sister knew what to expect when you ran away. You decided to explore other people's worlds, places where you didn't belong. You were bound to get into trouble. Our history is full of such tragedies.'

'But she couldn't have known that I would survive,' Shimon insisted.

'With prayer and her efforts to secure your release, she was able to achieve her aim.'

'You're saying that she manipulated me! She had no right to do that,' Shimon complained.

'We all have free choice, and you exercised yours. Miriam was merely instrumental, with the help of the Almighty, in ensuring that one day you would fulfil your destiny.'

'And this is my destiny, to remain here? I'm barely educated! You expect me to enter your place of learning and dismiss what happened to me as a necessary part of my development? A preparation for a life of purpose and meaning?'

'As I said, it has to be your choice,' the teacher reiterated. He stood up. It was time for him to return to his pupils.

'And what if I make the wrong choice?' Shimon asked. 'How will I know what to do?'

'The sooner you begin, the sooner you'll find out,' the teacher replied. He wrapped his shawl more tightly around his shoulders as he prepared to leave. 'And there's always the prize of my sister, if you're still interested,' he added.

Shimon thought about the olive-skinned girl and how much he wanted to see her again. 'You said that the man lucky enough to gain her had first to prove himself.'

'No one has yet,' Yochanan replied, laughing out loud.

An hour later, Esther went to the barn, expecting to meet the stranger. She desperately wanted to find out more about him. She was carrying a pitcher of milk and some dry bread to satisfy his hunger. But she was too late; the place was empty, and the visitor was nowhere to be seen.

Shimon had just entered the academy under the personal sponsorship of her brother, the *Rosh Yeshiva*, to begin a new life of purpose and meaning.

26

Apart from a few cursory glances, Shimon's appearance in the musty study hall caused little reaction from the pairs of shawl-clad students who occupied it. They were replicas of the master they were trying to emulate. Sitting at opposite ends of poorly lit wooden tables, in front of piles of different texts that they were straining their eyes to see, the young men were too immersed in academic arguments to notice the stranger who had entered into their midst.

Shimon looked around, feeling distinctly awkward in this austere place. Yet, for a reason that he didn't understand, it didn't evoke the same unwelcome sentiments as the hostile environment that he'd encountered when he entered the governor's household.

As he settled in and listened to the students talking, it seemed as if their unashamed competitiveness covered up a chronic fear of failure. If they didn't welcome him it was because of their insecurity. They feared him because they did not know how good a student he might become.

Shimon was only a few years older than them but manhood had been forced on him prematurely. He had not enjoyed their privileges, their protected lives. He had serious doubts whether the disparity between them could ever be overcome. Nevertheless, he had exercised his free will and had enrolled in the school no differently from any other new student. He had committed himself to the same unremitting regime of learning, where the sole aim was to attain spiritual excellence.

It seemed odd that he had chosen to re-enter a life that, as a boy, he found futile. Could he have changed so much that he was now prepared to abandon the attractions of the physical world and devote all his energies to the pursuit of a more meaningful life?

Unnoticed by many of the other students, Shimon made his home in the last unoccupied space in the cramped dormitory. As he waited for some form of instruction from the teacher, he began to feel increasingly anxious. He'd expected a routine to be drilled into him in the same way as when he entered the *ludus*. Memories of languishing for days in that dingy room in the governor's house, waiting for his mistress, Livia, to return and confirm his appointment, went through his mind. Surely this wasn't how it was supposed to be?

After several days, the master still hadn't spoken directly to him. It occurred to Shimon that the principal intended that he should initiate himself into the activities of the academy; perhaps it was a test of his initiative.

In the mornings, Shimon woke early and joined the others in the hall for morning prayers. The daily services were taken by the same tall, sly-faced youth who assumed that it was his right to recite the prayers at extra high speed. Shimon, visibly deficient in his reading, could see that the reader was putting on a display in front of his colleagues to gain their admiration. It was also an opportunity to mock Shimon because it was obvious that he couldn't keep up.

It wasn't any easier at mealtimes or during the brief respites from their studies. Shimon tried his best to befriend the other students but they ignored him. He remembered being subjected to the same silence when he entered the governor's household and then later, during the desperate moments of his two long years in prison. He was alone; an outsider who had again entered a world that was foreign to him.

Worse, he was still haunted by the same troublesome dreams. Sometimes he started screaming in the middle of the night, imagining that he was wrestling with the same faceless man, or lying mortally wounded in the arena.

He couldn't help feeling dispirited; he had entered a vocation for which he was totally unsuited. But he was determined to succeed. He had survived a far harsher environment and nothing was going to deter him.

And then one brief moment changed everything; a hitherto miserable existence was magically transformed into one of hope.

❧

Esther had wondered what had happened to the powerfully built stranger when she found the sheep barn empty. Her brother made no further reference to him so she assumed that he had gone on his way again. She was astonished when she saw him in the academy one day when she was delivering food to the students.

Shimon was standing alone, slowly reciting the morning prayers that he had been obliged to relearn. Suddenly, he raised his head and there she was looking at him from a few paces away. The same clear skin, slight smile and exquisite almond-coloured eyes. No further communication was necessary. In that briefest of instances, Shimon had found the motivation to continue and to prove himself worthy of the most beautiful young woman he had ever seen.

❧

Shimon returned to the cramped dormitory, exhausted from

another long *Torah* session. During his first few days at the school, Yochanan had been away visiting a close relative who had suffered bereavement. However, as soon as he arrived back at the academy he insisted that Shimon's tuition start in earnest. The master was eager to confirm his opinion that his new student had sufficient potential to achieve the required standard.

Adjusting from an existence based on physical strength to one of a spiritual dimension was a difficult transition. It took Shimon many weeks of hard work and perseverance to regain even the most elementary knowledge of his faith. Gradually, however, he found that he could memorise everything that he'd been taught; even the new, more complex texts that he was studying were not beyond his comprehension.

He also made a friend.

'My name is Shmuel,' a thin, pallid youth announced unexpectedly, when Shimon went into the dormitory and stretched out his huge frame onto the bed next to him.

Shimon wanted to sleep but he couldn't allow the opportunity of finally making an acquaintance to pass by. No other student had deigned to talk to him. It was evident that now the others were asleep, so Shmuel felt he could converse freely.

'That used to belong to Isaac,' the youth gestured, pointing to Shimon's bed. 'We wondered who would be the one to take his place. He was my best friend, but he suffered terribly when his wife lost their child and he was forced to leave.'

Shmuel handed Shimon Isaac's prayer shawl and *tefillin*. 'Isaac said that he had no further use for them. He lost his faith.'

Shimon affectionately touched the fringed garment and the two wooden boxes containing holy writings. He recalled the first time his father had shown him the correct way to position the phylacteries on his arm and head.

'What do you mean "forced to leave"? By whom?' Shimon

asked.

'The master,' Shmuel replied. 'You seem surprised. Few of us are permitted to stay here for more than a year or two. The master only bothers with those who are likely to benefit him. Most of the others never even get to talk to him before they're sent away.'

'But that's cruel,' Shimon replied, sitting up abruptly, suddenly wondering what type of place he had committed himself to. Why had Yochanan exerted so much effort in persuading him to stay if he might only remain for a short time?

Shmuel was curious about how Shimon, so different from the other students, had managed to get a place in the academy.

'My family hoped that I would follow in their tradition, but I wanted more for myself than a life working on the land and the endless hours of study,' Shimon said.

'So what brought you back to a life of learning?' Shmuel enquired.

'I realised that I'd been given another chance to achieve something worthwhile,' Shimon answered guardedly. He couldn't possibly expect the young student to understand the tribulations that he had had to endure.

After a short pause, Shmuel said, 'You need to be careful of Aaron.' He glanced towards the pupil that led the services, who was asleep at the other end of the room. 'He thinks of himself as our leader. He can be extremely devious if he thinks his position is being undermined.'

'And what exactly is his position?' Shimon asked, having often wondered what differentiated the tall youth with the unexceptional demeanour from the rest of the other pupils.

'He has been here the longest. He believes that gives him the right to special privileges. He has only a limited ability. He knows that the master will never select him as his assistant. But his family are very wealthy and insist that he be allowed to remain at the academy.'

'What are you trying to say?' Shimon asked.

'Without their donations, the academy couldn't continue,' Shmuel explained.

'But what reason could he have to feel threatened by me?' Shimon asked.

'The master only gives individual instruction to pupils with sufficient potential to be his study partner. It's obvious to the rest of us that that's what you're being groomed for. Aaron will do everything possible to discredit you, to ensure that you never achieve it.'

'But I'm not yet at your standard. That's the only reason for the extra tuition,' Shimon protested.

'Your humility is virtuous but, if you're as ignorant as you say, the master would never have allowed you entry.'

'So you're saying that Aaron is resentful because he thinks that the position of the master's assistant should be his?' Shimon asked.

'No, only the prize of being welcomed into the master's family,' Shmuel replied.

'I don't understand what you mean.'

'Do you think that you're the only one who has noticed Esther?' Shmuel remarked, smiling slyly.

Shimon was stunned. Had his feelings for the girl been so obvious? How could he have been so foolish? And why had he not realised that there would be others prepared to do anything to win the prize of a woman of such beauty? He'd been so immersed in his own longing for her that he hadn't thought about the other students coveting her.

Shimon was too unsettled to sleep. He reprimanded himself for believing that the girl could ever belong to him; all he could see now was her drifting away from him into the arms of another.

For the next few days, Shimon avoided returning Esther's glances. He tried not to think of her and nurtured his newly formed friendship with Shmuel instead. His young friend had a particularly sharp mind and easily mastered his studies, committing to memory most of the teachings and arguments that made up the content of the Oral Law. This was a subject in which Yochanan had established himself as the foremost authority in the land.

Shmuel, like Shimon, came from a poor family but he was descended from a line of learned rabbis in whose tradition he was destined to follow. The youngest of seven children, he was the only one of his siblings to gain entry to the academy. The master had imposed a restriction that only one member of a family was allowed to become a student.

Shimon soon discovered that he gained as much knowledge from his young friend as from his master. Shmuel had infinite patience with his endless questions. Shimon cherished the hours they spent learning together, either in their own corner of the study hall or, when the heat was too unbearable, under the shade of the white poplar trees overlooking the lake.

Shimon found that the guilt about his past, that had exercised such a strong hold over him for so long, was replaced by an insatiable desire for knowledge and a compulsion for self-improvement in accordance with strict *Torah* principles.

Time passed quickly. Shimon had been at the school almost a year and felt increasingly comfortable in an academic environment. His confidence grew, and he was far less reticent about entering into heated discussions about the Law with his teacher. He didn't want to win arguments or to enhance his status; his only concern was pursuit of the ultimate truth.

In his contentment, however, he was oblivious to the resentment that his continuing presence at the school provoked, particularly with Aaron and his followers.

27

'You may have been able to deceive the master but I knew immediately that there was something different about you,' Aaron said accusingly, pointing his dagger at Shimon.

Shimon, his mind still occupied with the lengthy discourse that he'd shared with Shmuel, had gone back to his quarters to rest before the teacher's Sabbath mid-afternoon study session.

'What are you searching for?' Shimon asked, bewildered. When he'd walked into the room, he'd been unexpectedly confronted by the tall youth rummaging through his possessions. 'I haven't done you any harm.'

'Oh but you have, Shimon, or whatever your real name is,' the boy answered back accusingly, not appearing the least concerned at being caught. 'And there'll be something here that'll show who you really are.'

'I don't know what you mean,' Shimon replied.

'A man like you isn't fit for a school. So why don't you go back to wherever you came from, where your talents would be more appreciated?' Aaron scowled provocatively. 'You're not wanted here. If you know what's good for you, collect your things and leave!'

Shimon had forgotten Shmuel's warning about the boy from the wealthy family. Now, all he could see were the sneering faces of the two assassins who had once attempted to rob him near the arena, Now, threatened once again, a rush of adrenalin flowed through his veins as the instinct to defend himself returned.

Shimon approached his armed assailant but, just as he was ready to inflict the first blow, he looked into the boy's eyes. Aaron had let the weapon slip out of his hand and was breathing erratically, his whole body stricken with fear. At that moment, Shimon was back in the fighters' pit, goaded by the cheering crowd. Socrates was down on one knee, fatally injured, the same expression of terror on his angelic face. In that briefest of instants, the need to lash out dissipated and was replaced by concern.

Shimon impulsively extended his long arms and drew Aaron towards him, holding him in a tight embrace. The unexpected act of affection startled the boy, who began weeping uncontrollably.

'The look in your eyes, I thought you were going to kill me,' Aaron cried, his thin frame trembling, convinced that he could only have been saved by divine intervention.

Shimon, as if stirring from a bad dream, looked down at the youth, horrified at the thought of what he might have done. The fact that he could instil so much fear into another person filled him with remorse. Despite all his efforts, he had not yet rid himself of his most basic instinct to fight.

'Where did you learn to be so fearsome?' Aaron enquired, full of adolescent admiration.

'Please forgive me, I didn't mean to frighten you,' Shimon replied, with sincere regret.

'Tell me! I want to know,' Aaron insisted.

'I don't want to talk about it. It was in a previous life, one that caused unimaginable suffering.'

'Did you kill someone?' the boy asked.

The question pierced Shimon more effectively than a trainer's dagger had ever done. He had worked hard to transform an existence dominated by greed and violence into a life of purpose and meaning. But however much he repented, he feared that he would always bear the scars of savagery and the guilt of breaking the sixth commandment and taking a life.

'Aaron, as you know, a person can suffer as much devastation by being reminded of previous sins as from a blow to the heart with a lethal weapon,' Shimon answered, trusting that the youth's inquisitiveness would be satisfied by the biblical analogy.

Without warning, Aaron suddenly said, 'You want her for yourself, don't you?'

Shimon hesitated, embarrassed by the boy's forthrightness.

'Is that the reason that you decided to discredit me?' Shimon replied, recalling that Shmuel had informed him of the lad's aspirations.

'Everyone can see the way she looks at you but she was promised to me,' said Aaron indignantly. 'I'm going to marry her as soon as my father has obtained the master's permission.'

'It's not a secret that the girl's suitor will be whichever of the students proves a worthy study partner to our master,' Shimon stated. He pondered for a moment. Aaron must be deluding himself to think that he could be selected; in the time he'd been at the school he hadn't been able to attain the most basic academic qualification.

'Shimon, you could help me,' Aaron suggested, sounding more hopeful. 'All of us know that either you or Shmuel will be chosen by the master as the next study partner. You two are the most knowledgeable students in the school. If you help me to reach the next level of my studies, maybe I could still be considered for the position. I'd be willing to pay you. Then my father will no longer have reason to feel disappointed in me.'

Shimon was amazed by the audacity of the young man. Only a few moments ago Aaron had been looking for ways to shame him; now he was trying to bribe him!

'I will help you in any way that I'm able,' Shimon responded, knowing that he couldn't refuse to help the boy, even though his intentions clearly showed a lack of principles. 'But there's a condition; use the money that you could pay me to fulfil the *mitzvah* of contributing to the poor.'

'Shimon, your help will not go unrewarded,' Aaron replied. He left for the study hall, confident that he had been able to remove the main obstacle that hindered his promotion. He would then no longer be denied access to the girl he had always loved.

Shimon honoured the arrangement and became Aaron's mentor. He established immediately that the boy was willing to learn but lacked the intellectual depth and tenacity that the master required of him. He decided, however, to conceal his doubts since he was aware from his own bitter experience how devastating the withdrawal of hope could be from someone with little else to depend on.

Another season of inadequate rainfall was followed by an exceptionally long period of sultry weather. The heat showed no signs of relenting. Shimon was in a reflective mood, thinking about how his life had changed. He was unrecognisable from the wild man, haunted by his past and with an uncertain future, who had arrived in the Galilee.

Not yet thirty years of age, his hair already thinning and his face a lined map of his tribulations, he had already experienced several different lifetimes. However, he had acquired a certain serenity; he knew that the life that he now lived in this place was intended for him.

He thought of his sister Miriam, but not as frequently as before. He prayed each year at her grave on the anniversary of her burial. She no longer appeared in his dreams, but he still revered her memory.

He put down his book of *Midrashim* as sleep swiftly claimed him. The next sound that he heard was from Shmuel, standing over him, wailing, his body swaying in prayer.

'My friend, what happened?' Shimon exclaimed groggily, sitting upright and rubbing his eyes. His companion had been absent for most of that day.

'It's Aaron,' Shmuel replied, immediately indicating that some form of tragedy had occurred.

Shimon had recently noticed a change in Aaron; the enthusiasm that had been evident at the beginning of their tutorials had waned without reason. Shimon thought that the particularly difficult nature of their present studies was the only plausible explanation and therefore wasn't too concerned.

'Is he badly injured?' Shimon enquired.

'He must have slipped. The ground is dangerously uneven in the mountains. In poor light, it could happen to anybody,' Shmuel said. 'It must have been an accident.' From the uncertainty in his voice, Shimon knew immediately that it might not have been an accident.

'His father summoned him,' Shmuel started to explain. 'Aaron confided in me. He said that he had to return home immediately but he asked me to promise that I wouldn't tell anybody. He was so ashamed.' The distraught student paused to wipe the tears from his face.

Shimon now understood the reason for his pupil's despondency. The young man had obviously known for some time that he was going to leave the academy. The fact that he only felt able to share his torment with Shmuel made Shimon feel that he had failed his protégé. Wasn't he also supposed to have been his friend? Shimon castigated himself for not being sufficiently sensitive to his pupil's needs.

'He realised that he'd disappointed many people,' Shmuel added.

Shimon realised that, unable to deal with the shame and upset that he had lost the opportunity of proving his love for Esther, Aaron had run away.

'The master will have to be informed,' Shimon asserted.

'We often venture out early in the morning,' Shmuel said, still visibly distracted. 'The master says that he finds that time particularly conducive for clarity of thought. Together, we've shared many stimulating discussions.' He paused and looked at Shimon, his closest friend, a lugubrious expression appearing on his face. 'We found the body this morning still wrapped in his prayer shawl,' Shmuel said, shaking his head sadly.

Word was swiftly sent to Aaron's family and, living within a short journey of the academy, they came to retrieve the body so they could carry out the burial of their son during the daylight hours, in accordance with Jewish law.

'The news must have been affected our teacher terribly. He's often said that we are part of his family,' Shimon remarked.

'Aaron was told to leave,' Shmuel disclosed. 'His family would happily have continued paying for his education.'

'Told by whom?' Shimon demanded.

'The master felt that it was his duty to notify Aaron's father that his expectations of his child were unrealistic. He would never be sufficiently knowledgeable to be granted *Semikhah*. The master could no longer justify taking their donations.'

'But the lad was progressing so well,' Shimon protested. 'He just needed more time.'

'My friend, on this occasion we must disagree. Having witnessed the consequences, perhaps we would be wise to learn a lesson from our teacher. Aaron's death is what can happen when acts of kindness are not tempered by a reality,' Shmuel responded. He could not hide his feeling. Shimon's benevolence towards Aaron had given the boy too much hope; Aaron could never achieve what he wanted. It would have been better for him never to aspire to such heights – and for Shimon to have refused to help him.

Shimon gazed at the empty bed opposite him, feeling profound grief. He picked up his book of psalms and prayed for the departed soul of his pupil

28

ANOTHER NEW YEAR arrived, leaving behind parched ground and withered crops, evidence of another harvest ruined by insufficient rain. The few remaining cattle were inadequately nourished and could not provide sufficient milk for the school. Esther was desperately worried that they would soon starve.

To add to their plight, the annual donation which they had relied on from Aaron's family had stopped after he died. Fortunately, Esther had been able to use her skill as a seamstress to take in additional work, though she often had to walk several hours to earn a little extra money. But she knew that unless they were able to delay paying the punitive *Fiscus Judaicus* that the Romans had imposed upon them, they would not survive.

'It's bad enough that you haven't arranged a marriage for me as you should have done,' Esther complained to her brother. 'But not providing for your students when you have a duty to their parents is unforgiveable.'

The Day of Atonement, the most holy of fast days, had just ended and Yochanan had returned home, weary from a whole day's prayer. Still in a sombre mood, he wanted to pass the rest of the evening alone meditating, not arguing with his sister.

'My work is to codify the legal discussions in the Oral Law and I can't be distracted by trivial domestic issues,' he said, unwilling to address Esther's concerns.

'Then you will have to continue without me. We no longer have the means to support the luxury of a school that's only being run for your benefit,' Esther replied sharply. 'I've devoted the last ten years of my life to supporting you and your dreams. What good has that done me? Now I'm no longer young, what man will want me?'

'Where will you go?' Yochanan asked, trying not to show his concern.

'I shall return to the place of our birth. Naphtali, our mother's brother, is a wealthy man. I shall ask him to take me in. He will honour the commitment that you made to our parents and then I shall find a husband.'

'I won't let you go. I am the firstborn and you are my responsibility until another man takes you for a wife,' Yochanan stated flatly.

Esther, once more impeded by his intransigence, was silent. She also knew that however angry she was, she was unlikely to carry out her threat.

Next day, Yochanan left early for the academy.

⁘

Once again, it was time to select the master's new study assistant.

'Now we shall see how much of your studies you have retained,' he said strutting into the hall for his evening study session with Shimon.

After the tragedy of Aaron's death, the school carried on as if nothing had changed. No further mention was made of the boy by the master or the rest of the pupils. Shimon, however, remained desolate, unable to comprehend Yochanan's callous attitude towards a young person who was so desperately in need of understanding.

'Master, I'm not sure that I'm sufficiently prepared,' Shimon objected. 'Shmuel is considerably more knowledgeable, especially on the laws of the Sabbath. With respect, he is more qualified than me. If you were to listen to his arguments, they are definitive.'

'I shall be the one to decide the topic, which will only be disclosed to you when you arrive here tomorrow,' Yochanan answered tersely, irritated by Shimon's modesty. 'By the evening, we will know which one of you will be fit to be my study partner.'

'Teacher, Shmuel is more accomplished than me. He's more worthy of such a prestigious position. Please, grant it to him so that we can avoid bad feeling between us,' Shimon pleaded.

This was the first time that the candidates to be the master's new study partner had been forced to prove their credentials in an open debate. Shimon couldn't understand how the head of the school could condone such a display, where two of his students would be paired against each other to prove their worth. One of them would be humiliated. It reminded him of the way in which he'd been forced to prove his worth in the arena; this time, he would be fighting for his spiritual survival.

'What makes you think that you're sufficiently qualified to make that assessment?' the teacher replied, angry that his authority was being questioned.

'I was only trying to say —' Shimon began.

'The discussion is concluded,' the teacher interrupted.

Scowling, Yochanan got up from the table. Shimon wondered if there was another unrelated issue that was making his teacher so irritable.

Shimon found Shmuel unresponsive and withdrawn when he attempted to discuss the following day's debate. It seemed that he was completely preoccupied with his family's expectation of him to succeed.

'Shmuel, what will happen to the defeated candidate?' Shimon asked.

'The master can only accommodate one study partner,' the young man responded without emotion. His expression revealed his grim determination to do everything possible to secure the position for himself.

Ironically, Shmuel's response jostled Shimon out of his contemplative mood. It was almost as if his friend's aloofness motivated him. Shimon now understood the true purpose of the years of study and the master's individual tuition; it was time to prove himself. In the safety of life in the academy, he had lost the competitive advantage that had kept him alive before, when he had been in physical danger. But he didn't know whether he wanted the position badly enough to fight for it, since he could no longer live with the consequences of employing his former ruthlessness.

He thought of Esther and wondered what had prevented her finding a husband. She appeared changed since Aaron's death, as though sadness pervaded her whole being. The youthful vibrancy that had first stirred him had departed, leaving her forlorn. Had she found love, he wondered, and then had it cruelly snatched away?

That night Shimon slept fitfully. His sister Miriam appeared to him in a dream. She was trying to tell him something, to guide him as she had so many times before when they were children, but he couldn't hear her words. He tried to grab hold of her but she disappeared, leaving him disorientated and insecure.

The day that would prove decisive for his future was to be like any other; the master had not granted either of the two competitors any special dispensation because of the evening's debate. Unable to approach his morning prayers with his usual commitment, Shimon decided to forgo the first meal so he wouldn't have to face the mutterings of the other students speculating about the outcome of the evening's contest.

Unnoticed, he left the school and went hastily down to the far end of the lake to the burial grounds and his sister's grave. There, he sat down on the same boulder where the master had comforted him during the painful period of his grief. He wrapped his white prayer shawl around his shoulders. Close again to Miriam, Shimon suddenly recalled her words of hope that sounded so empty during the bleakest moments of his despair. But hadn't her prediction proven accurate? He now understood that his imprisonment had enabled him to find the meaningful life that he was destined for. Shimon realised that he had an obligation to fulfil: to make his sister proud of him.

Shimon returned to the school revitalised. He had recaptured much of his old determination and resolve, which he firmly believed was still inspired by his sister. He passed the remainder of the day alone, meditating and attempting to clear his mind of negative thoughts so that he would be able to give a creditable performance and bring honour to the academy and its master.

After the evening service, seats were swiftly arranged in a semicircle around the periphery of the poorly-lit hall to accommodate the rest of the pupils who were eager to view the debate. Two small wooden chairs were placed opposite each other in the middle of the room for the two contestants. The imposing figure of the master sat perched high on a stool overlooking the proceedings, impatient to start the contest.

Both competitors were summoned into their arena.

'Will we remain friends, irrespective of which one of us is chosen?' Shimon asked, turning to his friend. He recalled the injustice that he'd felt when he had been paired against Socrates, and the devastation that threatened to overcome him when the person whom he had loved as a younger brother was killed.

Shmuel appeared nervous. He diverted his gaze from Shimon, too absorbed in proving his superiority to offer a response. Taking their seats, the two men waited, shoulders hunched, for the signal to commence.

Shmuel was the first, quoting several passages of teachings on the designated subject of the laws relating to ritual purity.

'Your argument is persuasive but where are the biblical sources to substantiate your claim?' Shimon retorted.

'The Oral Law is unequivocal on the subject.'

'Agreed, but where exactly is it stated?' Shimon interrupted, insisting on a specific response to his question.

'The sages have asserted in *Tractate Kelim* which articles must be passed through water and which through fire,' Shmuel replied, sounding more confident.

'True, but in the fourth book of the *Torah*, it clearly states the method by which a utensil shall become clean,' Shimon said.

'I'm aware of the section,' Shmuel answered curtly, and then abruptly stood up, angry at hearing his own words repeated by the man to whom he had taught them.

'I didn't mean to infer that you were lacking in knowledge.'

'However, you are obviously deficient in the intricacies of the *Mishnah*,' Shmuel responded forcibly.

'But your own discourses show deference to the divine source from which your argument is taken,' Shimon responded, remaining seated and not allowing himself to be intimidated.

'Which, if you had studied more carefully, you would have seen the anomaly that needs to be rectified,' Shmuel said, addressing his comments to the adjudicator. He knew that he was gaining the advantage.

'But surely you must see that it still does not permit you to say the Oral Law takes precedence over the *Torah*, which you must agree has to be the original source?' Shimon protested indignantly, pushing his chair aside to prevent his adversary from committing a desecration of the divine name.

'Since you failed to understand that both teachings are equally holy, you've obviously also misunderstood the essence of the debate,' Shmuel exclaimed superciliously, intent on winning the argument.

'Which I should gladly acknowledge as being preferable to a blatant transgression,' Shimon retorted. He had completely underestimated his opponent's resolve.

'Ignorance isn't compatible with a place of learning. Concede before you bring any more shame on our good name!' Shmuel demanded, confronting his opponent, convinced that he had inflicted the decisive blow.

'Better to be considered deficient in pursuing the truth than display arrogance in winning the argument,' Shimon responded, only now appreciating the extent of his friend's desperation for victory.

Expectation gripped the congested room. The other students were silent, awaiting the verdict of their master. Both challengers remained seated, their faces reflecting their different emotions. Shmuel's initial anxiety had transformed into defiance and confidence that he had secured the position that he coveted. Shimon, visibly drained, his tunic drenched in sweat, felt diffident and was prepared to submit to a more worthy challenger. Nevertheless he knew that, whatever the outcome, he hadn't wavered from his principles and would never cease in his pursuit of the truth.

The master, his huge face beaming with satisfaction, climbed down from his observation post and swaggered over to his two most accomplished pupils. 'Most entertaining,' he bellowed. 'You shall have my decision later this evening.'

Yochanan left the room to return home, leaving the hall to slowly empty. Many of the younger onlookers wondered when they might be granted the same opportunity to compete for the master's favour – and whether they would be ready for the challenge.

Shmuel ignored Shimon and sauntered out of the hall, confident that he would soon receive the call endorsing his promotion. Shimon remained alone, sitting in the empty, darkened room, contemplating the next stage of his life. The years in which he returned to study had provided him with incalculable rewards. He was now ready to return to the family that he had run away from and to devote the rest of his life to passing on the knowledge that he had acquired, helping others who, like him, had lost their faith. He had fulfilled his obligation to his sister. He hoped that one day he would be able to repay his teacher, who had invested infinite patience and care in him, by attaining the level of academic excellence that, at this moment, remained beyond his capability.

Shimon thought about Esther, the young woman he had desired for so long. He wondered whether Shmuel would now become her husband. He was happy that she would have at last found someone worthy of her.

He collected his few possessions from the empty dormitory and swiftly left the academy. Accompanied by his memories, he began the long journey back to the land of his birth.

29

'I THOUGHT YOUR days of running away were finished,' roared a voice from out of the shadows.

Shimon turned to see his teacher looking at him with the same expression of paternal love that he remembered from their first encounter in the burial grounds.

'I've brought discredit to the school,' Shimon explained, trying to hold back his tears. 'For the benefit of the other pupils, I should leave immediately.'

'Wait, there's no need to be so hasty,' Yochanan said. 'Come to my home; we can discuss it more sensibly there, and you must be hungry after such an exhilarating exchange.'

Shimon, wondering why the teacher had again been reluctant to let him leave, accompanied him to the small house.

'As you can see, my sister has been busy,' Yochanan remarked, referring to the piles of sewing that covered most of the small living room. 'She's already asleep so we can speak freely.'

He put food and drink on the table for them both, anticipating that their discussions would continue into the early hours of the following day. Shimon made the blessing over the food and the two men sat down to share their meal.

'You forgot that you came here with nothing but your bodily strength to protect you,' Yochanan reminded his guest, taking a huge mouthful of ground chickpeas from his plate. 'I could detect immediately that you were different from the others.'

Shimon didn't understand why his teacher felt it necessary to justify the kindness he had first shown him. He wished that he could be spared further shame and depart with dignity.

'You weren't afraid to question, nor prepared to relent until you received answers that satisfied you. And because you were not disadvantaged by misconceptions and preconceived ideas, I inherited an uncluttered mind that could be trained into a formidable assistant,' the master continued, oblivious to Shimon's unease.

'Teacher, I'm grateful for the special interest you showed me and the individual attention that you devoted to my education. I just regret that your faith in me wasn't justified.'

'The other students saw a wild man who couldn't possibly be worthy of entering into their exclusive domain. He threatened their existence. You took away the prize that they had been working for,' the teacher persisted. His words revealed that he was aware of the tension that his pupil's privileged position had caused. 'But you've clearly misunderstood what I have been trying to say to you,' Yochanan exclaimed, his round face beaming with joy. He stood up and stretched out his huge arms to his chosen student.

'What do you mean?' Shimon asked hesitantly.

'Why do you think that I invited you to my house?'

Shimon got up, slowly acknowledging what the teacher had been trying to tell him.

'And Shmuel?' he asked, after a brief pause, thinking first about his friend.

'Departed a few hours ago,' Yochanan answered.

'Why?' Shimon questioned. Shmuel must have been given the news immediately.

'Your friend said he wouldn't be able to deal with the humiliation of facing the students,' Yochanan explained, showing few signs of sympathy.

'He will be a great loss to the academy and to me personally. He was my closest colleague,' Shimon replied. The thought of the pain that his former study companion must inevitably be suffering filled him with sadness.

'He'll find another position, one that hopefully he's more suited to,' the teacher said, helping himself to another handful of bread.

'Isn't that a little harsh?' Shimon remarked.

'It's too easy to become intoxicated by this rarefied atmosphere and make the mistake of thinking that we are detached from the physical world,' Yochanan explained. 'There are always going to be those who will not succeed in their endeavours.'

'With their dreams shattered and their lives ruined,' Shimon answered, thinking of Aaron and Shmuel. 'Surely there has to be something more important than the recognition of spiritual prowess? Don't we owe it to our pupils to give them the opportunity and guidance to delve into themselves and to explore their unique gifts before they're turned away?'

'Your sentiments are very commendable, but standards have to be maintained if we're going to provide the quota of sages on which our people's future depends. Anyway, you succeeded!' The teacher smiled. 'It's a happy occasion, so we should rejoice.'

Yochanan poured out two full cups of wine and passed one to Shimon. 'To your health and a successful partnership.'

Feeling the effects of the wine immediately, Shimon relaxed, his spirits raised by his teacher's confidence in him.

'They were all just waiting for me to fail and looking for any opportunity to discredit me,' Shimon reflected.

'That showed you that if you wanted to gain their respect, you had to work harder and become stronger than them. You had to learn to compete with them by their rules and win.'

'My skin being torn from me wasn't what I expected.'

'We have to strive for excellence. However, I thought survival was your specialty,' the master responded sarcastically.

Shimon winced at the insensitive reference to his former life. 'I thought that this place was different.'

Yochanan looked at his student affectionately. 'But now you shall have your own pupils to call you Rabbi, and I shall have a study partner.'

It was almost daybreak when Shimon returned to the dormitory, still wondering if he had earned enough respect from the other students to justify his elevated position.

⁂

The cold months provided much-needed rainfall that increased the depleted levels of the lake on which their drinking water depended and helped ensure a healthier crop yield. Shimon's days were fully occupied supervising his pupils' study programmes, after which he would work for hours refining his discourses on the Oral Law. He was too busy to notice that Esther started to appear more frequently at the school.

'It's clear that you've researched the subject and gathered vast amounts of material, but the texts still need to be collated into the discussions of the sages before I can provide a definitive explanation of their judgments,' Yochanan announced, pushing aside the script that they had spent the whole night examining. 'But there is also another challenge that awaits you before you can fully assume your position.'

'Haven't I proven myself?' Shimon asked.

'You have provided me with some of the necessary tools to complete the task, but this is of a different nature. Although no less important, it is one which I believe you have been anxiously waiting for.'

'Teacher?' Shimon enquired, mystified by what additional test he was going to face.

'You are required to perform the commandment of having children, and my sister is waiting impatiently for a husband.'

'But I have no experience of such matters!' Shimon exclaimed.

'Together, we will study the part of the law that deals with betrothal. You will soon learn your marital responsibilities,' the teacher responded.

'But she doesn't know anything about me,' Shimon objected.

'My sister possesses all of the necessary facts,' Yochanan replied. He didn't reveal that he had withheld some of the more unsavoury aspects of his assistant's past from Esther. 'If I remember correctly, you once went to extraordinary effort to make her acquaintance.'

'Surely there must have been others more suitable than me?' Shimon questioned, thinking of Aaron who had been so desperate to have her as his wife.

'None that were worthy of her.'

Shimon's thoughts drifted back to when he first encountered Shmuel, and the mention of Esther's name. He had been devastated to find that the others had been captivated by her beauty. And now he was the chosen one, he doubted his suitability as a husband.

'I don't know if I can achieve what is expected of me,' Shimon said. Would his ignorance of domestic matters result in unhappiness and therefore jeopardise his position with his teacher?

'You will learn to love each other,' Yochanan assured him. 'The arrangements for the marriage have already been made.'

30

'BROTHER, IS IT good news?' Esther enquired, huddled at her workbench. Her swollen hands were bound with thread. The cold rains splashed heavily on the flimsy wooden roof.

Yochanan remained pensive for a few moments. He put down the letter he was reading and placed the coins in his pocket. 'You will now have the wedding that you deserve,' he said, looking affectionately at his sister.

'Even though he is not my first choice,' Esther answered back, resigned to her plight of sharing her life with a man she didn't really know.

'Aaron was not a suitable match.'

'Not sufficient for your purposes, but he would have made me happy.' Esther continued sewing without looking up. 'He was never given a chance.' Tears started to form in her eyes at his memory. She had been fond of Aaron and would have happily accepted marriage to him. But the young man had been unable to obtain the master's consent.

'You are mistaken,' Yochanan said.

'What do mean?' Esther put down her work and turned to her brother.

'Shmuel felt responsible for refusing to help Aaron with his studies. When he left the academy, he visited the boy's parents and informed them that their son had asked for help to achieve the required standard. He didn't want them to retain a low opinion of their son. He told them that Shimon agreed to tutor him. This money is a gift from Aaron's parents for the kindness shown to their son. Try and accept that it's a special person who places consideration for others before his own happiness. Shimon is the one. It has been worth waiting for him all these years.'

Esther looked at her brother, thinking that she should have been wiser than to doubt him. Perhaps she had misjudged her future husband.

�֍✋

Shimon returned from the late-night discussion with Yochanan, struggling to accept that not only had he become his teacher's new study partner, but also his future brother-in-law. A date had been set for the betrothal, when he would have to obtain Esther's consent to be his wife. The prospect of such enormous changes to his life made him seriously doubt his ability to achieve what would soon be expected of him.

The last weeks of cold passed without incident. Even though he had been officially installed as Yochanan's study partner and had the right to be addressed by his own students as 'Rabbi,' Shimon noticed little change in his relationship with his former master. He was still expected to provide the same quantity of analyses on the numerous texts that he'd researched, only for Yochanan to repeatedly criticise the work and then, after making a few perfunctory amendments, codify the arguments in almost the same form as they were presented to him.

The forthcoming meeting with Esther, even though it had not been referred to again, so dominated his thoughts that he became increasingly distracted and found it hard to concentrate on teaching his own pupils. He was obsessed with the thought that Esther might reject him and that, unable to live with the shame, he would be compelled to leave the academy.

Then, the day before his engagement, he woke up in the middle of the night. 'I've nothing to give to her,' he said to himself, beginning to panic. 'I can't get betrothed to the girl without giving her something of value. I'll have to inform Yochanan immediately.'

His heart started to pound. 'I'm not worthy to marry Esther,' he mumbled under his breath. What was he going to do? Would Yochanan seek another assistant who would be a more suitable match for his sister? Perhaps he should leave at first light. He didn't want to cause any further embarrassment to the master or to Esther.

Unable to get back to sleep, he thought of his sister Miriam and wished she were there to guide him. He suddenly reached for the sack in which he brought his sister to her final resting place; he hadn't touched it for a long time. Running his hands over its coarse material, he felt something hard lodged in the seam. He was amazed to find a gold bracelet belonging to his sister. It was caught in the stitching, almost impossible to detect. It was as if she had been waiting for the opportunity to present it to him herself.

Clutching the piece of jewellery tightly in his hand and hardly able to believe his good fortune, Shimon knew that the union he was about to enter had been preordained.

Shimon arrived at the house as arranged, keeping the bracelet close to his chest.

'Welcome!' Yochanan bellowed jovially from the open door, extending his arms. 'Your bride awaits you.'

Esther stood nervously behind her brother, next to the table that she'd set with several drinking vessels and a large jug of wine. Huddled together in the corner of the room were two grinning students from the academy, who had been given the honour of witnessing the betrothal.

Shimon stared at Esther and saw the same beautiful young girl whom he had encountered that first morning in the Galilee. He smiled and, slowly, she returned his gaze.

'Don't you have something that you would like to say?' Yochanan asked, impatient to start the first stage of the marriage proceedings.

Shimon had prepared himself many times for this moment but the words just wouldn't come.

'He wants to establish whether you will consent to the marriage,' Yochanan prompted, addressing his sister. 'That's the reason why you are here, isn't it?'

'Yes, I'm sorry,' Shimon replied hesitantly. 'I wish to betroth Esther as my wife,' he declared solemnly, clearing his throat.

'I give my consent,' Esther answered quietly, without any enthusiasm.

Shimon, relieved that his fear of being refused had been allayed, fumbled in his pocket for the bracelet and hesitantly handed it to Esther. She slowly accepted it, thereby committing herself exclusively to him under Hebrew Law.

Shimon looked at his bride, standing close to him, and was filled with joy. He had waited a long time for this moment, never allowing himself to believe that he might be good enough for her. She was now legally his and they were bound to each other.

Yochanan poured the wine, filling the tallest of the goblets. He made a blessing and instructed both of them to drink.

'And now we celebrate,' he pronounced. 'The *Ketubah* will be prepared and, under the contract of marriage, you will come together under one roof, which will be in the new month of *Ellul*. Six months from now, you will take your bride to her new home where you will consummate the marriage. The seven days of wedding celebrations will then begin.'

Shimon returned to the academy, already burdened by the

responsibilities of a married man. He wondered how he would to able to support his wife; unless he could adhere to the terms of the marriage contract, Esther would be entitled to demand that he write her a bill of divorce.

Shimon couldn't understand why Yochanan, who was aware of his circumstances, wanted the union to proceed. The only plausible explanation was that his brother-in-law must either have wanted him to ask for help, or to see whether in the six-month period he could use his own initiative to prove himself.

Shimon decided that he would use the rest of that evening to devise a strategy that he would present to his teacher so that he could fulfil his marital obligations.

After morning prayers the following day, Yochanan quickly left the study hall, which presented Shimon with the opportunity to approach him.

'Good, I find a companion can be much more rewarding,' Yochanan said, striding resolutely up the steep incline towards the mountains, not surprised that Shimon wanted to consult him. The two men continued their journey at a brisk pace, each waiting for the other to break the silence.

'If I'm to fulfil my obligations to your sister —' Shimon began.

'Look around you,' Yochanan interjected, pointing in different directions. 'The land is sufficient for all our needs. There is no reason to look elsewhere.'

'Are you saying that you are the owner of all this?' Shimon asked, halting abruptly, astonished at the huge expanse of the territory.

'The land belongs to God and even though I have a deed of purchase, I am only its appointed guardian. What I propose is really quite simple. The barn where you first stayed can be converted without too much work back into a comfortable home.'

'But I can't possible pay for it,' Shimon replied. Under the marriage contract he would have to own a property before he could provide for his wife.

'It will be my wedding gift!' Yochanan declared magnanimously.

'I don't know what to say,' Shimon responded, deeply affected by such an unexpectedly generous offer.

'Now we should return to that discourse of yours on agricultural law, where, if I remember correctly, you were being so pedantic,' Yochanan reminded his brother-in-law, knowing that he had just secured his loyalty.

※

Shimon spent the evening before the wedding ceremony alone, seeking guidance from the Almighty. Two strangers, even though they had seen each other almost every day for seven years, were now thrown together and expected to become one; he was again filled with feelings of doubt.

31

THE NEXT MORNING Shimon arose early. After taking morning prayers and adhering to the tradition of not eating on the day of his marriage, he instructed his pupils on their studies and left the academy. He was carrying the sack containing Miriam's letter and the trainer's dagger, the only remnants of a previous life tainted with violence.

He went down the steep path to the river and the pool, which served as the area for ritual cleansing. Attempting to sever all ties with the past, he threw the bag into the water, watching its contents disappear below the surface forever. He removed his clothes and, after repeating the appropriate blessing for spiritual purification, immersed his body completely in the depths of the cold pool.

Shimon closed his eyes and made a last effort to rid himself of the sins and evil thoughts that he had succumbed to in the past. He prayed for the well-being of his students and that he should be able to bring honour to his new family.

He didn't notice that, only a short distance away, Esther had entered her own part of the river for the same purpose. She had used the months productively since their betrothal, preparing herself for her husband. Her skin was soft from applications of oils and perfumes, and her flowing black hair was restored to its youthful vitality. Being deprived of her own father, she was grateful that her brother provided her trousseau.

Yochanan hadn't complained about the many hours that she'd spent away from her normal chores, preparing her wedding dress made from the finest linen. The work to refurbish the former barn, where the celebrations would soon take place, had finally been completed and she would now have her own home.

Esther felt revitalised as she allowed the cool water to cover her naked body. The doubts that she had harboured about her husband left her. Yes, she had once been infatuated with him. What woman wouldn't have been? His physical presence aroused a temptation that she had fantasised about succumbing to. But she'd never seen him as a suitable match.

She smiled to herself, astonished by her brother's intuition. What made him so sure that he could transform a man previously ignorant of any form of spiritual life into a deeply caring person and conscientious study colleague? Shimon could never replace Aaron in her affections; it would be unfair to expect him to. But he was a decent man and there was no doubt he loved her deeply.

Above all, she knew that she was marrying someone who would make a good father for the child that she was so desperate to bear.

Immersing herself one last time, she felt content; the last few harvests had produced a surplus of food and there was sufficient money to start married life without being compelled to take in extra work.

Despite the heat that had arrived early that year, Esther shivered as she put on her clothes and returned to her brother's house to continue her fast and to help with the final preparations. She was met by three young betrothed wives of students who had been assigned to her to fill the void resulting from the absence of her own family.

As dusk descended, Shimon, dressed in a white robe, waited

anxiously outside the small house to claim his bride. Eventually, responding to his summons, Esther appeared accompanied by the three maidens. They were holding candles, ready to escort her to her husband. The entourage, led by the groom who had been enclosed by a band of his students appointed to witness the marriage, walked up the steep path to the barn.

The groom's arrival was heralded by great excitement among the remainder of his pupils, who had gathered for their teacher's marriage. Shimon, embarrassed by all the attention, felt like a king reluctantly being led to his own banquet. Vivid images of a cheering crowd throwing money at him in appreciation of his victory in the arena passed through his mind, unsettling him. But then he looked up and saw Esther approaching and his mood changed dramatically.

Her lithe figure, enveloped completely by a pure white tunic that accentuated her natural beauty, enthralled him. Shimon stood, mesmerised, as his bride approached him, the contours of her face barely visible through the veil that covered her head.

Shimon, adhering to the custom of ensuring that the bride was his betrothed, gently lifted the veil. Esther then began circling him seven times, signifying the start of the ceremony.

Yochanan, his ceremonial robe encompassing his huge body, as if feeling it necessary to reaffirm his own status as the *Rosh Yeshiva*, pushed his way through the throng of guests to the front of the room. The tumultuous din was suddenly replaced by a respectful silence.

In his loud voice, the master began to recite the seven biblical wedding blessings. He passed two cups of wine to the bride and groom for them to drink. Shimon, without needing to be prompted, moved forward and stamped on one of the small goblets that was placed under his foot, shattering it into small fragments.

Now he had to complete his nuptial obligations. The room

filled with music and the dancing began. He nervously led his bride to the wedding chamber that he had carefully prepared. Standing together, Shimon was suddenly filled with desire for his new wife. Effortlessly, he carried her in his arms and, placing her down tenderly on the virginal canopy, she allowed him to love her.

⁂

'I hope that this is not the end of our friendship,' Shimon said later, emerging alone from the wedding chamber and approaching his mentor, conscious that the seven days' celebrations would cause substantial disruption to their work.

'My new brother-in-law, this is just the beginning!' Yochanan was unsteady on his feet from the effects of too much wine. 'We will have many stimulating discussions, of that you can be assured.'

'I only wish that Miriam could have seen her wishes fulfilled,' Shimon remarked sadly, thinking of his sister and hoping that she would have approved of Esther.

'She would have wanted her good name to live on through you,' Yochanan answered.

'I shall have to do my best not to disappoint her,' Shimon replied, pondering the meaning of Yochanan's strange comment.

Yochanan laughed and, stretching out his arms, drew his brother-in-law to him and embraced him. Together, arms across each other's shoulders, they joined in the wedding celebrations.

Esther, feeling abandoned, suddenly appeared from the wedding chamber. Looking at the two men, she wondered whether she would ever have a normal marriage.

32

Esther, having endured another evening without her husband, had gone to bed early. The sense of well-being that accompanied the first few months of her marriage proved short-lived. Shimon soon devoted all his attentions to his brother-in-law, feeling the need to justify the faith that been bestowed on him.

'There's soup on the stove,' she whispered drowsily an hour later, hearing the sound of her husband arriving home. 'You must be hungry and it has to be nearly daybreak.'

The fire from the hearth had long since gone out. The barn was bitterly cold, exposed as it was to the chilling wind that penetrated its poorly insulated walls.

'We're expecting at least a hundred of the most eminent scholars in the land and I must have lost sight of the hour,' Shimon said excitedly. He was still preoccupied with the arrangements for the forthcoming conference that he would be jointly hosting.

'First it was the new *Torah* scroll, then the all-night studying, and now the symposium. When was the last time you saw your child?' Esther asked, looking over at the young lad lying next to her.

Shimon sat down at the small wooden table and poured some lukewarm soup into a bowl. 'I'm sorry that, with the responsibilities for my students and the extra work with Yochanan, I have forgotten my family obligations. Please forgive me. Try and go back to sleep.'

Shimon knew that his wife had good reason to complain but he didn't want another confrontation. When they were first married she had accepted his absences; she understood how indebted he felt to Yochanan and that her brother had to remain his first priority.

He remembered how things started to change when, unable to conceive, she became disillusioned with their marriage. She proposed that he write her a bill of divorce so that he would be free to pursue his true love of a scholarly life. She said she didn't want to force him to choose between her and his work. Even now, the memory made him feel ashamed.

He looked over at the child asleep curled up next to his mother. After five long barren years, their prayers were suddenly answered. He thought that his wife had found contentment again, devoting herself to her baby son.

'We hardly have enough to eat. Reuven is no longer a child. Soon he will be starting school. Where's the money going to come from?' Esther complained.

The plentiful harvests that marked their early years of marriage were followed by a famine that threatened their existence. If Esther hadn't been so prudent in storing the surfeit of grain that they had accumulated when food was available, the students would have starved. There were signs now that conditions were returning to normal, but the experience of such a long period of deprivation had damaged her confidence. She didn't believe that any improvement in their living conditions could be sustained.

'My hands have become useless from the cold. I can no longer make clothes for our son. I'm not yet thirty and I'm an old woman,' Esther whispered. She began to cry.

'The Almighty will provide for our needs,' Shimon replied, continuing with his meal.

'But you have a family that relies upon you.'

'I'll take on more students. Things will improve, you'll see.'

'What's the use, when the ones you have don't have enough money to pay?'

Shimon, feeling uneasy, went to refill his bowl, forgetting that he had eaten the last of the food. Unable to suppress his own feelings that he'd failed her, but also acknowledging that he was neglecting his duties to his students, he got up quietly to go back to the study hall.

'Where are you going at this hour?'

'My pupils are waiting for me; I must look after them.'

'How long are you going to keep running away?' Esther asked.

'But Yochanan depends on me!' Shimon shouted, unable to control himself.

'And so do we!' Esther answered back, more forcibly than he had ever heard her speak before.

'I owe him a debt that no amount of money could possibly settle. I was lost and he saved me from myself. He believed in me. If it hadn't been for his kindness —'

'You gave him your life. Isn't that enough?' she screamed, waking their child, whom she drew closer.

'What do you want of me?' Shimon demanded, exasperated.

'A husband and a father for our child! Is that too much to ask?'

'I'm sorry.'

Shimon gathered his books and, with a deep feeling of shame, left his home for the study hall.

The argument with his wife affected him deeply and that morning he couldn't concentrate on teaching his students. He appointed Ephraim, a small youth with an intelligent face and the most able of the young scholars, to deputise for him in arranging the day's study programme. Ephraim had replaced Shmuel at the school; he had already been ordained and, despite his affable disposition, he had a resolute determination to succeed.

To avoid any further domestic upheaval, Shimon decided that he would remain at the academy and resume his former position in the dormitory. He was upset that he'd brought unhappiness on his home but how could he allow family disharmony to compromise his position with his students? Surely Esther would understand that they also depended upon him?

Too submerged in his own thoughts, he didn't notice the murmurings and spiteful comments that accompanied his return.

He assumed that, since his pupils had always showed him the utmost respect for his knowledge and voiced their enthusiasm for his teachings, they would welcome him living among them again. But he had underestimated their capacity for deviousness. Rumours about the breakdown of his marriage soon circulated the confined living quarters. There was talk that Yochanan had found him deficient and wanted to replace him. Speculation festered as to which one of them the master would now summon to the prestigious position of his assistant.

'Teacher, it's too much for you, you are looking tired. Permit me to take the study session so that you can rest.' Ephraim sounded genuinely concerned for his tutor's well-being.

Shimon looked up from the text he was researching. His young protégé was eager to be given the chance of elevating himself in front of his peers.

'It will provide you with valuable experience,' Shimon replied. He gave his consent without hesitation, unaware that his authority was about to be challenged. 'It will give me more time to prepare my own discourse with the master.'

Following the exhausting three-day conference, where Yochanan had outlined his new text detailing his definitive analysis of the *Mishnah*, Shimon was fully occupied working on the next *tractate*. His work helped to distract him from his feelings of guilt about his family.

In his solitary moments, he thought about the numerous disagreements he'd had with his sister when he was young and obtuse and only thinking about himself. Now, after years of self-improvement, he realised that he had again wilfully discarded those closest to him, who had shown him unconditional love. In the most sacred aspects of life, he had proved himself to be deficient. Shimon had been apart from his family for six months. He knew now that he had to return.

He had again awoken early. The dreams that plagued him had returned with even more intensity. His son Reuven was screaming with fear and trying to run away from him. When Shimon thought that he'd eventually caught him, it was Yochanan who turned around, laughing, and wouldn't release him to find his child.

His pupils were still asleep. Shimon left the dormitory and visited the pool; submerging himself in cold water helped to clear his mind. The exceptionally cold weather had been replaced by an extended period of warm sunshine and the trees that lined his path were in full blossom.

Walking along the bank of the river, he heard the sounds of someone bathing in the *Mikvah*. He recalled the day when he first arrived at the Galilee; in the same place, the day he had met Yochanan, the man who was destined to change his life.

Shimon continued on the same track, unaware that he had been noticed.

'I suppose that I should have expected to find you here,' Esther said from a short distance away, now she was sure that the man was her husband. Shimon turned around and was surprised to see his wife standing behind him, adjusting a scarf on her still-wet hair.

'I was just about to take my own bath,' Shimon replied.

'Perhaps it was destined that we should meet by this part of the river,' Esther commented sadly. 'If you remember, this was where we first encountered each other.'

Shimon thought back to the young barefoot girl moving gracefully towards him. The possibility that she might one day become his wife had helped him to survive the hazardous months when his life was in danger in Bosra.

The girl had become a woman. As he looked at her, as if for the first time, he was intensely stirred by her beauty. He approached her, desperate to take her in his arms again. But at the last moment, when he was confronted by Esther's expression of almost unbearable sadness, he realised that he was trying to recapture the past. At that instant, he was aware of the extent to which he had been responsible for her suffering.

'Your son has been asking after you. He has grown since you've been away. You would barely recognise him.'

'Esther, I've been very foolish. I should like to return home if you'll have me. A child should have a father and a woman of such —'

'Husband, even after all these years, there is much that we are ignorant of about each other,' Esther interjected. 'If we are to make our marriage worthy, for the sake of our child, that is something that we shall have to correct.'

※

Reuven drew the last bucket from the well and, using all the strength from his puny frame, emptied it into the trough. He turned around and saw his mother approaching in the distance with a man that he didn't recognise. As they came closer, his heart began to beat wildly.

Reuven threw down the empty bucket and, shouting '*Abba*! *Abba*!', ran into his father's outstretched arms. Shimon lifted his son onto his shoulders and carried him the short distance to their home.

'Please, *Abba*, let me read to you,' the boy pleaded as soon as they went in the door.

'We've been learning together,' Esther announced, proud of her son's achievement. 'He will soon be ready to commence *Mishnah*.'

Shimon noticed the attachment that the lad had forged with his mother during the time he was living in the academy. The innocent child, deprived of the presence of his own father, had grown. Shimon felt ashamed that he'd allowed his life at the academy and his work with Yochanan to take precedence over the only stability his son had ever known.

Sharing their first meals for many months, he realised how much he had missed his family and vowed that he would never abandon them again.

He was not, however, aware that his assistant, Ephraim, had left the school for a meeting at the *Rosh Yeshiva's* house. Representing the other students, he felt obliged to make the master aware of their disillusion with their teacher. The student's leader intended to make full use of the opportunity to establish his own claim as the master's next study partner.

33

'WHY HAVE YOU never wanted to talk about your past? How you just happened to appear as if you'd just walked down from the mountain like Moses at Sinai?' Esther asked, as she cleared away the evening meal. She suspected that her husband would soon have to return to the academy and she wanted to detain him, if only for a short while.

'You know I was destitute. My life had no meaning,' Shimon replied.

'After the Romans destroyed your village and you were separated from your family?'

Shimon looked at his wife, astonished that somehow she'd been told a different version of events of his previous life. It occurred to him that Yochanan must have purposely omitted the worst details of his violent past. At that moment, his admiration for his brother-in-law rose again; he would always be indebted to him.

'Do you really believe it was just fate?' Esther probed, giving Shimon the impression that she perhaps knew more about his past than she had revealed.

Shimon thought back to the degradation that he'd experienced during his time in the *ludus*. 'I nearly didn't survive,' he said, more in response to his own thoughts than to Esther.

'My brother was always searching for new devotees to enter his academy so that he could safeguard the future of his precious life's work. When you came here, he saw that you were more interesting than the rest. He looked upon you as a challenge; a wild man that would test even his capabilities and perseverance. But the same fate always awaited those pupils whom he designates as "special". When they are no longer useful, drained and bled dry and unable to deal with the shame of being told that they're never going to be good enough, they are sent away.'

The image of Aaron, her one true love fleetingly entered her mind. She had never had chance to exchange some final words with him. She couldn't forgive her brother for that. 'And now,' she added, 'you have to prevent him from treating you in the same way, before it's too late.'

'My sister wanted this to be her final resting place.' Shimon continued with his own tale; he was not prepared to hear anything detrimental about his mentor.

Esther could see that her warning had gone unheeded. If they were going to salvage their marriage, she would have to accept that her husband's allegiance to her brother would always be stronger than their ties to each other.

'I carried her the whole way on my back. Four days and nights without sleep across the mountains. I arrived exhausted, more dead than alive. But the day after I buried her, while I was picking fruit from the trees to satisfy my hunger, the most beautiful girl I'd ever seen ran towards me. I knew then that one day I would return.'

'But you disappeared and I thought that I would never see you again,' Esther answered, in a lighter mood, having abandoned any hope of instilling any sense of reality into her husband.

'I had some unfinished business that needed my attention, although it nearly cost me my life. I was drawn back to the Galilee, to a young woman who I'd unsuccessfully tried to impress. And then, when I eventually decided to settle here,' he continued, 'I remember making any excuse to be in the study hall when I knew you would be delivering our food.'

'You weren't very discreet,' Esther said smiling.

'I was just relieved that your brother never discovered my intentions.'

'In this place, there is very little that he is unaware of,' Esther replied caustically.

'He never mentioned anything.'

'Yochanan can be very secretive and always knows more than he reveals. Knowing my brother, he was just waiting for the right opportunity.'

'You mean that our marriage was already decided?'

'Probably from the first time that he met you.'

Shimon was confused. He couldn't contemplate thinking badly of his brother-in-law. But what if his wife was right and, like many others before him, he'd been manipulated? He just didn't understand what the reason could have been.

Esther saw her husband's look of unease and realised that he might finally have begun to question his own judgment. 'I've been trying to tell you that there's a great deal you don't know about my brother,' she stressed.

'My students have remained patient long enough,' Shimon said tersely and got up from the table. He didn't mention that his work with Yochanan would again continue until the early hours of the following day.

Esther couldn't stop herself thinking about the unfortunate young woman buried in the cemetery. She wondered why her brother had never mentioned her before, and concluded that it could only have been because he hadn't wanted anyone to know the woman's identity.

Her prayers that evening took on a greater than usual intensity; she was grateful for her husband's return and the look of contentment on the face of her sleeping son. She was happy that they were a family once again.

She prepared her bed and wondered, while her menses still flowed, whether she would be granted another child. She remembered her husband's panic when it was her time. She had woken him in the middle of the night to fetch the midwife from the next village. And then, the hours of painful struggle until their beautiful son was born later the next day. She recalled the young, inexperienced nurse and how she differed from the confident woman whom she had assisted. She still wondered how her life would have changed if her brother had allowed her to become the midwife's apprentice.

The young woman's face suddenly appeared in front of her eyes with such clarity that she could have been present in the same room. Then it came to her; her features and skin colouring were similar to those of her husband. Surely it wasn't possible? But their mannerisms ... they were too alike for it to be just a coincidence. That midwife, carried on the long journey to her final resting place, was the sister-in-law that she was destined never to have.

Yochanan would also have established that family connection; he had formed a close relationship with the midwife. Miriam – that was her name. They had shared such a mutual respect and love of learning that when it was time for Miriam to leave, it had affected Yochanan deeply. She remembered feeling that Miriam would have made him a good wife.

Her brother must have been overwhelmed with sadness when he realised what had happened to the young woman. Not revealing what he knew to her husband would have only accentuated his grief.

Lying awake, waiting for her husband to return, Esther was convinced that Shimon had somehow been used to suit her brother's purpose. She worried how seriously it might harm him should he ever find out the truth.

34

'YOUR MIND IS obviously elsewhere,' Yochanan said, trying to find an excuse for failing to get Shimon to agree to his interpretation of an ambiguous section of text that they'd been toiling over for the last week. 'I suggest we return to it tomorrow, when hopefully you'll be able to think more clearly.'

Yochanan yawned and got up from the table strewn with manuscripts and writing materials, and stretched his massive arms upwards.

'The principle will remain the same', Shimon replied with unusual fervour, feeling that he had to assert himself.

'Dear brother-in-law, always in pursuit of the unattainable.' Yochanan started to clear away the night's work, indicating that their session had ended.

'But truth is something that can never be compromised. Surely it is our duty to instil that same ethic into our students,' Shimon insisted, making no attempt to leave.

'Not if it takes us away from our everyday responsibilities so that we can't relate to them on their level,' Yochanan responded, openly critical of his study partner.

Shimon had found his students unusually argumentative and unreceptive in the early evening learning session. He had been particularly disappointed with Ephraim, whom he regarded so highly. Unaware of his protégé's plans to undermine him, Shimon blamed himself and was prepared to acknowledge that his teaching methods had become stale. He needed to become more stimulating in order to regain their enthusiasm. But he would never be persuaded from what he believed to be right, or from his pursuit of the truth of the *Torah*.

'What exactly do you mean?' Shimon asked, regarding his friend's comment as a personal affront to his zealousness.

'It's nearly light and your family needs you,' Yochanan replied curtly.

'I'm not prepared to rest until we've agreed on the last point!' Shimon announced and faced his brother-in-law.

Yochanan, irritated at having his authority challenged by his former pupil, was unable to contain his temper. 'Naturally, if it were only a question of when a blade becomes pure, *Resh Lakish*, one would have presumed that you were the undisputed master. That's what I'm going to call you from now on! *Resh Lakish* – "Head of the Bandits"!'

Shimon looked at Yochanan aghast and wondered what he could have done to warrant such a virulent attack. 'I thought we were friends and could argue as equals,' he protested. 'If I'm not permitted to question without you reminding me of my past, then I've achieved nothing.'

Yochanan's smile dispelled any doubt that he knew that he always held absolute control. 'It seems that you have completely failed to appreciate what we're supposed to be achieving at this place. Do I have to remind you again that, however commendable time devoted to learning may be, we have been charged with something more realistic: nurturing future generations of sages to carry on our work of providing a practical legal framework by which our people can continue to live in the physical world?'

Shimon moved back to their worktable, dispirited. 'I thought that I could rely on you. All the years we have spent together, first as your pupil and teacher and then as colleagues, what was it all for? Haven't I earned the right to disagree?' He looked at his brother-in-law, even now desperate for his approval, but Yochanan remained impassive.

Shimon suddenly remembered his sister's warning: the last words spoken between them. How readily he had put his faith in the *lanista* and the governor, who he believed had shown him compassion, only later to discover that he'd been used for their benefit. 'Why did you go to so much effort to persuade me to leave my old life, unless all you ever wanted was someone to help you increase your own knowledge so that you could claim the credit? At least in prison there was no pretence. You knew exactly what you had to do to survive.'

Despite the cool air, Shimon's entire body was drenched in perspiration.

'Who was the one who nurtured you, that brought you back to a life of learning and restored your faith in the Almighty? I supported you. Even when you were shown to be deficient,' Yochanan snarled venomously.

'What did you say?'

'The contest with Shmuel? I only let you think that you had won.'

Shimon was stunned as if he had unexpectedly suffered a heavy blow to the head. He was back at the inn, and he heard the *lanista*'s voice goading him. 'Don't you want to know how you were able to walk away?' the trainer kept repeating over and over again.

'You mean that I've been living a lie?' Shimon looked pleadingly at his mentor, unable to absorb what he had just heard.

'You couldn't lose,' he heard the trainer say again, continuing to mock him.

'You hadn't yet reached your full potential,' Yochanan answered, attempting to justify his deceit.

Shimon covered his face with his hands. 'I took away what was rightly Shmuel's.' He felt a sharp stabbing pain in his chest at the impact of these words. He had difficulty breathing and his complexion turned the colour of snow. 'I wasn't good enough,' he muttered unintelligibly.

Yochanan hesitated, then moved awkwardly over to his brother-in-law and offered him some water. 'You don't look well. Our differences will have to wait until tomorrow,' he said, concerned that his words had been misinterpreted and caused more harm than he had intended.

Shimon, summoning all his strength, managed to get to his feet and staggered unsteadily out into the light of the early morning. He wandered aimlessly for hours until his son Reuven, who had just finished tending their flock, saw him. Frightened by the strange expression on his father's face, he led him home.

35

'I TRUST THAT you're now satisfied,' Esther exclaimed, facing her brother.

'You shouldn't have come,' Yochanan replied. He continued writing at the table that had once served as the workbench for her clothes making.

'My husband has been asking after you. What am I supposed to say to him, that all the years at your side have meant nothing?'

As soon as she'd seen the tormented look in Shimon's eyes, she could tell that he had been exposed to some hidden secret. Her worst fears were confirmed.

Shimon had completely withdrawn. His once-broad frame crumbled and his handsome face shrivelled as his will to live abandoned him. In just a few weeks, he was transformed into an old man, dependent on his wife and child to look after him.

'Attending to his family won't do him any harm. He'll soon recover his faculties and realise that he overreacted,' Yochanan replied. 'It was a simple misunderstanding.'

'Brother, please. He refuses to talk about your disagreement, but for the last few days no food has passed his lips. He's fading away in front of our eyes.' Esther started to weep. 'If you don't want me to be left a widow and our son fatherless, go and make peace. He thought that you were his friend. How can you now be so heartless?'

'I will not belittle myself,' Yochanan replied, displaying his usual intransigence.

'I gave up everything so you could study.'

'If you remember, we needed the money,' her brother answered back nonchalantly.

'Only because you decided to neglect a perfectly good living because you thought a blacksmith's life was demeaning,' she reminded him. 'Grandfather believed that you were going to look after the business, not sell everything as soon as he died.'

'As the firstborn, I could do with it as I wished.'

'So that gave you the right to give away our inheritance and subject me to a life of poverty? What did I receive in return? Your family is your students and your life is the academy. If I'd been strong, like your wife, may she rest in peace, I would have refused and let you go and follow your own dream.'

'You are not to mention her,' Yochanan retorted, angry at the reference to his own unhappy marriage.

'Why? Because she demanded that you grant her a divorce? She had good reason. She knew that there wouldn't be any money after you built your school and that you wouldn't be able to support her and the child. She only did what any reasonable wife would do.'

Yochanan had never told anyone that, with the proceeds of his grandfather's business, he had purchased a huge parcel of valuable land in Tiberius in order to establish it as the primary source of learning for future generations.

'Your memory is conveniently short,' he retorted, attempting to divert attention from himself.

'I was young and in love,' Esther replied. She had often wondered how different her life would have been had she remained in the place of her birth.

'Raphael wasn't suitable for you,' Yochanan said, passing judgment on his childhood friend.

'That wasn't what you said when you were his study partner. Then, if I recall, you couldn't speak too kindly of him. Why did you insist on running away?'

'It wasn't the same when our master, of blessed memory, died.'

'It wasn't the same because you knew that you weren't going to succeed him and take over his school,' Esther said abruptly.

'It was a good time for me to start my own school,' Yochanan replied, feeling increasingly uncomfortable with his sister's incessant delving.

'Only so that you could avoid the humiliation of being discarded because Raphael was the one that he'd chosen.'

'You had nothing to prove. You were never told that you were expected to continue the family line of scholars. I had no choice. The new master didn't even give me a chance.'

'What are you saying?' Esther asked, affected by her brother's rare display of emotion.

'There were many occasions that I envied your strength and tranquillity,' Yochanan revealed. 'But I fulfilled my obligation.'

'To whom?' Esther asked, anticipating that she was about to hear her suspicion confirmed that he had made a pledge to Miriam.

'I provided you with a husband that you so longed for, arranged your marriage and gave you a home.'

'Who is now being taken away from me,' she replied. 'The demands you made of him were too great; I often wondered whether you did it to spite me. A husband in name only, strangers to one another, that wasn't how it was supposed to be, but it made him happy knowing that's what you expected. No one could have shown you greater devotion.'

'I've heard all you have to say. There is no point in continuing with this conversation. Tend to your husband.' Yochanan gestured with his hand that he wished his sister to depart.

'Or is it because he was the only one that was prepared to challenge you?' Esther continued, unwilling to be dispensed with. 'You demand excellence but are afraid of the competition. If that is what you instil into your pupils, you'll never achieve your own true potential.'

Yochanan, seething with anger, got up to confront his sister, who had effortlessly uncovered the weakness that he had never been able to admit to. Then, without any concern for herself, Esther reached up and slapped her brother hard on the side of his face, sending him reeling backwards. It was her reaction against a lifetime of frustration and disappointment, which she considered he had subjected her to.

'My husband repaid you with his life and became the man you could never hope to be,' she scowled, her eyes aflame. 'Unlike you, he knows the meaning of remorse!'

Esther looked at her brother. His vulnerability was finally exposed and she was suddenly full of pity for him.

Yochanan, watching his sister disappear into the dark night, was tempted to follow her but after a short distance he hesitated and turned around before going back to await the arrival of his new young assistant.

36

'Do you think that providing me with confirmation of my own words is supposed to impress me?' Yochanan shouted irritably, throwing the student's work back at him, still affected by the bad feeling between him and his sister.

'Master, I thought that I'd done what you asked,' Ephraim replied meekly. He had not expected such a scathing response to the hours of work that he had undertaken in preparing his dissertation.

'That's the problem, you didn't think. You were too afraid to use your own mind so that you wouldn't be deemed wanting. But remember that, not so long ago, you had sufficient conceit to think you could replace your teacher.'

The young scholar looked downcast.

'You're no better than any of the others, expecting praise for telling me what you think that I want to hear. *Resh Lakish* never came to me unless he had thoroughly researched every aspect of the text beforehand and then with questions that could only come from an intuitive mind. That is how we learned together, both of us increasing our knowledge. You can't possibly expect to replace a man of that quality. You're not even worthy to sit in the same chair. So go and study and only return when you have something new to say that I haven't heard before. Get out!' the master shouted.

The assistant, humiliated by having his inadequacies so easily exposed, got up quickly. 'Master, I'm sorry to have disappointed you,' he said. 'I'll do my best, but I don't know if there can ever be another Shimon ben Lakish.'

Yochanan extinguished the remaining candle and sat in the silence of the darkened room. He knew what he had to do. He began praying with extra intensity, beating his chest and begging for forgiveness for the iniquity for which he had been responsible. Finally he left his house and travelled the short distance up the steep path to see his friend, hoping that there was still time.

Esther, hearing footsteps, recognised the familiar figure of her brother approaching.

'My husband is sleeping,' she said, leading her brother over to Shimon's bed. 'He will be happy that you have decided to come.'

Esther drew up a stool near the bed and placed a candle on the table between them so that the two men could talk privately. Yochanan took hold of Shimon's emaciated hand, trying not to show his shock at his friend's rapid deterioration.

Shimon opened his eyes and his face filled with joy, seeing that the person he had loved unconditionally was again by his side.

'Dearest friend,' Yochanan began. 'What have I done to you?'

Shimon tried to reply but the words wouldn't leave his lips. However, the expression in his still-vibrant eyes was one of conciliation.

'Do you remember the first time we encountered each other? I was bathing in the *Mikvah* and there you were, appearing out of nowhere suddenly with your arms around my neck. What an introduction. Who would have predicted you'd become my closest friend? I thought you might have guessed, but it wasn't purely a coincidence that we met.'

Shimon forced a smile and tried to sit up. He coughed, emitting a small trickle of blood from the side of his mouth. Esther rushed over with a cloth to wipe his face and a cup of water, which Yochanan took from her so that his friend could drink.

'Brother, my husband is tired, please let him rest,' Esther pleaded. But Shimon tightened his grip, indicating that he wanted his friend to continue.

Yochanan, knowing that he had to satisfy his conscience by seeking his brother-in-law's forgiveness, looked for confirmation and his sister nodded for him to remain.

'The letter from your sister, which you treasured so dearly, was the sign that I'd been waiting for. You see, your sister and I had met when you were in prison. She came here to deliver the baby of a student's wife. I could see immediately that she was an exceptional woman. Bringing life to so many, she asked nothing for herself except one favour. She asked that if you should find your way to the Galilee, that I would give you the opportunity to lead a decent life.'

Esther, hearing her brother's story, began to wonder what the real reason had been for the disagreement between them and whether she might have judged her brother too harshly.

'It was only when you began to trust me that I learned of your suffering. But I also realised that you'd shown extraordinary effort and dedication to carry your sister the long distance from your home to fulfil her final wishes. That entitled you to the opportunity she had requested. And when you demanded that I let you become acquainted with Esther, what choice did I have to refuse a man of such passion? Miriam left me her bracelet with no instructions, except that I would know when the time came for it to be put to appropriate use.'

Shimon, completely lucid, stretched out for his wife's hand to examine the piece of jewellery that had mysteriously appeared the evening before his betrothal. So it had been placed in the sack by his brother-in-law to secure Shimon and Esther's marriage.

'I didn't appreciate that you would apply the same intense feeling, first to your studies and then later to our partnership. Never prepared to compromise, always in search of the ultimate truth. Your capacity for work is immense. I could never have coped without you and yet you permitted me to think that I was the more learned. My friend, we both know that hasn't been so for a long time. Those unfortunate words that passed between us? Can you forgive them?'

Shimon, gasping for breath, summoned all his remaining strength and placed his ice-cold hand on his brother-in-law's lips to prevent him from speaking further. He had heard enough. With tears in his eyes he looked adoringly at the person whose recognition he had so desperately desired. At the last moment of his life, he found contentment.

Yochanan tore at his tunic and stood facing his widowed sister. They were equal in their grief for the man who, in their own ways, they had both loved. Providing comfort for each other, they knew that their main priority was now the sleeping boy who had just been deprived of his father.

His huge body swaying back and forth in prayer and his eyes closed, Yochanan began to wail, unable to reconcile himself to the loss of the friend whose body he was watching over. An overwhelming sense of emptiness engulfed him.

The next morning, Shimon, accompanied by his distraught family, was carried from his home. Ephraim and his fellow scholars led the procession to the burial grounds and to a grave that had already been prepared as soon as the news of Shimon's passing reached the school. His shrouded body was placed in the earth next to his sister Miriam.

Yochanan, supported under his arms by two of his students, recited the eulogy in a broken voice:

'How have the mighty fallen
In the thick of battle
Jonathan, slain on your heights!
I grieve for you,
My brother Jonathan,
You were most dear to me.
Your love was wonderful to me
More than the love of women.
How have the mighty fallen,
The weapons of war perished!'

The entire community, immersed in their own thoughts, slowly filtered out of the tranquil cemetery for the start of the prescribed seven-day mourning period, wondering how they would continue without the man that had left such a unique impression on their lives.

Shimon

Epilogue

REUVEN, HIS PRAYER shawl wrapped around his powerful body and laden with texts, struggled to keep his footing on ground sodden from the deluge that had affected the whole area. He had just left the study hall to go back to his home. He had taken the same steep path as his father had so often done.

Even though it had been more than ten years since his father died, Reuven could still visualise his kind face, as if he were there standing over him and patiently teaching him. He prayed that Shimon would have approved of his achievement, for he was now the *Rosh Yeshiva* presiding over an academy of a hundred students. The school was now the foremost establishment of rabbinic learning in the land.

Reuven had been tutored by Yochanan, his uncle. Together they had completed the work that Shimon had started and produced the text that was now widely recognised as a definitive explanation of the *Mishnah*.

Reuven smiled to himself, remembering the hours of learning and the interruptions during their lessons when his teacher would suddenly stop. Yochanan would roar that the boy's incessant questioning reminded him of *Resh Lakish*. He knew that his uncle had never recovered from losing Shimon. Yochanan remained profoundly troubled; until his own recent death he regularly did *Teshuvah*, as if feeling that he had in some way been responsible for a terrible deed for which he had never adequately atoned.

Entering his house and hearing two people in conversation, Reuven was surprised to find that they had a visitor. From his forlorn appearance and voracious appetite, he appeared to have undergone a hazardous journey.

'Reuven, this is your cousin David!' his mother exclaimed. 'He has something to ask you.'

She was stooping over the man. Reuven studied him curiously. The stranger shared a strange likeness to the teacher he'd just been thinking about.

Glossary

Abba: Hebrew word for father

Cena Libera: Banquet provided to gladiators on the eve of their fight

Damnatio ad Gladium: Sentenced to be killed by the sword in the arena

Denarius/Denarii: Roman silver coin(s)

Domina: Mistress

Ellul: Sixth month of the Jewish calendar

Fiscus Judaicus: Tax imposed by the Romans on the Jews

Fortuna: Luck

Iugula: Term meaning 'kill him'

Kelim: Section of the *Mishnah* (Oral Law) that deals with the ritual purity of utensils

Ketubah: Hebrew marriage document

Lanista: Trainer

Ludus: Gladiatorial school

Ludi: State-sponsored games

Medicus: Doctor

Mikvah: A ritual bath for purification in accordance with Jewish Law

Midrashim: Rabbinical texts commenting on scriptures

Mishnah: First concise presentation of the Jewish Oral Law

Mitzvah: Jewish commandment

Munera: Privately sponsored games

Nissan: First month of the Jewish calendar

Rosh Hashanah: Jewish Day of Judgment for the New Year

Rosh Yeshiva: Principal of a religious Jewish academy

Sacramentum Gladiatorum: Gladiatorial oath

Salve: Welcome!

Semikhah: Rabbinical ordination

Sestertius/Sestertii: Roman silver coin(s) worth one quarter of a *denarius*

Tefillin: Two black boxes with straps containing scrolls from Jewish scriptures that are attached to the head and arm during prayer

Tehillim: The Book of Psalms

Teshuvah: Hebrew word for repentance

Torah: Jewish written Law

Tractate: Section of the Oral Law